W9-AAM-197

THE SADDLEBAG

BHS SOUTH LIBRARY

THE SADDLEBAG
A Fable for Doubters and Seekers

Bahiyyih Nakhjavani

BEACON PRESS
BOSTON

Beacon Press
25 Beacon Street
Boston, Massachusetts 02108-2892
www.beacon.org

Beacon Press books
are published under the auspices of
the Unitarian Universalist Association of Congregations.

© 2000 by Bahiyyih Nakhjavani

First Beacon Press edition published 2000

All rights reserved

Printed in the United States of America

05 04 03 02 01 00   8 7 6 5 4 3 2 1

This book is printed on acid-free paper that meets the uncoated paper ANSI/NISO
specifications for permanence as revised in 1992.

Library of Congress Cataloging-in-Publication Data
Nakhjaváni, Bahíyyih.
The saddlebag : a fable for doubters and seekers / Bahiyyih Nakhjavani.—1st Beacon
Press ed.
p. cm.
ISBN 0-8070-8324-9 (cloth)
1. Bahai Faith—Fiction. I. Title.

PR6064.A35 S23 2000
823'.914—dc21
00-034226

To *The Dawn-Breakers*

THE THIEF

There was once a Thief who made his living by stealing from pilgrims along the road between Mecca and Medina. He was a Bedouin who had been born among the dunes and had never known a father. The priests too were alien to him and he cared nothing for the Prophet or his laws. Since he had been raised by several mothers who had all died before he learned the art of picking pockets, he had received little love and no schooling. But he had always been free.

Freedom, for the Bedouin, was the desert air he breathed. It was that open space of possibility between the known and the denied, that uninhabited place of expectation between apparent facts. He had been born to this inheritance of emptiness; it was a legacy that had been left him gratis. Even as a boy he knew the value of it but he still had to define this freedom for himself. City dwellers, he discovered, did not trust such freedom: they bound its myriad meanings within human wills and walls. The only place he found its vestiges in huddled towns and squalid villages was in those secret gardens where sweet fruit trees bloomed. The wilderness still flourished there, like the memory of orange blossom, within a courtyard, by

1

a pool; even there the seeds of freedom grew, in spite of confined space. But it was not enough for the Bedouin. He longed for vast immensities.

This was why the desert was his charter. To guess remained a birthright here and lack of proof was evidence enough of immortality. These rolling sands permitted endless interpretations; these hills and valleys provided infinite opportunity for conjecture. And though he had been orphaned young he had never felt forlorn in the desert, for his head had always echoed with its various voices. It had been a mother and a father to him, a teacher, a lover and a guide.

Despite his illiteracy, the desert made a scholar of him too. He discovered whole treatises hidden in sandstorms; he read a thousand poems inscribed across the wide horizon. When his soul was unsullied, at the hour of sunrise, he could understand the language of the sand. By the age of twenty, he knew the secret paths along the creviced cliffs and could read the riddles in the moving dunes. He analysed each cloud of dust according to its hour, read the moon's messages in all her seasons and could tell the voice of every star. The wind was his religion and the planet Venus was his love and he had found the traces of their will in rocks and desert valleys. Above all, he knew how to hide and steal and disappear along the gullies of the road between Jiddah and the twin holy cities. And it was for this reason that he had fallen in with a group of bandits who used him as their guide.

It was an easy step from picking pockets to serving the bandits. Since boyhood, the Bedouin had spied on those who stopped by wayside shrines and eavesdropped on their conversations by the village wells. He learned about their purposes, assessed their weaknesses, and ambushed them along the pilgrim road. Sometimes he even hired himself out to them as a special guide. But it was not always pockets that supplied the greatest treasures. As a young boy he had been fascinated by one man prostrate on the sands whose habit was to pick his nose tranquilly throughout his prayers. He had been barely old enough to finger his presumptive beard when another propositioned him in the coffee house and gave him more than he had bargained for. And on a third occasion in his early youth, the sheer extravagance of a pilgrim's hypocrisy had caused him to flee from the man without retrieving a single coin. In fact, he owed the pilgrims less for his livelihood than for a certain ability he had learned from them to distinguish between social piety and sincere faith.

In all the years he had been a thief, he had not found many who valued their faith above their financial worth. Most of the pilgrims seemed to address a cipher whom he could not recognize as the One who made him shiver with ardour on the edge of a quicksand or tremble with fear at the lip of a precipice. Their religion demanded much external gesture but showed little evidence of that terror by which he judged the presence of the Divine. Since he concluded that the pilgrims' god was not his god, he had no qualms about stealing from them.

But life for a lonely thief was hard and there had been times of extreme indigence when he too had been tempted to ask for alms under the guise of devotion. It was from this terrible compromise that the bandits had saved him. They had found him begging on the road to Mecca and shamed him with their oaths in which he sensed no blasphemy. They also offered him protection, for the dangers of the desert lay less in quicksands than in men. In exchange for his help as a guide, the bandits protected the Bedouin from harassment at the hands of savage tribes. Their chieftain needed this desert lizard to alert him to the presence of the richer caravans before his rivals, and to some extent he needed them. He made a bargain with them then and served them in order to be safe from them; he gave up his liberty because he was still young enough to believe himself free. And as a result of this contract, he had stayed true to his cherished dreams so far. For he hoped, one day, to be as wealthy as a prince.

Such dreams, had they been shared, would have shown the other bandits that this Thief not only lacked shrewdness, but was a naive and eccentric fellow. It was not immediately apparent, however. His eyes were narrow and as sharp as a hawk's, and of a disconcerting colour: vacant as the blue sky to reflect what might be seen on the horizon, green when he turned his gaze on the human face. At times they held a strange tincture of yellow which people remembered afterwards with unease. His nose too was like a hawk's beak, and his skin was leathered by the sun and almost black. His hair, prematurely grey with dust, was tangled in ragged tufts and tied back with a band which had once been an indigo blue. He moved with the speed of light and barely left a tread behind him, for he was not tall or heavy but small, agile, wiry and subtle. He was a wild man.

But despite his disturbing eyes and sharp nose, despite his savage and ruthless appearance, he was a dreamer, this Bedouin. He was a romantic. He heard the voices of his freedom in the wind and in the sands; he was attuned to them at all times. The other bandits said he was a coward because he would not stand and fight a man: he preferred to turn and run. They did not understand that this was because he loved his freedom absolutely. For his voices told him never to compromise with anyone but only to serve the stars, the moon and sun.

He listened to the voices of men too, however, in order to better serve the bandits. And though he was deaf to the voices in the mosque, he was alert to the ones in the marketplace. When the pilgrims put aside their prayer books and spoke in their own voices, he followed them all the way. For these reflected their worldly concerns and provided a road map of their anxieties. When they argued with each other, when they bargained, when they complained, he could distinguish between their wealth and poverty, their loss and his gain. He had become an acute listener and could follow the voices of men all the way from their lips into their pockets.

One evening, after several years in the service of the bandits, the Thief heard rumours at a roadside inn of a rich merchant and his caravan, which was expected to pass by in the next few days. So abundant was the wealth of pearls and jewels in his train, they said, that the shimmer of it caused the sun to set and forget to rise again. So laden were the mules and camels in this caravan that they carved a track of pure gold through the rocky paths. Here was silver that outshone the moon, they murmured, and all the wealth of the Orient contained in a few saddlebags. Here were sweets and spices fit for a wedding feast as well as a funeral! According to some, this merchant came from Shiraz and was performing his *hajj*; according to others he was from Bushire and was en route to Damascus in order to conduct his business affairs. All contradiction about where he came from and conjecture about where he was going converged, however, in the general conviction that his wealth was vast and worth stealing.

Of course, there had been many such rumours and many

subsequent raids over the years. None had proven as enriching in fact as in anticipation. But the Thief felt that this particular story was different from the rest. For some reason, the lure of this treasure seemed more enticing, this merchant sounded more wealthy, his caravan promised more opulence than ever dreamed of by the bandits. Anticipation made them drunk. And the Thief drank with them too.

That evening by their desert fires, as they planned an ambush, the chieftain called the Bedouin to his side. He had begun to love this guide of his, with his sinewy torso and ropelike legs. You could not call him a man, exactly, but he had spirit, unlike the rest of the jackals. Before all the others, he embraced him and gave him to drink from his cup. It was an unprecedented honour. They would share the stolen goods among them all, as was the custom, but this time the Bedouin was led to understand that he would gain the lion's share. The lion's share, that is, after the chieftain had taken the bulk of the booty, as was his personal due. It was a sign that he, the Thief, the Bedouin, was becoming a member of the band.

The bandits cheered lustily and spat secretly at the sand at their feet; they cheered loudly and cast each other sidelong glances of distrust. Their smiles were dim as they shifted around the fire, slapping arms, envious of warmth. There was something in this honour that they did not like.

It was said that each kiss received from the chieftain was worth a fortune and might cost one too. His embraces were more valuable than jewelled daggers and as dangerous. In the past, the Bedouin had yearned for such distinction and such love. There had been a time when this token of trust would have thrilled his pride as much as the escapade itself would have excited him. But something had changed. What ailed him now? What was his trouble?

His voices were restless. They whispered of the quicksands at the bandits' feet and the poison in the chieftain's kiss. They murmured of the solitary dunes, for they had become impatient with his life of compromise. They urged him to part company with these men and reap the rewards of theft alone. And they reminded him of a secret place to hoard his coins where none might find them. It was not the lion's share he wanted; it was not to share at all! It galled him to be allocated anything. As the chieftain embraced him, he felt himself drawing away. 'Run,' whispered his voices, 'before you lose your freedom ever to run again.'

He sat beside the chieftain watching him gnaw the lambs' bones and toss them one by one into the darkness beyond the firelight. This man would have the choice of three women in his tent tonight and the fairest from the raid. The Thief watched him lick the grease from his lips and pick the shreds of meat caught in his teeth and he remembered his own far different loves. 'There is more passion waiting for you under the naked moon,' murmured his voices, 'than in the chieftain's dreams.'

He scrutinized the circle of bandits round him too, and knew that their souls had been seized and possessed already. He watched their sullenness beneath the radiant stars, listened to their unhappy laughter like the hoot of night owls round him, felt their rapacious jealousies in the flickering darkness full of sparks. 'They are accustomed to envy what they'll never have,' muttered his voices, 'and they will always hate you because you do not envy them.'

The new moon rose limpid over the dunes and a chill night breeze tugged at his tangled hair. The moon had one message; the bitter breeze another. She was his advocate;

the breeze his accuser. She bore witness that the contract had changed, the time had come. The breeze whispered that this moment had been long coming and the terms of the contract were overdue. And as they argued, the desert was filled with their voices.

'A fine coward,' whistled the breeze harshly. 'A better hypocrite than any pilgrim, a worse liar than any mirage!' The bandits were drinking with wild abandon and were becoming rowdy around the fire which the fierce wind whipped into their faces.

'But it was different before,' murmured the moon, and her argument was so compelling that the chieftain lifted his face to her momentarily. 'Then he was a boy and now he is a man,' she continued, but it seemed that the chieftain was unconvinced by this lunar logic, for he turned away immediately as one of the bandits told a vulgar joke.

'If there is a difference between what he feels and what he does,' sneered the breeze, 'what difference is there then between him and those he so despises?' The Bedouin shuddered at the accusation and pulled his jellaba closer round him in the shadows. The wind had grown bitter. 'How can he rob the pilgrims when he's worse than they are?' it mocked.

'His original bargain had been to exchange his freedom for protection,' replied the moon quietly, 'but now he prefers liberty at any price.' And she pulled herself loose from a last tag of cloud to prove it, and sailed eloquently into the dark dunes of the uncharted universe.

The Thief heard the breeze betray him, but it seemed the bandits did not. He heard the moon defend him, but it seemed the chieftain did not. Even when the stars gave evidence, one by one, citing examples from far-off suns, presenting proofs from the passing seasons, no one but the

Bedouin seemed aware that the time had turned, that the terms of the contract had shifted, irrevocably altered.

But there was a reason why the Thief had not abandoned the bandits yet. He feared revenge. His fears buzzed in his head like flies in swampy watering holes; they emitted sharp cries, like the carrion birds above. The chieftain had an insatiable appetite for vengeance and was ruthless with traitors. The Bedouin knew that if he ran away the chieftain would hunt him down and kill him; he would not deviate from this course. He knew the bandits would track him down wherever he might hide, would stab him in the back and slit his throat and cut his tongue and manhood off and plunge their hands into his liver and his heart. They were a bloodthirsty and pitiless lot. Each time he thought to flee, his voices hissed that it would be towards his death.

There was only one way he could buy his freedom back and live, and that was if he were rich. It was perhaps the greatest sign of his naivety that he thought this. It was more like faith than thought, in fact, and had an ardent, simple voice. Full of the day's hope it gathered in the valleys of his heart. Fresh as the morning dew it assured him there was a way out of his dilemma. It told him that if the lure of stolen wealth were sufficiently great, if he could steal enough of it alone, if he could bribe the bandits to give him his freedom, then he need be no man's servant: he could command the absolute freedom he desired.

And now it seemed the opportunity was at hand. Since he had earned the chieftain's trust and been singled out for special favours, the bandits would have no reason to suspect his betrayal. If the caravan was as laden with wealth as they all seemed to suggest, he might have the chance to steal enough to bargain with. Mesmerized by possibility, the Bedouin succumbed to his restless voices. That very night, after serving the bandits faithfully for several years and finally earning their acceptance, after being specially favoured by the dagger point of his chieftain's love, the Thief stole away from his masters and vanished into the desert.

For the whole of the first day of his freedom, he lurked in a valley of treacherous dunes ahead of the other bandits. If they follow me, he thought, I will lead them into the quicksands. But they did not follow him.

On the second day, he waited on a narrow pass near the edge of a deep ravine, well hidden by a rocky range. If they follow me now, I will push them over the pass and escape into the mountains, he thought. But they did not follow him.

On the third day, he came upon a lonely well on a barren stretch of road between Mecca and Medina. It was a place where pilgrims often paused, for there had been a shrine here in the old days; it was the perfect spot to pilfer from the unwary caravan before it reached the main ambush ahead. There was a roofless ruin and an old, dry well on the edge of a gully where he could hide among the rocks, and a new well gushed on the road nearby, tempting travellers to stop and drink their fill. If they find me here, the Bedouin thought, I will climb down the old well and escape into the gully below the ruin, where they won't see me from the road. But they still did not find him. Maybe they were not even following him. And where was the caravan?

The Bedouin began to grow frustrated. No caravan laden with riches came by and no roving gang of bandits hunted after him. He began to ponder deep in his heart and question the rumours he had heard. And he began to fear, fear the stalking footsteps that were bound to dog him now for the rest of his life, fear the vengeance of the chieftain. Worst of all, he began to doubt his voices, doubt the desert which had told him to hide himself in this barren valley between the high cliffs and the ruined shrine. Should he perhaps have stayed at the caravanserai one *farsang* back? There he might at least have double-checked the rumours. But there too he might have risked encounter with the bandits. Or should he have lingered closer to their ambush? During the long, hot hours of the third day he brooded over how his companions might even have invented the rumour of the rich merchant and his caravan just to trick him, how the chieftain of the bandits had probably made promises just to dupe him, and how they had all plotted his death because they no longer needed him. As the sun sank listlessly in the western skies, his heart grew as dry as dust on his lips and the sands bleared his yellowed eyes. That night the Thief was not visited by the beauties of the evening star as he sat cramped and cold near the well. He was courted by the spectre of despair.

Finally, on the fourth dawn, just as he was about to give up, he glimpsed something coming from the direction of the sacred city. Something like a call from the distant horizon, an appointment with sunrise. He could see little at first. Then the watery mirages of early morning relinquished their meaning and he gradually made out three figures approaching. Three notes struck against silence, the call of the coming dawn. The figures shimmered, beckoned, blurred and then emerged at last: three men on the far horizon.

This was a different language from that which he had been led to expect. Hardly the grand caravan he had hoped for. But he hid himself hurriedly in the ruined shrine and waited, counting the pulse beats in his throat. As they drew near and solidified from the quavery haze, he saw that one of the three travellers was a young man dressed in pilgrim's robes, riding a camel. Another was a youth who held the bridle of the camel and walked barefoot as if before a person of great importance. The third was a black slave.

There was no entourage and no wealthy train, but the rays of the rising sun gilded the straps of a fat saddlebag which had been loaded on the camel, and the sharp eye of the Thief saw a pearl hanging in the left ear of the slave. There was no entourage and no wealthy train, but he was struck by the signs of marked deference which the youth showed towards the pilgrim riding the camel, a young man whose nobility of bearing was distinguishable even from this distance. There was no entourage, no train but – here's a pompous young pimp off on his pilgrimage, the Thief thought, here's a rich charlatan disguised to look as poor as I am to escape attention. Here, if this eye of mine is to be trusted, is a clever little hypocrite who has put all his wealth into a single saddlebag. But he can't fool me! He must be the merchant!

It was the hour of morning prayer. As the Bedouin's hopes revived, he raised his tawny eyes towards the sky. Venus glimmered like a last kiss on the velvet horizon and his heart sang with desire. He thought his lady Fortune had abandoned him, but perhaps she loved him still. He breathed an invocation to her that this merchant was devout and willed him, with all his heart, to stop.

His eyes grew as green as the turban wound about the young man's head, while the camel approached closer and closer. Most people had forgotten the significance of the ruined shrine when the old spring dried, and few had learned about the freshly dug well. But since it was the first day of the holy month of mourning, perhaps these pilgrims would want to pray? If they prided themselves on their devotions, perhaps they would stop here and find pure water?

As luck would have it, the merchant stopped to perform his ablutions. It seemed to the Bedouin, in his joy, that the well overflowed with jubilant voices, shouting their delight. His excitement was such that he half expected the travellers to turn round and see him. But they did not. While the black slave unloaded the camel, his master dismounted and approached the well. Then he washed his face and hands in the singing happiness of the waters and knelt down to pray with the youth in attendance. As he did so, he laid the saddlebag on the ground beside him.

The Thief eyed it greedily, his body taut as a spring. So far, so good. This pilgrim was devout at least in word. If he were devout enough in deed, he thought, it would be even better for the state of his soul. Everything depended on the perfect combination of prayers and stealth. Let me tread softly and the fellow pray himself blind! thought the Thief. Who knows but that this saddlebag might put out the sun? It looked fat enough and seemed heavy enough; its voice was thick and hummed with mysteries. If his luck held out, it might be all his own. Now, he thought, addressing himself wryly to the suspect deity of pilgrims whom he had learned to despise, let their false god be true for once and make me a test of their devotion.

He waited for the three travellers to prostrate themselves before he slipped out of his hiding place, like a snake. Within seconds he had snatched up the saddlebag and started to run. The merchant was absorbed in chanting his prayers and seemed unaware of the theft, but the youth was momentarily distracted. Huh! thought the Bedouin, the sands scalding the soles of his feet. So much for your

piety, my boy! He exulted at the heaviness of the saddlebag. But his action had already caused the black servant
to leap up and take a lunge towards him. Ah! thought the
Bedouin, slipping between them like a whisper of wind.
The slave's prayers are not more pious! But his heart beat
with fear at the hot breath of his pursuer on his shoulder.
Just at that moment the merchant, still chanting his prayer,
raised a hand in admonishment. His voice never wavered,
his chanting never faltered, and his eyes remained closed,
but he raised his hand and beckoned the slave back.

The Bedouin saw the gesture from the corner of his eye.
So peremptory was it, so compelling, that he wanted to
obey, despite himself. He found his limbs growing heavy,
his legs slowing down. 'Don't run!' whispered his voices
treacherously. 'Don't even try to run! Freedom is obedience!' He almost dropped the bag.

How was this? Who could command his voices? The
Thief was half stunned. The sands mocked him; the rolling
dunes laughed at him heartlessly; the high cliff above gave a
shout of scorn that shook the crumbling foundations of his
confidence. It was only with the greatest effort of will in the
world that he forced his feet to keep running. 'This man's
prayers are the strongest of all,' he muttered to himself, 'if
they can master my voices!' He was terrified. At any
moment he knew the slave could reach out and lay a hand
on him, but to his astonishment, the man suddenly ceased
giving pursuit. He had obeyed! The youth resumed his
devotions too as if nothing had taken place. And the prayer
continued.

The Bedouin slackened his pace for a split second to
glance over his shoulder, incredulous. All three were prostrate on the sand. The youth had bowed his head and
moved his lips mutely now, eyes closed. The servant had

thrown himself flat on the ground, his long black fingers stretched on the sand before his bared head. The merchant, who had never ceased from his melodious chanting, had reached an invocation at that moment. He lifted his face upwards in rapt devotion and raised his palms in prayer. He was calling on the name of the Ordainer, the Almighty. He was calling on God, the Forgiver of sinners, the Most Compassionate –

The beautiful words seemed to rise like the freshness of pure water from cracked earth; like a ripple of water from the wellspring of the vast horizon. They flooded the early morning dunes with the light of dawn. The merchant's face, as he uttered the sacred supplication, was illumined by the sunrise. It was so bright that the Bedouin was forced to turn his eyes away, half blinded. He felt a familiar shudder of awe pass through his being; it told him of unmentionable powers, of infinite presences. He felt a terror which told him that this was the voice of the One who ordained his voices. And he fled.

He ran like a pelting stone towards the high cliff on the other side of the valley, his mind echoing, his feet torn by the imprecision of rocks and fear. He was confounded. It had taken no more than a few seconds for him to question everything in his life, to realize the futility of his past and the poverty of his future dreams. The sound of the morning prayer followed him like a finger of light as he fled into the foothills, along the shadowy edges of his own secret paths, hugging the saddlebag to his pounding heart.

Once out of their sight and out of hearing, he began to babble to himself incoherently. Surely they were mad, these pilgrims! Not to stop their confounded prayers, not even to chase him! Pursued by a panic that he could not name, he began to laugh hysterically as he picked his way across the valley, keeping hidden by the hills; he began to weep helplessly as he clambered up the sharp rocks on the other side. The shadows under the tall cliff were menacing and whispered warnings to him, but these were nothing to that nameless terror which stalked at his heels. He threw himself against the near-vertical incline and began to scramble higher with a demonic sense of urgency. He had strapped the saddlebag to his back in order to dispel the feeling of ill omen that dogged him, but it could not be shaken. Although he could see, across the valley near the well, that the three travellers had not moved from their place of prayer, he still felt pursued. They had let him go and yet he felt as if he had been caught forever.

What goaded him was that the merchant had permitted him to steal. He had stolen the saddlebag because the merchant had allowed him to. He had been given this freedom by the merchant, rather than taking it as his right. The difference was immeasurable, and his whole world tumbled into the gap that yawned between the two. This was not what he had intended at all when he had taken to his heels and run from the bandits, when he had fled from the chieftain and his 'lion's share'. He had wanted no share in sharing, but had he not just been given one? He had not imagined this possibility. 'That merchant gave you his blessing,' muttered his voices insidiously. 'It was his prayer that enabled you to escape; it was perhaps even his will that you could steal! What kind of freedom is that?'

He shook his head to free himself from the disturbing chatter in it. The vast desert opening inside his mind threatened to crack the confines of sanity. 'The man must be a lunatic,' he shouted at the listening rocks. 'And his companions stupid!'

16

'Stupid!' replied the rocks, mockingly. And the echo caused him to shudder so much that he almost lost his grip and had to cling immobile for a moment to the sheer rock face, lest he slip and fall. Had he tested the merchant's devotion or had his own just been tested? Was he not more stupid to imagine he could steal what was freely given? The idea gave him such vertigo that he knew he would fall in earnest if he looked below. So he kept climbing.

But the miracle of it gradually grew warm on his back as he scrambled higher. His glad animal spirits returned as the sun rose. If he had been given permission to steal, why, let the consequences be damned! Was he not the luckiest devil this side of death? Even if he had only been granted a portion, it was surely more than his share among the bandits. Even if he had proven the pilgrim's prayer true and himself mistaken, wasn't he finally free? As he scrambled to the safer paths halfway up the cliff, he began to laugh aloud at his good fortune, at the folly of pilgrims and the dull wit of bandits. Here was booty at last that was all his own!

He climbed without glancing to the left or right but only upwards for some time, and finally reached the windy prominence of the precipice. He was at the top of the high cliff, above the valley where he had been lurking for the past three days. He had to crawl now, for a man could be seen for miles from up here, and could see for miles too. The wind was cruel. The abandoned shrine where he had stolen the saddlebag was a dizzying spot below. The three pilgrims had already finished their prayers and had vanished into the dunes. Opposite lay the road along which they had just come. And if he had gazed towards the shimmering eastern distance where the sacred city lay, from this great height his keen eyes would have seen the junction where the pilgrim road was joined by camel routes from the sea. If he had lingered long enough to look that far, his eyes would have turned green.

There was a caravan coming now along that road, glinting in the distance, a mere *farsang* away. It was a sizable one at that, but the Bedouin had no time to consider it. Flat on his belly he slid like a lizard along the edge of the precipice till he reached a narrow chimney of rocks. Here he let himself down inch by inch, feeling for each foothold, till he worked his way into a cave set in the sheer rock overlooking the valley. It was a perilous ledge with a stark drop on one side and a shallow hollow on the other into which the wind surged like an ocean. From it he could see the top of the precipice, but unless one knew where to look, no one could see into the cave. One false step could lead to instant death and the only way up was the way he had come down. This was the lair which he had kept private from the bandits. Hidden here under the rocks he could store his secret wealth. At last he was safe! No one could find him here!

He threw the heavy saddlebag down and tore it open eagerly.

But what was this? For a few seconds the Thief swayed against the side of the cave. He did not know whether the murmur in his ears came from within his own head or from inside the saddlebag. He looked more closely. It was packed with bundles and packets and rolls, some bound in silk and others in parchment. All were tied with fine string and knotted carefully. Ah! This merchant was taking no chances! The Thief wet his cracked lips with a ragged tongue and imagined the bulging purses, the fabulous jewellery and the ingots of gold inside these careful bundles. Murmuring love to his lady Fortune, he fumbled with the knots but his nails were cracked too and his hands craggy with the knowledge of rocks. He could not untangle them. Finally, in frustration, he used his teeth and one of the bundles burst open.

His heart contracted with disbelief. The roll of parchment he had just ripped free fell open at his feet revealing a wad of paper, thin blue paper, covered in writing. Gossamer writing, so fine it looked like the threads of spiders spun across translucent space. Could he read this stuff? No. What did he care for writing? Nothing! But inside the roll of paper he found a narrow box. Ah, was it jewelled, perhaps? No. Was it covered in gold leaf, like the precious box the chieftain had once given a favourite concubine? No. It was a simple wooden box, illumined with coloured lacquerwork, and it had a sliding panel which opened –! His heart thudding with excitement, he slid open the lid, expecting finally to discover the string of pearls, the diamonds clustered within.

But he was bitterly disappointed. There was nothing in the box but a collection of reed pens. They were sharpened and ink-dipped, well used and ordinary. A pen case. He found a little knife, too, in the box, a simple penknife with a piece of glass lodged in the handle which promised nothing more than what it was, for it could hardly cut a throat. The only other mystery was a porcelain cup containing a curious dark powder. He smelled it. He tasted it and his tongue became black. Ink.

Was this all then? Pens? Ink? Scribbled paper? Words! Choked with dismay, he ransacked the saddlebag. Bundles, nothing but bundles and packages, doubtless nothing more inside them than pens and ink and paper and words. No wonder the merchant had not stopped him! No wonder he had gestured to his slave to let him go! It was he himself, fool of a Bedouin, who was stupid. They were letting him run off with what was worthless! Swearing furiously, cursing his luck, and stung with humiliation, the Thief reeled from the blows of his mocking voices. He stared at the remaining packets in the saddlebag, uncertain for a moment whether he should tear them all open or simply throw them away. Did these elusive bundles all contain the same rubbish? Were there no jewels here? No ingots of gold wrapped up in these silks and parchments?

But his voices were merciless. 'How can you be sure?' they murmured. 'Shouldn't you open all of them, one by one, before you throw them away, just in case?'

At that moment, as he hovered at the cave ledge, poised at the abyss of indecision, he heard a shower of pebbles falling from above him. His anger had blinded his usual instincts of caution. His voices had deafened him to the world. Swinging round, he saw above him on the clifftop that he had been encircled indeed. There were the bandits whom he had abandoned! And the chieftain whom he had betrayed!

Could they have been following him? How was that possible? Had they actually clambered after him and hunted him to this place? How else would they have known where he was? But that could not be, for he would have heard them, seen them below him!

Suddenly it seemed as if the desert itself had betrayed him. It had conspired against him. It had guided his enemies to his hiding place. Nothing was sacred any more and there was nowhere left for him to go. In a flash he understood that he would either die famished in his cave or be stabbed to death, if he tried to climb out. No alternative, no freedom remained, except the chasm below. The Bedouin saw cold anger glinting like a knife in the eyes of the chieftain and knew he was finally trapped.

But the point of that knife was not more sharp to him than his own rancour, and his rancour no less bitter than the chance of freedom lost. All possibilities between the known and the denied were taken from him, but he still held one mystery for his own. All expectations were gone but this one. It lay still at his feet, bulging with hidden hopes, wrapped in secret bundles. He would not give up this legacy for all the world!

Hadn't the youth with bleeding feet unloaded the saddlebag with an unusual reverence and the black servant run after him with great urgency? Hadn't the merchant – and now the Thief was certain of this – had not the young pilgrim let him take the saddlebag because he was himself as rich as a prince of the realm? And didn't the bandits also believe the saddlebag contained a fabulous sum? Hadn't they hunted him to his lair in the hope of stripping him of his prize? Maybe it did contain the wealth of the world! Infinite possibilities lay in its very lack of proof. Let them kill him, let them watch him dry up like a lizard, let them ransack his secret cave, but he would keep the saddlebag! This treasure was his own!

Quite forgetting his bitter disappointment of a few minutes before, the Bedouin thrust the pale-blue papers and the little pen case savagely back inside the saddlebag and clutched it to him. It seemed, in that moment of extremis, that this torn piece of dusty leather contained his very soul. Abruptly then, and with a cry that chilled the bandits and their chieftain, he leaped with it over the edge of the cave, crashing from rock to rock, until he plunged headlong several hundred feet over the precipice and into the valley below.

The bandits watched the saddlebag and the man soar in an arc, black as ink against the blue. They watched them falling, a curve of calligraphy against the papery sky. They watched them crash down in the gully directly opposite the well below. And then their eyes caught the glint of a caravan approaching along the road from Mecca to Medina. A mere *farsang* away . . . The merchant's caravan!

Minutes later, they had dispersed and were riding wildly through the narrow files and treacherous passes of the mountain, with the curses of the chieftain in their ears. The Thief was forgotten. And although he searched for several hours the following day, the chieftain never found the stolen saddlebag among the rocks below.

The Bedouin lay broken as a reed on the rocks below, splintered like words on fine blue paper. Memory thundered through his veins and burst in his shattered brain with one last pulse. He saw three men prostrate on the sands and heard the words beckoning him like a long finger of light. He saw the faint trace of ink on the desert page and tried to decipher the words that beckoned him like a long finger of light. His eyes filled with tears of pity for his illiteracy, as he stumbled, step by painful step, towards the light. In the brief moment before death, he knew that if he could just make out those beckoning words, he would always be free.

With a piercing sweetness that stopped his last breath, the voice of the merchant at the well came to him, chanting. The voice of the merchant came from the well invoking the mercy of God. He was praying in the name of the Ordainer. Praying for him, the Thief. The Bedouin.

It was clear now. He heard the words of the merchant as he began to read them spread across the blue scroll of the sky. He read the prayer as he heard it, spanning the heavens like a bridge of light. Clear-sighted and wide open he died then, as rich as a prince of the realm, with eyes the colour of angels' wings.

THE BRIDE

W hen the Bride saw a man with flaming wings dive down from the top of the precipice above the caravan, she knew it was an angel with a message. It was an angel crossing the bridge of separation between heaven and hell, between truth and denial, but she had no immediate premonition of the message. Whether it was a fiery angel of light from Ahura Mazdah or a dark angel of Ahriman, she did not know either, at first, for she was half blinded by both possibilities.

The other angels she had seen in her brief life of fourteen years were less scarred, less agonized, but she recognized this one as an angel immediately, because of the wings. They flamed vibrant from his shoulders and made the air hot with joy. He fell in a pure arc from the top of the precipice up ahead and she read her fate in the word he carved against the cloudless sky. At a glance of the high sun, her heart was pierced by the iridescent message he was carrying, and then no shadow of a doubt remained, for she realized the plume of fire in his hand was blazing with the truth. She let out a cry and fainted at the sight.

The Bride had always been prone to visions. As a little girl she prattled comfortably to people who were not there

⌐BHS SOUTH LIBRARY

and often sang songs she claimed she had been taught by unseen spirits. Her mother tried at first to punish her when she invented this kind of nonsense, fearing it would be whispered about that this pretty child of the Gebr merchant of Kirman was mentally defective and that would damage their family reputation. Worse still, it would be murmured among the neighbours that the girl was constitutionally weak because of inbreeding and that would destroy her chances of a good marriage despite her father's wealth and her own marble skin and green eyes. For everyone suspected that these Gebrs, like the Parsees over the border, may have retained their Zoroastrian faith after their forced conversion to Islam.

Unfortunately, her mother had to admit that there was inbreeding in the family. They were wealthy Zoroastrians from the eastern borders of Persia, and cousins had been marrying cousins for generations between Kirman and Karachi. Why, she herself was her husband's maternal cousin by a third wife who had actually been something more like a sister. Since the word 'illegitimacy' was no less disconcerting than the idea of incest, one did not speak of these matters, of course. No more than one allowed one's religious preferences or the extent of one's assets to be noised abroad. For faith and wealth had been retained by intermarriage and both had been kept assiduously concealed.

The girl's angels were a far more serious matter. They were too scattering bright, too noisy, and they attracted the attention of the Muslim neighbours. Some murmured that the Gebr child was epileptic, others that she was possessed by demons. But whether the girl was slightly mad or simply a mystic, her mother's pride had suffered enough from both real and imagined discrimination all these years, without the stigma of any further indignity. She did so wish her daughter would not advertise these otherworldly visitations.

The girl was her father's darling, however, and in his eyes could do no wrong. Several children had died in infancy, and he had never been blessed with a son. But when this daughter had been born, a Zoroastrian soothsayer had told him she would be the first of her people to recognize the saviour Saoshyant, who would appear in the fourth epoch of time, after nine millennia of struggle between good and evil. Since this seemed far enough into the future to be safe, the Zoroastrian merchant took it to be a good omen that his child would live longer and remain healthier than the others and named her after the spirit of salvation, Haurvatat. He lavished his attention on the baby and spoiled her in flat contradiction to the self-restraint he expected from the rest of the family. Whenever her mother scolded her, she ran and told her father of it and there would be scenes in the women's quarters. After a while diplomacy dictated that even though the child might be telling lies, it was not politic to admit so. Her mother pursed her lips and pretended not to hear her daughter's ravings or her neighbours' gossip. Gradually the family became accustomed to her visions and in time, to her mother's unmitigated disgust, even the neighbours began to consult her opinion.

The year the plague broke out, the child named after Haurvatat insisted that she saw great birds flying over her father's house each dawn. No one else saw them, but after a while people began to whisper that it was the vultures who had come down from the high rocks where the sun worshippers abandoned their dead and were hovering over the living to protect them from infection. For, miraculously, no one in her family succumbed to the dreaded malady. No one under the roof of the Zoroastrian became sick with the pox which took its death toll of thousands in the town and left twice as many of the living hideously marked. No one, that is, except the girl's mother, who was one of the first in town to die of the plague and did so, people said, to prove her daughter's visions wrong, once and for all. For she died laughing. The only other person who was infected in the home of the Zoroastrian merchant was an Abyssinian slave who was immediately put under quarantine, with her newborn baby.

The year her mother died and she was nine years old, the girl's father took another wife. The new wife was even less partial to her stepdaughter's visions than her own mother had been and began to nag the merchant to arrange an early marriage for the child. The second month had hardly passed before the presumptuous little creature began to trumpet her dreams about, announcing to everyone that her father's new wife was carrying an old turnip in her belly. Feelings of offence ran high in the women's quarters. The new wife became hysterical, lost her baby and blamed her stepdaughter for it. The neighbours murmured that the girl was bewitched and her visions were becoming danger-ous; a nasty rumour began to spread in the Zoroastrian community that the child was crazed because she had been raised addicted to the narcotic *haoma*, which was the cause of her hallucinations. No man in his right mind would want to marry such a freak. The Gebr merchant tried to placate his wife, but she became even more irascible and issued an ultimatum that if he did not treat her with more respect and send his daughter away, she would go back to her father's home.

The merchant agreed to her demands and began to search for a husband for his daughter, for he certainly had no intention of disturbing his business connections with his new wife's relatives. The multiple impediments he faced, however, made his task an exercise of virtuosity in negative constructions. The prospective groom had to live far enough away not to have heard the nasty rumours, not to be prejudiced against the little Gebr. But while the Zoroastrian merchant did not wish to undermine his daughter's chances of a wealthy marriage, he did not plan to lose her for ever either. He decided that the only solution would be to seek out a husband for her who would not live long, so that his lovely girl might soon return. And thus, in years to come, he never forgave himself for what ensued, for he knew he had been planning as much for a funeral as a wedding when he began to look for a bridegroom for his daughter. It was in the year of the plague that negotiations began which would ultimately lead to the complicated marriage contract between the little Bride and a wealthy old Turk living in Damascus.

The negotiations were necessarily long and protracted. The girl was still young and her father saw no harm in involving several middlemen whom he employed as much to delay the proceedings as to conduct the discussions about the dowry with the Turk. One of these go-betweens was an Indian who introduced himself to the Zoroastrian as a fellow tradesman from Bombay. He was short and fat and oily and each time he came to the house he excited a series of double and triple visions in the girl. She claimed that she had seen him standing naked by the side of a river which turned to manure at the touch of his foot. She said she had read tattooed on the skin of his sagging belly the warning that he was a *druj*, one of the People of the Lie in the scriptural Avestas. She had heard the Trumpets of Righteousness resounding, she said, to tell the world that the short, fat Indian had rubbed his oily hands on the law of trustworthiness and rendered it impotent in the land.

This vision later proved to be entirely correct. The Hindu who said he was from Bombay was a charlatan from Calcutta already engaged in shady deals with the Turk, who thought he was a devout Muslim from Karachi. After ingratiating himself with both parties in the course of negotiating a marriage contract, he absconded with the engagement gifts from the groom to the bride and disappeared, much to the indignation of the girl's father.

When this treachery was discovered, it confirmed the little Bride's visions, caused her stepmother considerable chagrin and enhanced her standing in the women's quarters as well as the entire neighbourhood. But it led to severe complications and growing antipathies between the Zoroastrian and the Turk, who preferred not to suspect his own middleman. The result was that the marriage plans were cancelled and the merchant's second wife suffered another miscarriage.

At that point the old Turk fell seriously ill. Rumour had it that he might have died but for the girl named after Haurvatat, the spirit of salvation. Her visions saved him. She insisted that angels had come to her in a dream with instructions that the old man be sent nine bolts of pure silk and nine barrels of rose water for his burial, all strapped on the backs of five Cypriot donkeys. She would brook no opposition to these divine instructions so her father was obliged to comply with them, despite his hurt pride and his private preference for vultures at the hour of death. When, by a miracle, this unexpected gift arrived intact, the Turk was so surprised that he instantly recovered from his illness and found a new zest in life. He determined then to marry the little witch, whatever it might cost him and her father.

And it cost a lot. The marriage negotiations that began in the year of the plague were resumed during the spring of her first sign of womanhood and finally bore fruit when the girl was fourteen. The gifts her father sent to Damascus matched to the last gold coin the presents that he received from the Turk during the extended courting period.

That same year of the plague, the Zoroastrian also gave his personal slave her freedom. Though the Abyssinian had taken to the veil after her illness and had hidden her once beautiful face, his second wife was a jealous woman. His first had learned detachment through her daughter's visions and had been ready, long before dying, for high places of silence. But the new wife was anything but silent, and had no intention of dying. Besides she had brought her own servants with her from Bombay, a flighty bunch of Parsee popinjays who spoke a silly mixture of Hindi and Persian and filled the women's quarters with unfamiliar smells and spices. They shrieked with laughter at the Bride's visions, which slightly mollified the new wife's pride, but they could not dislodge the sombre Abyssinian from the altar of her devotion. Despite being discarded, the freed slave chose to stay in the Zoroastrian's household. She was trusted for her discretion and became the girl's nurse first, and then her maid.

From that time on, the little Bride had a confidante. She grew up under the watchful care of her maid, who believed in her visions and understood the bright language of angels by the flickering shadows they cast on the flat contours of everyday life. There were days, for instance, when the girl refused to look into a mirror for fear she would see the shadow of the dark angel Ahriman where her face should be. Once she broke every mirror in the house to the loud indignation of all, leaving nothing but a polished silver tray in the women's quarters for people to reassure themselves of their identity, because she was convinced that this fatal shadow could slip through the glass and attach itself to her feet, forever. There were nights too when she could not sleep because, she whispered, the flaming crystal of Ahura Mazdah had replaced the moon and midnight had become high noon. Should such things be denied, she said, judgement would fall on all the family. She was a difficult child and took orders from none but her angels.

She had frequent conversations with Ameretatat and Haurvatat, who were her particular familiars. These angels, of immortality and salvation, filled the maid with dread for they often carried the marks of death and decay in their wake and told the girl secrets that she would not share. She whispered these secrets to the little rings she wore on her fingers, however, and one time, when the rings mysteriously disappeared, the little girl drooped and grew wan and perilously thin. Nothing the doctors did or said had any effect and the Zoroastrian became desperate. When, quite by chance, the maid found the rings buried in the orchard, under the mandarin trees, it was their discovery that eventually restored the child's appetite although it also provoked terrible tantrums. She wept and screamed and tore her hair and demanded that they be returned to their shallow graves immediately. According to the angels, she had to sacrifice her desire to tell them her secrets so that they might grow to be the rings of creation, she said. Without such sacrifice, she sobbed, how could the fingers of Saoshyant be adorned? Her maid made a deal with her then, to eat one mandarin each day in exchange for telling her secrets to the silent trees, in order that the rings might grow beneath them undisturbed and become worthy of the saviour of the world.

Her angels made the child promises, too, which gave her such palpitations of joy that the maid was obliged to soak her little feet in orange water for hours afterwards, in order to calm her pulse. One day, when she had just turned thirteen, her maid found her in the summer house, with a bowl of peeled pomegranates spilled in her lap. The bowl had tumbled to the ground and broken, and a mass of rubied fruit, tender and vibrant, had scattered across the chequered sunlit floor. She was in a trancelike faint and was trembling violently. The angel of the divine kingdom, Khshathra Vairya, had come to her, she breathed, and touched her with his wingtips and given her a terrible pain here, she pointed, in her groin. He had told her that the time had come for her to become a woman. She, of course, obeyed.

She had a great celerity in responding to her angels. Her lustrous hair grew long and was dyed deep henna red when she began to menstruate. By the time she was fourteen, she was stunningly beautiful, with alabaster skin and jewelled eyes. Her maid adored her with a blind devotion known only to dogs.

When the time finally came to send the little Bride to Damascus, as was expected, her faithful maid accompanied her. There was no one else who knew so well how to take care of the spoilt and eccentric girl, and no other woman she would accept to serve her. When she had her visions, there was no one else who could control her either, for there were times when her angels were downright tyrannical and difficult to contain. They rampaged through the women's quarters, leaving trails of telltale syrup, shameful patches of squashed fruit and charred spots on all the carpets. They had even been known to penetrate as far as the male quarters, or *biruni*, and had apparently experimented with the *qualun*, dropping tainted water and scattering ash from the hubble-bubble across the best silks and satin cushions. Her good spirits and her bad required a regular entourage of servants to do their bidding.

It was decided, for her wedding journey, that she should travel in a luxurious *takhteravan*, an elegant tent constructed on a wooden platform and supported on the backs of four mules. She would be accompanied, moreover, by twelve armed horsemen, a train of nineteen donkeys and camels, and a *farrash-bashi* who would be responsible for the animals and the half-dozen male servants. But for her special and more intimate needs, besides the three female attendants he had allocated in her dowry, her father also provided, in goods, in linens, and in silver coin, all that was necessary for the freed slave, who would accompany the little Bride as a personal maid.

To the astonishment of his neighbours, who had never suspected the extent of his wealth from the parsimony of his habits, and to the righteous indignation of his wife, who was driven to the limits of jealous petulance by his extravagance, he spared no expenses and economized on nothing in his preparation for this bridal journey. His daughter should be fit for a king and decked like a princess. For over a year, the seamstresses had come in a steady stream to the house, sewing little gold coins to the multilayered hems of her many petticoats. For over a year, an opulent trousseau had been prepared for her: sheets of pure damask silk and covers from Kashmir; exquisite carpets from Kashan and chests of silverware. She had a samovar of pure beaten gold from Russia and her mother's seed pearls, over two thousand and fifty-five, not counting the black pearls from Ceylon which had been laid aside for her on the day of her birth. She would want for nothing and would possess much more than she would ever use.

In addition to the luxuries intended for her personal pleasure, her father had prepared gifts too for the Turk: a chess set of ebony and ivory, a fine piece of calligraphy depicting the sun, in the name of the supreme deity, invocations to the Prophet illumined with azure blue and gold, a brocaded rug for wintry hours and several crates of sugared apricots, which he knew his daughter loved. Since the Turk was old and dropsical, there was no harm in planning for his daughter's widowhood. She would inherit everything: that at least he had succeeded in negotiating, and already he had his eye on the prospect of a prince from Rajastan for a second marriage. He might allow his darling to go far this once, but he intended that she would stay closer to home next time so he might benefit from grandchildren. His second wife, a neurotic woman, had not proved fertile.

There remained only the problem of the route. The quickest way from Kirman to Damascus would have been up the Persian Gulf and through Basrah across the Syrian desert. But this was not a well-worn pilgrimage route and to send a bride with her dowry all alone across the Najd wilderness would be madness. Normally, he would have sent her by land along the regular roads of Persian pilgrimage through the western provinces of the country and across Kirmanshah to Iraq. But recent turmoils of a religious nature in that region filled him with concern; there had been altercations in Karbila and Najaf between the Turkish and Persian authorities and he did not want his daughter trapped in Baghdad among narrow-minded

Shi'ias. The alternative route, south by sea, was even more problematic for after the tedious voyage it entailed an additional journey through the Arabian Desert. Though technically Muslims, it would be tempting fate for the Gebrs to come too close to the holy city of Mecca where they might be at the mercy of fanatical pilgrims who could suspect the Bride of being an infidel. Besides, there were equally worrisome rumours that the standard of revolt had been raised against the weakening Ottoman pashas by wild tribesmen in this region. The other long overland route, from the north through Tabriz and across Armenia, was not much safer, however. What should be done? Perhaps the wedding should be celebrated in Kirman so that the Bride might travel to her new home in Damascus under the protection of a husband?

When he ventured this suggestion, despite his wife's fit of sulks and the risk of losing an excellent bargaining position with the Turk, he was gratified by the latter's prompt response. The old man was determined for reasons he did not divulge to celebrate the wedding in Damascus and instantly sent word that he would seal his nuptials with his *hajj* and would himself provide safe custody for his bride through the terrors of Hijaz. He would escort her personally with pomp and privilege through Mecca and Medina, he promised. The desert, he said, would bloom as she passed. At that point the Zoroastrian stopped his dithering and decided to take the risk of sending his daughter by way of the sea route to Jiddah.

Since it was to be such a long journey, the Zoroastrian was determined to accompany his daughter as far as Bandar Abbas. This was where the boats from Bushire frequently stopped before rounding the Arabian Peninsula, and here he planned to bid her farewell and send her on her way through Muscat and Mocha with the pilgrims bound for Mecca. He set aside all his business dealings, allowed himself the luxury of losing his temper with his wife, and travelled in the *takhteravan* with his lovely daughter from Kirman to the humid port of Bandar Abbas. There he learned that the boats this winter would board pilgrims only at Langih, and so he was obliged to continue further up the coast and wait at this smaller port for her crossing to Arabia. At every step he extended his journey; at every stage he conceived of another excuse to delay his return. And all along the way he redoubled his doubts and his guilt.

The desert journey beyond Jiddah, after the sea voyage, gave the Zoroastrian much reason for concern. It was a route notorious for bandits and rife with fanatic Muslims. Despite the Turk's promises to be there to protect his gilded darling, he feared the worst. His days, as they waited for the next pilgrim boat, were itchy with anxiety; his nights, in the fetid port of Langih, were sweltering and sleepless. Should he continue with her further?

Owing to his second wife's machinations, and much to his private chagrin, he had found no male relative or trustworthy friend in the Zoroastrian community willing to act as his daughter's chaperone on this long journey. This was itself proof of the necessity of her marriage to the Turk, but was a source of hurt pride to her father. Cousins, even of the second and third category, were not forthcoming, nor any uncles whom he trusted. He feared treachery among the horsemen, guile among the guards and un-adulterated incompetence among the footmen accompanying the mule train. There was no one but he who could shoulder the delicate task of protecting the little Bride. There was no other person he could trust. But his affairs were in a critical condition at home and demanded his immediate return. He did not dare risk a longer absence. His wife was already in a frightful pique. What should he do? Being a rather ineffectual man and not gifted in the art of decision-making, the Zoroastrian spent a small fortune on sweet lemons for his daughter as he dithered once more over this dilemma. And they missed the boat.

His daughter was entirely oblivious to the crisis, however. All she wanted was baths. She drove her female attendants to distraction by demanding complicated ritual baths while they waited. Sucking on sweet lemons and afloat for hours among the rose petals, she lay languidly on her back in the Langih public baths and giggled helplessly as her maid painted the soles of her feet with scrolls and arabesques of henna. The Zoroastrian was obliged to pay for the use of the private apartments in the baths for seven consecutive days to accommodate her fastidiousness. It caused a scandal in the town that was remembered for decades. The people of Langih even incorporated the wonder of it into their local dialect and girls who lingered too long in their baths were scoffed at for years after as 'brides on their way to Damascus'.

Finally, when they had been waiting for another vessel in the unrelenting humidity for over a week, a dubious solution presented itself to the Zoroastrian during his last day in Langih. The Hindu from Bombay who had so badly cheated him before, introduced himself again through the intermediary offices of the local *kad-khuda*. Obsequious to the point of slime and behaving as if nothing at all had soured in their relationship, claiming to have resumed intimate business dealings with the Turk of Damascus and introducing himself as a moneychanger who was now, as it happened, on his way to Mecca, he offered to be a chaperone for the Zoroastrian's daughter and a private spy who would notify the worried father of their progress at every stage of the journey. He promised that he would devote himself to the safety of the little Bride, would sacrifice himself for her honour and would immediately tell her father if anything untoward occurred. In the unlikely event that there might be a crisis, he purred, he would send word immediately to Kirman and the Zoroastrian could dispatch a rescue party at once. At the very least. Or rather worst. He spoke in confidential Gujarati, in a repellent and conspiratorial fashion, so that none of the Arab sailors or Persian pilgrims might understand.

It was not an appealing solution nor one that provided much assurance to the uneasy Zoroastrian. Indeed, it entailed as many risks as it proposed to solve. But complex anxieties often beg for the simplest elucidations. He was prevailed upon to trust the fellow by the *kad-khuda*, who claimed that the Indian had undergone some kind of religious transformation since he knew him last. He insisted that the Hindu had become a holy man, almost. The Zoroastrian was a doting father and inclined to be blind. In his dread not to have done enough to protect his daughter, he made the fatal error of doing too much. He paid a handsome sum to the new-minted moneychanger, and unhappily committed his daughter to hands that were too smooth and waves that were too rough.

The only comfort to him was that the Bride had no visions of imminent disaster during this journey. On the contrary, she had seemed oblivious to discomfort and absurdly happy in the hot and dusty *takhteravan* with her father; she had giggled at the jolting mules and buzzing flies trapped by the gaudy striped silk curtains, and, once in Langih, had applied herself with unappeased zest to the

ritual baths and the sweet lemons. To her father's astonishment, she had not murmured a word against the Indian.
In fact, the night before he was offered this uncertain
proposition, she had what proved to be the last of her
visions for a while. She dreamed that the Spirit of Righteousness passed by bearing glad tidings and a simple
bargain.

'He'll cut out the tongues of all who wish to use their
eyes to see the truth,' she announced joyfully to the women
in the public bath the following day.

Despite her claim that this would be an irrefutably
efficacious method for resolving conflicts, the splendid
offer did not appear to attract many candidates for truth
among the ladies in the baths. The little Bride was rather
saddened that they were so disinclined to take it up. It was
the only time during her journey that she drooped and her
spirits seemed to be dashed.

Later that evening, when she heard that the Indian
would accompany them, she grew cheerful again, however,
and to her father's boundless relief made no objection to
the idea. She had no anticipatory dream that night of
manure or other forms of excrement, no warning vision
about being submerged in dirty water or drowning in silt.
Surely, thought her poor father, if anything untoward was
going to occur, she would have sensed it? Unlike her
sceptical mother, the Zoroastrian had unbounded faith
in his daughter's visions. He had even bargained with
the Turk on the strength of them, for he felt she was no
ordinary girl. She had been touched, he was convinced, by
the truth of fire, and the spiritual needed its material
expression, surely? She was only part human; the other
part was flame. And therefore expensive.

But it seemed the flaming part was quenched in her

during her bridal journey. Though the Spirit of Righteousness had offered a bargain of speech for insight, the
Bride appeared to have taken her cue from the other
women in the public baths, and chose to sacrifice her
visions to a stream of chatter. On her last day in the
company of her father, she was frivolous and full of foolish
fads, and behaved with the abysmal normality of any other
fourteen-year-old. Even when he finally bid her farewell on
board the cramped pilgrim boat bound for Jiddah, with her
entire entourage aboard a sister vessel which was carrying
twice its prescribed load, she neither trembled nor wept
nor gasped nor fell into a trance of palpitations, but smiled
at him prettily and showed a dimpled cheek as her father
turned away with an aching heart. In fact, she was incon-
ceivably callous, hardly indicating evidence of normal
sensitivities, let alone supersensory awareness. He was
relieved, in part. And sorely bewildered and sad at the
same time. The combination protected him from both
extremities.

During the dreadful voyage that ensued, when the
narrow *dhows* with their uncertain sails threatened at
any moment to capsize and one load of pistachios was
lost in the deeps, when their laboured progress from port
to port along the southern coast of the Peninsula was
delayed by storms and sailors who threatened mutiny
because their water had turned brackish, the little Bride
was so sick that her maid feared she might lose all consciousness, but she had not so much as a single vision.
Even when they arrived in Jiddah and found no evidence
of the Turk or his promised escort to accompany them to
Damascus, she seemed quite unperturbed. It was a very
grave situation, grave enough, certainly, to merit some
premonitory dream, some visionary insight. But none was

forthcoming from the usual quarter. The Indian made great show of sending messages in all directions but no replies came from the Bride's familiars. When there was an uproar among the devout Muslim pilgrims as a result of the delay caused by the bridal train, the girl still remained untroubled. Finally, when the Indian claimed that the Turk wanted his bride to proceed directly to Mecca in spite of the dangers, she accepted this suspect instruction too without a single tremor. It was as though her angels had deserted her.

They were just about to leave for Mecca when a dashing escort of Ottoman infantry appeared on the horizon, with a fanfare of trumpets and enviable self-regard. They stated that the Turk had already performed his *hajj* and completed his pilgrimage while the Bride had been delayed in Langih, and that he was now in Medina, waiting for her to join him. They announced they had been instructed to escort her to his eminence along a detour that, for reasons of security, skirted safely round the sacred city. And much to the Indian's discomfiture and in flat contradiction to his claims, they produced sealed documents to the effect that she should on no account proceed into the sacred city itself without the protection of his person.

Although this clarified certain matters, it complicated others. Since the main caravan had by then already left for Mecca without them, the idea of taking the dangerous desert detour alone made the Turkish escort nervous and highly susceptible to the Indian's suggestions. The ways were wild and dangerous, he averred, and they were vulnerable to reprisals from the tribesmen at every pass. They had to guard the honour of the Bride, certainly, but should their honour not be protected too? The Turkish soldiers thought it should, and so at the last minute the

Indian convinced them to have bodyguards themselves, which he naturally proposed to find. As a result, there were more delays.

But the little Bride was as light-hearted as a songbird and not in the least disturbed by this further deferment. She simply took advantage of the procrastinations to have a second round of baths. Jiddah provided a wider choice and much better quality of public baths than Langih, and she established her residence in some of the most elegant near the city gates of Bab Mecca. They were spacious and light-filled and famous at the time for their indigo-blue tiles. To her maid's consternation she ordered that several loads of sugared apricots be sold in order to pay for a particularly pretty little private alcove of white marble which she established as her own. Here she had her hair re-dyed with henna and arranged that all her bodily hairs be carefully plucked in preparation for her wedding night. And here, smooth as a new-laid egg, she held forth for several hours each day, in quaint Arabic, on the subject of cleanliness, to the astonishment of dozens of Jiddah housewives. It was at this time, too, that she stopped eating garlic and refused any more meat. She also developed a strong antipathy towards the *qualun*, to which the Indian was especially partial. But despite her squeamishness, to her maid's mounting annoyance she never said a word against that odious man nor expressed any qualms about the sincerity of his motives or his reasons for creating this delay.

The maid herself had begun to betray signs of nervousness as the days went by and could ill conceal her revulsion against the Indian. She had irritated him, in turn, by seeking out the leader of the Turkish escort and urging greater haste. Finally, when the Indian's prices were too high for the Turks, her appeals were heeded at last.

Economics compelled action where a woman's words could not. One week after the pilgrim caravan had left Jiddah without them, the bridal train and its skittish escort embarked on a wide detour around Mecca with the intention of joining the pilgrims on the other side of the holy city. They travelled ignominiously in the wake of a small trade caravan along the unfrequented camel route to the northwest of Mecca, expecting to encounter bandits and robbers and wild tribesmen all the way. And they had no bodyguards. But the Bride was perfectly placid about these arrangements too.

The conditions of travel were extremely difficult along this route and baths were soon a mirage in the memory. There were no *khans*, no flea-infested caravanserais where they could lodge at night beneath the crumbling arches constructed in a quadrangle around a central well. There were no mud brick rooms where the bridal party could take refuge from marauding tribes, men holed above and beasts below. Instead they were obliged to camp under the open sky, at the mercy of the elements, huddled close to the trade caravan for protection. Some of their supplies of fuel and food found their way mysteriously into the personal baggage of the camel drivers, to the mounting irritation of the Indian, and their camels too became ill-tempered and fractious, for watering holes were few and far between. It was very uncomfortable.

But the Bride hardly seemed to care. Her maid was disconcerted by her serenity. She had expected the girl to fuss and fret at every turn, had dreaded that her angels would make impossible demands, was ready each day that she would require them to empty all the water skins for her personal convenience, but the little Bride never made a murmur of complaint. Although she had no more than a cup of tepid liquid for her needs each day, she still had no premonitions of disaster. She had no dream and no fainting fit until they had bypassed the holy of holies; she had no vision of any kind until after they had joined the main caravan that was travelling from Mecca to Medina with its usual freight of pilgrims, dead and alive. She gave no sign of physical discomfort or mystical awareness until the fourth morning of their journey, a few hours after they had left the caravanserai of Khulays. At that point, with her shriek and subsequent swoon, the entire entourage, corpse and camels and all, were obliged to halt. For that was when she saw the angel falling.

When her maid had chafed her temples with eucalyptus balm and brought her back to her senses with a sniff of *arak*, the little Bride tossed about in her stuffy *takhteravan*, writhing and delirious. Some strange consuming passion seemed to have taken hold of her. Her eyes dilated, her hair unravelled and was drenched in sweat. She was hysterical, wildly excited. Nothing could calm her. She claimed that an angel had fallen from heaven to bring a message to her. She insisted that the message was waiting for her at a well. She said that it was vital that she read it, quickly, now, without delay, for the angel had brought her tidings from the saviour Saoshyant. And he was waiting, waiting for her, in the midmost heart of the frostbound mountains up ahead.

'He has left a message for me where the dead and the living drink together!' she wept. 'He has remembered me in this, his latter manifestation! And I am unprepared!'

She insisted that her maid should send for the message immediately. If she lost her chance to read the angel's message, she shrieked, her whole life would have been wasted. She would go mad instantly. Breathless, spent with her own screams, she whispered to her maid that she had seen the angel's face, she had seen his wings, they had touched her body, all over. Look! And she ripped the pearl buttons off her little blouse to expose the budding breasts, aroused and pink with desire. When the maid tried to soothe her agitation, she shrieked again and swooned in her arms, shuddering from head to foot like one possessed.

Despite her vigilance beforehand, the poor woman had not reckoned with a crisis such as this, in such a time and place. The drivers were losing patience and the wealthy passengers were calling for explanations as their camels sneezed and snorted in the sun; the poorer pilgrims were having difficulty with their braying donkeys and the mule train had lost its direction. The caravan had to go on. A group of footmen, who had been employed to guard a stinking corpse which was being taken from Mecca to the cemetery of 'al Baqr, together with its offerings for the holy priests, began shouting abuse. The emasculated Indian had ridden close to the *takhteravan* and was talking in Gujarati through the curtain, asking in a wheedling voice if the *khanum* was all right. A young Shi'ia priest, who had distinguished himself from the other pilgrims by his insufferable arrogance and fanaticism, dismounted from his camel and was beginning to hover rather too close for comfort, complaining about women who overstepped the bounds of propriety. Finally, the leader of the caravan pushed roughly through the bridal train to enquire, gruffly, the reason for this unscheduled halt, and at that point the maid, in desperation, was at last obliged to place a sliver of quince drenched in opium syrup under the tongue of the girl to quiet her down. It was only a tiny dose, just enough to calm her for the next hour. Her shrieks were too coherent.

There was indeed a well, the caravan leader stated flatly, a disused well in a ruined shrine in the valley up ahead, nothing more, but they could pause there briefly to accommodate the ladies' needs. It could not be for long, however, because the evening caravanserai was still some hours away, and there was a chance of dust storms. The winds that whistled through the mountain passes they could see looming on the horizon could be treacherous. The paths were strait and narrow up there, and the caravan would have to move slowly, one beast at a time, so he could not afford to linger long. But he promised they would stop.

Before sinking into a stupor, the Bride made her maid promise to send someone ahead, quickly. She begged her to send someone to find the message from the angel at the well. She made her swear, on her life, that she would do it. 'Tell him that I am ready though I'm not yet prepared!' she breathed, and her head lolled on the cushions like a lily on a broken stem as the caravan began to wend its way forward, slowly through the steaming mounds of camel droppings.

Just before midday, the caravan arrived at the well a bare *farsang* beyond. It proved to be neither disused nor dry. To the caravan leader's surprise there was a newly dug well near the old shrine, which afforded cool, sweet water. Scanning the horizon anxiously, he gave orders for a pause of one hour. They should avail themselves of this unexpected blessing and fill the water skins, but they could not stay longer to water all the animals, as a dust cloud was approaching. He wanted to press on through the craggy passes ahead before the day's light dimmed.

When the caravan stopped, the Bride revived from her opium haze and, to her maid's consternation, the memory of the angel had survived intact. She showed no signs of having bitten her tongue and was not foaming at the mouth but the fit had passed without being forgotten. In fact, she had become fiercely lucid. She was no longer hysterical but impatient for the sequel of the vision. She had no doubt of its urgent significance and she enquired immediately if her maid had kept her promise and retrieved the message from the well.

What next ensued was inexplicable, though the Bride showed no astonishment. Whenever the maid thought of it during the course of that day, she could not repress her shudders at the girl's uncanny prescience. There was indeed a message for her, from the angel, in a saddlebag. And it was carried by the eunuch.

Despite this unlikely conjunction of circumstances, the Bride accepted the saddlebag in a manner that seemed to suggest that the Indian had been put on earth to carry messages from angels; he existed for this purpose alone. She gave him an imperceptible nod and stretched her arms out wordlessly to receive it as her maid lifted the curtains of the litter. She barely even glanced at him as she clasped its dusty leather flaps and broken straps close to her breast. She did not waste a single breath on thanks, as though it were self-evident that such a deed as his bestowed its own reward. The fellow seemed tongue-tied anyway. After he handed over the saddlebag, he stumbled from the *takhteravan* and was never seen again.

There were some dozens of messages inside the saddlebag, all wrapped in silk and bound with twine. The little Bride pressed one of them to her lips, muttering feverishly. She tore the twine so savagely that it cut her tender fingers and the sheets of paper, when she spread them on her lap, were smeared with her blood. There were pages and pages in the little packet, covered in fine, whispering calligraphy.

Touching them lingeringly, the girl became utterly tranquil and calm. The rage was gone. A quiet descended on her spirit, like a balm.

She commanded the maid to leave her in solitude, refusing all offers of food and only accepting to drink water from the well. She ordered her to prepare the copper bathing bowls and warm the well water for a ritual bath. She said that she wished to administer the most complicated procedures of absolution and purification to her body now. Immediately. In the middle of the desert. And then she closed herself in her *takhteravan*, and read the pages from the angel alone.

The Bride's instructions were followed to the letter. Water was drawn up from the well and a fire was made in the ruined shrine, out of the wind. To the surprise and comment of all, perfumed odours from a bridal bath rose in the middle of the desert. The moist miracle of orange blossom encircled everyone in a cloud of sacredness. It was a fragrant sacrifice of wasted tenderness, a fragile ceremony tossed lightly into the arid air, lingering much longer in the mind than the perfume itself remained among the undulating dunes. The relief it offered would not be forgotten by those who lived to remember it.

But the procedures were complicated and could not be completed before the signal came for the caravan to start up again. At that point, the Bride insisted on continuing the rituals, whatever the circumstances. She ordered her maid to set up the bathing bowls right there in the jolting *takhteravan* with nothing but a swaying curtain between her nakedness and the world. It was inconceivable that there be any further delay; the purification rites had to continue, she said. The pungent odours of perfumed oil and water were so strong inside the *takhteravan* that they quite overpowered the stench of the corpse. And the preparations were so all-consuming that every other concern was utterly forgotten for the next three hours. Nothing could distract the little Bride from her task.

Not even a sandstorm.

For the caravan had not travelled more than a *farsang* further when a sandstorm hit them and they were brought to a halt for the third time that day. But even this additional disturbance had no effect on the young girl's concentration. It seemed that the very elements conjoined with her to uproot all other thoughts and notions from the mind and efface all memories of the past in preparation for some new and terrible beauty. Buffeted by the sandstorm, and barely barricaded against it, she stripped and washed herself meticulously in the dusky light inside the *takhteravan*, spilling water all over the embroidered quilts and silken cushions as they swayed and staggered at the mercy of the wind. And when the bath was over and her fingers and toes had been freshened with henna, she insisted that her maid roll up the silks and satins and throw away the cloths and covers of her *takhteravan*, throw them all out with the water, by the wayside. For they were soiled and spoiled now, she insisted, they were wet and unworthy for her purposes. They were tainted with her old self, she said, and should not sully her new soul.

When the maid tried briefly to reason with her, tried gently to remind her that these silks and satins were part of her dowry, that they were priceless and rare, that it was the custom for a girl to treasure these embroidered cloths till she could pass them on to her own daughter, the Bride became pale and angry. She raised a small peremptory hand, the tips of whose fingers were bright as flames, and slapped the older woman's pockmarked face. She told her shrilly to hold her tongue. The maid did not utter one word in protest but bent over, doubled up with pain. The slap had been slight but it seemed to have stunned her, broken her in half. The little Bride looked at her coldly for several moments, without any sign of remorse.

'The time has come to change the customs,' she said crisply.

Then, with her flaming hand still raised, she gave a flick of a slender wrist that sent six months of labour and several hundred yards of embroidered damask out into the storm. She had always been hard to discipline, hard to control, but this new tyranny was something more than adolescence, something worse than mere wilfulness. Even her angels had been mild compared to this. There was a terrible certitude in her decisions, a fearful and absolute conviction in her commands that caused her maid to shake with trepidation.

After she had thrown the sodden cloths and bathing bowls away, the Bride ordered the woman to search among the huddled mules in the blinding wind and sand in order to retrieve the wedding sheets from their careful bundles and packages. She ordered her to spread them out in the *takhteravan* instead of the old cloths she had rolled away: wedding sheets spun from the busy silkworms that had fed on the fat mulberries of Kirman, silk wedding sheets all laced with bay leaves and cardamom to protect them against the onslaught of moths in the Syrian hills. Then, as the *takhteravan* rocked under the howling storm, she lay down on the sheets and anointed herself in all her private places. As the wind whipped the sand against the huddled caravan, she decked herself in her gowns and trousers, layer upon layer, coin after jingling coin. Finally she submitted her long, tangled hair to the oils and combs to be twisted and coiled into bridal braids. Her maid, as she dressed the gorgeous locks and threaded them with seed pearls, was trembling so much and was so distraught that the little Bride was obliged, finally, to take her hands in her own and murmur endearments to her. She pressed those thin, cold fingers in her little flaming ones, and kissed them till the older woman became calmer.

She asked her maid to forgive her then, for all her former and more recent tyrannies, for all her unjust actions and her many cruelties. This new turn was more terrifying to the woman than any of the fits and phases she had had before. The child included everything but the slapped cheek in her litany. With this notable omission, there was not one act of callousness that she did not remember. With deadly accuracy, she enumerated all the petty and unreasonable demands she had made of her maid since the age of nine, she reminded her of all the times she had stamped her foot and screamed at the parrots and thrown the carp out of the courtyard pool. And she asked her maid's forgiveness for each and every one of these acts of selfishness. Kissing the chill and narrow hands of the trembling Abyssinian, the little Bride told her that if she were not forgiven, she would be unworthy of the angel. If she were not forgiven, it would be as if the baths had been wasted and the soiled satins had left their taint upon her. And at that point she hung her head in silent shame. Knowing that if the bright tears began to roll, the antimony would have to be repainted round her lovely eyes, the maid forgave her, with all her heart.

When the Bride was ready, it was one hour before sunset. The storm had finally begun to show some signs of abating its fury. She sat serene in the *takhteravan* with the wind still screaming round her and her maid shaking at her feet. Her hair was coiled about her head, her body was

51

perfumed and in her right hand lay a bundle of silk in which was wrapped a sheaf of papers. It was the angel's message. The writing on the paper bore the seal of the Promised One.

The angel, she told her maid, with exquisite patience – for the woman seemed on the verge of nervous collapse and the girl was obliged to speak to her very gently, very quietly now, so as not to ruffle her disturbed spirits any more than they already were – the angel, she repeated, had told her to be ready for his summons. He had told her, in his message, that the world had entered upon the fourth epoch and Saoshyant was at hand. He was sending a messenger to bring her to the presence of the saviour, for the struggle between good and evil was finally over. She was at pains to explain to the maid that since it had taken nine millennia to reach this single, sacred moment in history, the least she could have done was to be fully and entirely prepared. And having completed her explanation, she kissed her maid on the lips, placed a carnelian ring on her little finger that was as radiant as clear tea, and bid the shaking woman farewell. Then she commanded her to rejoice, for the only reason ever to weep again in this world would be if Saoshyant did not remember to send for her.

Her maid's love was absolute. Moulded from the clay of obedience, she was faithful to her mistress in this last command as well, and pressing her face against the curtain of the *takhteravan*, she began to laugh hysterically.

When the bandits descended like another storm down the slopes of the ravine, just as the sun's bleary eye was setting through the veils of sand, the Bride was ready. When they attacked the caravan several *farsangs* beyond the ruined well in the last rage of the howling wind, she was waiting. She was dressed and perfumed, sitting quiet at the heart of the tempest, and prepared. Calm as a plucked peach, she turned her green eyes edged with antimony towards her maid and simply said, 'You see, he did not forget!'

What her maid saw in the gathering dusk under the distorted moon were horrors without name. As the torches began to flare, she lifted the silken curtains on a thousand gleaming teeth and axes of a thousand savage men. Nine millennia of struggle between good and evil could not have contained the hell she saw. What her maid heard through the whine of the sandstorm were the voices of the damned at the end of time, and her own shrieks were loud among them. Nor as she choked with fear in the darkness could she not avoid the heavy blow of the bandit who rode by like a fury and felled her from the *takhteravan*. But the little Bride noticed none of these things. She heard only the Trumpets of Righteousness announcing the arrival of the King of kings. She saw only the lights of the Concourse, and the Hosts of the angels gathered to dance at her wedding feast. And her heart sang with joy.

When the whooping bandits surrounded the *takhteravan*, the maid had already been laid low beneath the trampling hooves of the terror-stricken mules and did not see how the chieftain's eyes glinted as he looked within and found the little Bride waiting. She did not see what would have been worse than death for her to see, the violation of her lovely girl. But she did not see either what might have raised her, in astonishment, from the dead who lay groaning all around her: she did not see the girl's expression as she lay back on the silken cushions, waiting for life and death to come for her.

When the Bride saw the chieftain, she instantly recognized the messenger sent by the angel who had fallen from the sky above her. She knew he was sent from Saoshyant, the saviour of the world, and was coming to take her to her lord. In his gleaming eyes she saw her saviour poised in the midmost heart of a frostbound mountain. In his straight limbs she saw him moving along a middle path in this, his latter manifestation. On his right the People of Righteousness; on his left the People of the Lie; and she was ready to throw herself beneath his feet. She saw a flame before him that she knew was God, Ahura Mazdah, and a shadow behind him that she knew was Ahriman, and she wanted to be all that lay between. He was a mirror placed before the sun and she believed in him. He was crystal placed before the fire and she accepted him. He asked nothing of her that she did not instantly desire. He said nothing to her that she did not intimately understand. Like a mass of ruby, tender and vibrant, she saw Saoshyant leaning forward to embrace her soul, and she knew she would die to be the ring of creation on the finger of just one of his servants. As the chieftain pushed apart the curtains of the *takhteravan*, at the turning point of the ninth millennium, in the fourth epoch of time, she offered herself to him with all her heart, that he might take her to her well-beloved, instantly.

Confounded by the expression on her face and the look in her eyes, which he was destined to remember all his days, the chieftain slit her throat and backed out of the *takhteravan* with a vulgar oath. He seized a torch which smouldered on a heap of slaughtered donkeys and within seconds had set the *takhteravan* on fire. As the flames lapped up the curtains, and the water skins began to hiss and steam, he strode away, his nostrils scorched with the perfume of unprecedented shame. But not before he had given a staggering blow to the head of a dead man lying

wrapped in his winding sheets nearby. He would afterwards, and with some surprise, remember that inglorious
incident in which he killed a corpse because he could not
rape a virgin.

A laden mule sneezed nearby, shook its head with a faint
jangle of harness and flattened its ears as the smoke of the
Bride's *takhteravan* engulfed it. Surprised by the pungent
odours, it turned aside as the chieftain blundered past;
unseen by the bandits, it nosed its way into the darkness of
the dunes. And thus, by a miracle of martyred perfume in
the desert, it suppressed the instinct to bray and escaped
being disembowelled.

THE CHIEFTAIN

T he next day, when the Chieftain looked for the
broken body of the Bedouin down in the gully, he
found a heap of charred ash and the remnants of burned
bones. Indecipherable. And the saddlebag was nowhere to
be seen.

The Bedouin had always been something of a cipher for
the Chieftain, an enigma, a riddle. He had never known
how to read this guide of his, although in other respects he
considered himself to be a knowing man. He certainly
knew the weaknesses of other men. He had been told once
that he was born under a fortunate star and had always
believed this to be true, though he prided himself on
commanding the stars rather than conforming to them.
Women feared him, men obeyed him and leadership was
his destiny. And this, he felt, was due to his own will and
effort, nothing else. He owed no one anything, for his life
had been hard.

As a young man he had been bound in service to a
ruthless sheikh for several years and once, in a fit of wild
fury, he had killed a man and had been forced to flee for his
life. After that, he determined none should give him orders.
And he roamed the lonely passes looking for revenge

against the rich and powerful, for he was set on having his own sheikhdom in the wilds where he would be the one who gave the orders. As time passed, he gathered a band of reckless ruffians round him whom desperation had made outlaws, but whom fortune had not graced with a similar will to power. They were his thralls and he became not only his own lord, but theirs as well. It was gratifying, but not a matter of surprise. He expected no less from life than to determine it.

He had a quick wit, a clear mind, a strong body and teeth as white as his beard was dark. Although he had reached his fortieth year, there was not a grey hair on his head and he had collected concubines from all his raids who were fairer than any found in the sheikh's palaces. He had strong men in his tribe, too, who were willing to die at a word from him. And for years now he could plunder pilgrims along the roads between Mecca and Medina because he had a Bedouin guide who knew the secrets of the dunes. His Bedouin could lead him to his prize before his rivals even knew there was one, and could bring him out of danger before his victims even knew they had been robbed. This was probably why he had the reputation of being a knowing man. But he could never fathom the nature of the Bedouin. It was a mystery to him.

When this guide abandoned him one night and vanished into the desert, the Chieftain felt a fear in his heart that came from somewhere deeper than the dread of danger: he began to doubt, for the first time, that the stars were at his command. He had trusted this lizard of the desert. He had honoured him and planned to give him special gifts that would tie his wandering spirit irrevocably to his own. It filled his mouth with bitterness and his throat with gall to remember that he had even permitted the slave to drink from his own cup the night he ran away. He had wanted to manacle this man to his service forever but something in the Bedouin eluded him. Something in him escaped the Chieftain's control. The rest of his men were servile, but not this one. He could not put his finger on it, for the fellow was weak-limbed and lily-livered when it came to physical combat. He had no guts to fight, no heart for blood. He could not even ride a horse. But he could run.

After the Bedouin's desertion, the Chieftain swore to take revenge but did not really believe in his own oaths. He knew the Bedouin had never been among his followers; he had not violated any trust. He had been their amulet, their token of good fortune, like a gift. But he had never been possessed. Why he should desert them now, at such a time, when they had the possibility of rich booty waiting for them, was a mystery that filled the Chieftain with foreboding.

But there were gains ahead of them, and the rest of his men were still his thralls, despite this enigmatic loss. A fabulously laden caravan was expected and although the rumours were contradictory, the Chieftain did not want to lose any opportunities. There was talk of a bridal train crossing the desert by the camel routes from Jiddah and a corpse coming from Mecca; there was some talk too of a merchant, but no one was certain whether the purpose of the latter was trade or the *hajj*. No one was sure when the caravan was expected to reach the coastal road to Rabigh, either, because of delays. But the Chieftain had his eye on the dowry of the bride and the goods accompanying the corpse to heaven. And even though the extent of the merchant's wealth was uncertain, he was determined to ambush the caravan at a time and place where he had every possible advantage and where nothing would be left to chance.

The bandits had plotted with their Bedouin guide to set an ambush one hour before sunset some *farsangs* from the mountains of Dafdaf and the valley of Khulays. It was a perfect place and isolated between two caravanserais, or *khans*, on the road between the holy cities; it lay along a narrow pass in the mountains from which they had access through secret paths across the dunes directly to their camp. There would be no chance of assistance from Khulays and little possibility, at such a time, of rescue from the *khan* of Towal either, the coastal caravanserai where caravans camped at the crossroads to Medina. The Bedouin had been the one who suggested this place and time of ambush and the Chieftain saw no reason to change these plans, even after he found that his guide had vanished.

To overcome his doubts and give the appearance of an independent decision, however, he made immediate plans to double-check the details of the ambush. He ordered some of the bandits to ride into the mountains of Dafdaf to warn him if any travellers were coming from Jiddah and Mecca. The small caravanserai at Khulays was the fourth stop on the road from Mecca, and this was where he sent his scouts. He also sent a few men on towards the fifth stop, at Towal, to alert him in case anyone was approaching from the direction of the coast. He would wait, he told them, at the ambush point, in the windy mountain passes of Dafdaf, in full command of the situation. There would be time enough for revenge later. Let the traitor be pursued by his own fantasies first before he felt the edge of the knife. The Bedouin was a fool, he said; he might have become wealthy from this raid, had he stayed with them.

For three nights and days he and his men waited for the merchant and his caravan in the appointed place. For three nights and days they did not pursue the guide who had abandoned them. But no one of any significance passed by. True, word did come back on the third night from his scouting party that certain travellers had arrived at the *khan* of Khulays on the road from Mecca, but these were evidently pilgrims from their white robes and seemed not to match the description the Chieftain had been led to expect. There was no rich merchant, apparently, no sign of any accompanying train of donkeys, and only one camel. The saddlebag with which it was loaded appeared to be of little significance and the travellers were carrying only the barest provisions for the journey: a bundle of charcoal, a kettle, a bag of dates and a sagging water skin. He ordered his men to let them proceed on their pilgrimage undisturbed.

He was growing impatient, however, and rode up to join the scouting party himself that third night. They hid one *farsang* away from the *khan* of Khulays. Not in the usual place the Bedouin guide had shown them, at the ruined shrine of Abwa' beside the new well, but on the other side of the valley, at the foot of a high cliff under the mountains of Dafdaf. It was always deep in shadow there, the Chieftain said, and safer.

On the fourth dawn, he saw the three travellers dismounting beside the ruin across the gully. They had doubtless left the caravanserai in the cool hour before dawn and appeared to be preparing for their morning prayers at the well. They were, as had been reported, poor and insignificant. Although the black servant accompanying the pilgrims on the loaded mule may have brought a good price in the markets, the Chief had already sold enough slaves that year, and there was talk of the trade lessening. The youth who walked had bleeding feet and the one mounted on the camel in pilgrim's robes was worth nothing at all, despite the greenness of his turban which denoted some presumptive lineage with the Prophet. The Chieftain signalled silently to his men that they should be left in peace.

But as the pilgrims prostrated themselves in prayer, a shadow stole out from behind the ruined shrine. A thin, scrawny shadow, ragged and dark. A shadow with a long arm and legs that melted like a mirage. It seized the saddlebag lying on the sand beside the prostrate pilgrims and then, to the consternation of the bandits and the fascination of their Chief, ran straight towards them. It was the Bedouin! He was running at them with the saddlebag in his arms! Either he's a fool, the Chieftain thought, to be risking his life for a bag of pious papers. Or he's faithful after all, and is bringing the booty back to me.

The bandits muttered nervously among themselves. The Bedouin would be upon them in a few seconds. He would draw the attention of the travellers to them! The Chieftain signalled that they stay motionless among the early morning shadows. Had the thief seen them? But he ran on. He did not stop. He was talking wildly to himself, in gulping, incoherent phrases. He seemed unaware of their presence and was certainly not behaving like a hunting hawk returning to his masters. The bandits stirred to attack. Again the Chieftain made the signal not to move, as they seethed impatiently. The thief ran so close to them that they could see the whites of his eyes; they could hear his panting.

The Chieftain watched, hewn out of stone. Nothing moved but the circle of his eyes. The travellers had let the thief go. They were obviously more interested in prayer than in pursuit. Even the black servant did not persist in his chase. His assessment was right, the saddlebag was worthless. But why had his guide deserted him to so little purpose? Was this some folly or a more nefarious design? He could never be sure with that subtle Bedouin.

His followers fretted in bewilderment. Why was their Chief letting the fellow escape? Why was he behaving like the pilgrims? Why had he not ordered them to seize the guide and kill the traitor on the spot? Even if the saddlebag was worthless, what about revenge? They smouldered, sensing injustice, jealous of preferences, afraid.

But the Chieftain had a longer tooth for revenge than anything as simple as a stab in the back. He watched intently as the Bedouin strapped the saddlebag to his back. He watched, implacably, as the fellow began to scramble up the side of the cliff, his feet slipping on the slope. A cruel, lazy smile spread across his lips as he watched. The Bedouin climbed upwards, painfully and slowly. The cliff-side was almost vertical. The rubble gave way under his feet. He was scrambling on all fours, clinging to the unforgiving rock face, babbling to himself, cursing. The line hardened along the Chieftain's jaw and fixed his eyes like sculpted rock; the smile left a scar on his face, almost as grim and ruthless as the cliff itself. If he had loved a little, he was able to hate a great deal more. 'So,' he murmured through set teeth, 'the little sand snake tried to cheat me, did he? He thought he'd slip out of my hands as easily as he fell out of the palms of pilgrims? Let him rot and be picked by vultures for as long as it takes for him to realize his folly!'

He spat a silent oath at the rocks and whispered swift orders to his men. He would follow the Bedouin secretly from behind; he would climb up the cliff face after him, he told them. Let them ride like the wind through the short-cuts of the mountain defiles round to the other side of this cliff of Al Daf, and let the whole gang gather as silently as owls at the top. If the traitor heard him following, he would trip his heels and dangle him from the rocks above. If he succeeded in following him without his knowledge, they would know where the traitor was hiding and could slit his throat when he least expected it.

Disconcerted by his savage looks and disoriented by the events, the bandits did not dare remind him of the caravan or the raid. When their Chieftain gave orders, they were to be obeyed.

By the time the thief clambered into his cave, the Chieftain had him trapped to perfection. He had waited until the Bedouin had disappeared into the rock face and was safely hidden in his cave before he had worked his way round to the clifftop after him. There he had joined his men and had brought them where he knew the thief's hideaway was situated. It was a sweet revenge indeed, for the fugitive could not come out without being butchered and his only other choice was to starve to death in the hole below. The Chieftain saw no third alternative.

A treacherous creature, that Bedouin guide. As slippery as a hot snake in the rocks. He had never understood him after all, pondered the Chieftain. When the incomprehensible fellow flung himself and his saddlebag over the cliff, all possibilities of revenge evaporated.

The Chieftain was left at the mercy of his doubts. Why the man had chosen to destroy himself in such a fashion and to take a worthless piece of leather with him was a mystery that was even deeper than his desertion in the first place. Why he had tied his life to this piece of horsehide only to pitch them both into the abyss was beyond all logic or reason. What in the world was in this saddlebag that he should so covet it? Either he had lost his wits or else there was more to that bag than met the eye, after all. The

Chieftain felt a sickening jolt as he watched his guide crash on the rocks below. An unpleasant taste soured his mouth as he realized what a fool he had been. That saddlebag must be filled with treasure!

At that very moment something else caught his attention, glinting on the far horizon. There was a blemish moving on the distant dunes. There was something forgotten approaching along the route from Mecca, at the turn in the road from Khulays. Only then, as he sensed the treasure of the Bedouin slip from his grasp, did he remember the far greater treasure he had been expecting. There was the promised booty they had been waiting for! There was the gold that could wink out the sun! By the looks of it, they might be lucky enough to find a corpse on board, and that meant wealth enough. And those gaudy litters could only be a bride's, and that meant dowry gifts. The caravan!

So fierce had been his thirst for vengeance and so deep the doubt caused in him by his guide's desertion that he had quite forgotten the caravan till that moment. It must have halted for the night in the desert before arriving at Khulays, or else reached the small caravanserai after his scouts had taken shelter under the cliffs. Now it was only half a *farsang* away, if his eyes did not deceive him. They should be down below, poised at this very moment and ready to attack. There was not a moment to waste! They might lose their chance for ever if they were seen from up here.

Reckless with a sense of impotence with which he was not familiar, he ordered his men to ride hard through the dangerous mountain passes of Dafdaf and come back around the foot of the cliff across the *wadi* from the well. He gave no further thought to the Bedouin or the saddlebag. They would have to launch an attack at the well itself, immediately, in case they had been seen. They would have to change their plans and attack then and there, he said, at the ruin of Abwa'. There was no other choice. It was not half as good a place for an ambush, but it was too late to follow their first plan now. He would divide his men and they would attack the caravan from both sides of the *wadi*. He hazarded a guess that even if they had been seen, the caravan would not have the time to prepare properly to defend itself. But he had lost his best advantage and the risks were great. He cursed his lack of judgement in following the Bedouin.

By the time they rode round the mountains and reached the well in the valley of Khulays, he expected the caravan to be upon them. Judging from its distance and their speed, it should arrive at any moment. He split the band in two and waited on the two sides of the *wadi*. In silence and with beating hearts, they watched the horizon. No one came. Still they waited for another half an hour. Still nothing.

This was inconceivable! Had they missed it? Had the caravan leaders seen them when they stood exposed on the high cliffs and taken a detour to avoid the ruined shrine? Had they turned north and cut across the desert on the unfrequented camel routes towards Buraykah and Hamamah where he knew the tribesmen of Harb were often lurking? And would he therefore lose this booty to his rivals? The Chieftain ground his fine white teeth in rage against the Bedouin – may his body feed the carrion birds! The collapse of his plans was all the fault of that fellow. Why, they would have all been ready and he would have been in perfect control of the situation but for this lizard who lured them from their place of ambush. Was it possible that they had missed an opportunity to raid a jewel of a caravan, stocked with barrels of oil and bags of rice, goods fit for a bride and bribes enough to send a corpse to heaven, just because of some fool's gold of a saddlebag?

Without losing another moment, he sent two scouts to double-check in both directions once again: one towards Mecca, the other towards Medina. And once again he waited for what felt like an eternity.

On the road going to Medina, his scouts reported breathlessly, there were only the same three travellers of this morning, still several *farsangs* away from the caravanserai of Towal; but on the road to Mecca the caravan had been spied, standing stock still in the middle of the desert, just half a *farsang* away from the *khan* of Khulays. It had pulled up short under the beetling brow of the mountains of Dafdaf and stalled there. It had not moved from where they had seen it from the top of the cliff.

The Chieftain was disturbed. Why this unscheduled stop? Why had they called a halt between the regular caravanserais? Was it an omen? Did it play into his hands or was it a sign that something had slipped out of them? He narrowed his eyes and looked across to the other side of the valley, beneath the sharp escarpment of the overhanging cliff. He could not see anything from where he was, because of the shadows among the rocks at the foot of the mountain, but the carrion birds were circling high above. He was satisfied. It was a good omen. The booty still lay within his grasp. He ordered his men to wait and scanned the eastern horizon with mounting excitement. Any moment now the prize would come!

But instead of the train of camels and donkeys, instead of the soldiers and guards and pilgrims the bandits were expecting, instead of the caravan, a single man appeared on the horizon. As he drew near, the Chieftain saw it was a short, fat man riding a mule. The mule appeared to be charged with no other bags, no other load, than the considerable one posed by the rider himself. It was a man with an unsettled air who looked frequently about him. He scanned the red-rock mountain range of Dafdaf to the left and peered at the white, hot valley dunes of Khulays to the right. He seemed not to know where he was heading.

The Chieftain watched suspiciously as he drew close to the well. The fellow seemed nervous and cast repeated glances towards the shadows under the cliffs. He muttered to himself and swore aloud. Then he drew out a drinking bottle of some sort from his pockets and gulped it down and turned his mule towards the very spot where the Bedouin's shattered body must be lying.

The Chieftain and his men shifted uneasily. Where was this man going? Why was he heading for the cliff? Did he know something about that saddlebag? Or the Bedouin? As he began to clop away, the Chieftain gave the signal for two of the bandits to pin him down. Alive.

They dragged the fellow kicking and crying into the ruined shrine, together with his mule, and began to question him. He seemed to be a foreigner, neither Arab nor Persian nor Christian nor Jew, and he was clearly terrified. His protruding eyes rolled about in his head as he gaped at the Chieftain; his chins shuddered as he goggled from one bandit to another; his mouth drooled saliva as he struggled to speak, for they had caught him and held him tightly by the throat. He was just a humble moneychanger, a poor honest Sunni from Karachi, he gasped, on his way from his *hajj* at the most holy of holies. He was just a simple man who wanted to pay his respects at the shrine of Medina. May God strike him dead if he lied, but truly he had abjured his trade in order to purify himself for pilgrimage and had nothing to give them, nothing, see, save these few poor silver coins . . .

The fellow stank of *arak* and hypocrisy. They kicked him a little, for the sake of form, stripped him to his skin and, to the Chieftain's surprise, found he was telling the truth. His pockets contained a few silver coins and he had nothing else of value but some cheap trinkets around his neck and a gold bangle on his arm, which they ripped off without further ceremony. The Chieftain was not interested in his eager offer to supply the bandits with forbidden alcohol, which he promised he could provide at an excellent bargain from Parsee merchants that he knew. Across his sagging belly was the tattoo of a badly rendered rose. But he had already been deprived of the only remaining articles the Chieftain would have bothered to remove from a man of his type.

The Sunni from Karachi vehemently denied knowledge of, no, nor any loss of, no, a saddlebag. But eagerly confirmed, yes, that he had been travelling, oh yes, with the caravan. He was loquacious on this subject, moreover, and knew exactly how many horsemen, how many footmen, how many soldiers and guards and camels and mules and servants and female attendants were coming towards them along the road from Mecca, just one *farsang* away. So why had he left them behind and why was he riding ahead? He had no precise reply to this pertinent question, no clear reason, and he mumbled nervously, even blushed slightly, when pressed. And they certainly pressed. But they could get no more than a little helpless scream from him on the subject, which culminated in floods of tears, and some incoherent accusations against Zoroastrians and Jews. In exchange, however, he could certainly tell them about the bride's wealth. It was fabulous, he wheezed. And the corpse! He waxed eloquent about the corpse. The guards

about it, he said, were fierce and from Luristan. But the
wealth on board was no less significant than that of the
bridal train, whose escort of effete Turkish soldiers, he
assured them, would put up no resistance. He was more
than willing to tell the Chieftain everything he asked and
much he did not wish to know and, with the significant
exception of his motives in riding ahead of the caravan,
needed no threat of torture to speak. His Arabic was as
cheap as the trinkets round his neck and he had a slight lisp.
The reason for the delay, he said, and here he permitted
himself an uncertain smirk and a knowing wink, the reason
for the delay was the bride, who was young and ripe for
marriage, he could vouch for that. It had been her desires,
he intimated huskily, that had obliged him to come ahead
of the caravan. It was to satisfy her passions that he had
risked his life –

The Chieftain ordered his men to push the odious fellow
against the side of the old well in the ruined shrine and then
gave him a choice. 'There is a dead man under that cliff,' he
murmured, pointing. 'You can either join him now or let
me cut out your tongue so you won't have to join him later.
Which do you want?'

The implications were clear. If he were to try to warn the
caravan of an impending raid, he would be dead. If he did
not, it would be because he was fortunate enough to be
dumb. Weeping and blubbering, the man from Karachi
submitted to the second alternative. They trod heavily on
his soft shoulders to hold him down, but it was hardly
necessary for he did not resist. He was even accommodating enough to present his tongue to them, with revolting
acquiescence. The Chieftain shuddered at the flaccid nature of the fellow. He sharpened his dagger against the stone
lip of the disused well and they threw the tongue into it.

Afterwards, they let him go free. They even allowed him his mule, which the Chieftain considered an act of great magnanimity. With such a treasure coming towards them, what did they want with another mule anyway? The Chieftain did not like to be seen as small-minded, especially in front of his men. That was why, for the second time, he resisted the urge to send one of them to retrieve the Bedouin's saddlebag from where it must have fallen at the foot of the cliff.

The last they saw of the Sunni from Karachi, he was heading towards the rocks on the other side of the valley of Khulays, where the carrion crows were circling lower and lower. He seemed to have lost all sense of direction. Much good may the saddlebag do him, thought the Chieftain, even if it contains the greatest treasure in the world. Of what use was gold or silver if you could not bargain with it? At any rate, the Chieftain was in no mood to think of saddlebags for the present. He was satisfied that he had all the information about the riches of the caravan and wanted to concentrate his whole attention on a perfect ambush. He was not going to make the same mistake twice. And besides, there was a dust cloud approaching on the southern horizon. Another omen? But he was determined to make this one bend to his will.

The Chieftain was a godless man but he believed in the power of omens. Originally of the Wahhabi sect, he gave the Prophet more credit for being human than divine. The Prophet was a pragmatist, in his opinion, and a leader of men. If he taught people to worship a divine fiction, it was in order to govern them better. But he saw no reason to be thus governed himself. The Chieftain considered the veneration of gods to be a sign of weakness in people. Most men were weak and few were strong and those, like himself, who had been born to command, had no need to feel craven before fictions. The importance of the Prophet, in his estimation, lay in his practical and political ability to bend the hearts of his followers, as well as the omens of the world, to his all-powerful will.

Omens were a political tactic as far as the Chieftain was concerned. They could be employed to maintain power over others. They were tools. By their means, he interpreted the circumstances and opportunities of life much as he commanded men and controlled women. They served to show how well he could anticipate the games of fate. That was really all that it amounted to. Either one played the game like a man, with the dice in one's own hands. Or one constructed a fictitious god to play it, and gave the dice over to others. The Chieftain felt he had mastered the game and was in control of the dice and so far, circumstances had proven him right. His men, who shivered at his blasphemies, were secretly thrilled by them. They feared and believed in his strength. He knew this and despised them for it. And since they were craven before the power of omens, he interpreted omens to prove his power over them.

It was for this reason that when he saw the dust cloud rolling in from the south he changed his mind again, for the third time. A dust cloud would limit the visibility and serve his ends and he could interpret it as an omen to prove his control over fate. He reverted to the original plan. He determined to send his men back with all speed to the rocks at the original point of ambush on the road to Medina, five *farsangs* ahead in the mountains of Dafdaf. With a dust cloud at his command, there was time enough for his men to hide themselves in their appointed places and be ready for the raid one hour before sunset, which would be the caravan's expected arrival at Towal. Now that he had ascertained exactly the number of soldiers and guards, the quality and quantity of their arms, and the extent of the booty, they could use this unexpected circumstance to their advantage. They could ride along the road and return to their original place of ambush with greater speed instead of picking their way slowly through the wild terrain above the caravan route. For the dust cloud would slow the caravan's progress and cover their traces. This omen had played into his hands.

As the sun climbed high overhead and the first glint of the approaching caravan detached from the horizon and drew near, he gave the signal. One piercing whistle, and his bandits hidden among the rocks on both sides of the *wadi* rose as a single man, leaped on their steeds and took off along the road towards Towal. Within seconds they had disappeared in their own cloud of dust. They rode like the mountain winds towards Medina for over an hour until they were one *farsang* from the coastal crossroads at Towal. It was a classic point of ambush in a narrow pass high in Al Daf. When everyone had been carefully briefed, when everyone was installed in his appointed hiding place and knew exactly how and when and in what order he should attack, the Chieftain finally felt he was in control again. There was nothing left to do but wait for the caravan to appear.

And then, without warning, it seemed to him, the sand-storm struck.

Nothing happened according to plan. The Chieftain had never in his entire career conducted a raid as chaotic, as mismanaged, as doomed as this one. When he remembered that fatal ambush years later, he had not a moment's doubt that the wealth they stole was far less than the honour he lost that night. And when he thought about his decisions during the course of it, he could never understand what had governed his choices. Or who. His calculated moves, in retrospect, seemed totally irrational. That ambush marked the moment when he began to lose his power.

They said the mother of the Prophet had died here centuries before, in this valley, between these mountains along this desolate stretch of road between Mecca and Medina. Her name was Amanih and the shrine of Abwa' by the well had been built long ago to honour her. It had fallen into disrepair, however, and for years had simply been a ruin in which the well had gradually filled up with dust and become dry. Then, recently, an ardent Turk had made a vow to rebuild it. He had been a zealot, they said, and had interpreted it as a grave dishonour to the Prophet that his mother's shrine should be so disregarded. The primitive building had been restored with roof beams blackened against decay, and slaves had been brought all the way from Djibouti to rebuild the walls. It was at this time that the new well had been dug nearby.

But the tribesmen of Harb, considering this act of re-paration an infringement of their independent rights and outraged by any sign of Ottoman interference in this region, had laid waste to the shrine just months before. They had burned the roof down and torn the walls asunder and reduced the shrine to its original rubble, as much to snub the Turk as to insist on the insignificance of places associated with the Prophet. For like most of the Saudi tribes they had been converted to the sect founded by 'Abdu'l-Wahhab and were offended by insistence on the Prophet's divinity, and considered it a sign of idolatry that the holy places in Mecca and Medina should be preserved and treated as objects of worship. It was only weeks before that they had attacked the shrine at Abwa' and left it in rack and ruins again. The desert had completed their work. And though the Chieftain had laughed when he discovered that his rivals had expended so much energy on wood and stone which might have been better used to procure themselves wealth in a raid, he too had played his part in the demolition of the building. He had followed in the footsteps of the tribesmen and scavenged what had not been totally destroyed by fire. Wood was a costly commodity in the desert, and there were a few carpets too, under the rubble, which he salvaged for his own purposes.

Although he had not initiated the destruction of the shrine to the Prophet's mother, he always afterwards associated his own downfall with its demolition, and afterwards referred to his subsequent loss of power as 'Amanih's Revenge'.

But whether it was the revenge wrought by a long-dead mother, or the reversals of irony rendered by her son who might have been a divine messenger after all, there was no doubt that the agency of vengeance was the desert itself. And the sandstorm was its instrument. It came upon them with a fury no man could have anticipated. There were frequent dust storms in this region, for the winds in the mountain range of Dafdaf were fierce and raised red whirlwinds with banal frequency. But the cloud he had seen on the horizon when they were waiting by the well had been accompanied by a clear blue sky, without any sign of an accompanying storm of sand. It would have been sufficient to dupe the camel drivers, but not a desert eagle like himself, who had always known in the past the difference between storm and cloud. Or else had always known because the Bedouin had warned him in the past, for that man had been able to read the horizon. Now, to his dismay, the Chieftain was taken unawares. That morning he had let anger blur his judgement but by noon he had succumbed to the seduction of complacency. His eyes had been dimmed by the proximity of success. He had cut out the eunuch's tongue with a dagger that had dulled his wits. He cursed the clown from Karachi now, as well as his guide, for his mistake.

As it was, long before the caravan was expected to arrive at the place of ambush, the winds whipped the sun into a blur of sand and the desert threw its wicked vengeance at them. What should he do? Stay in the mountain pass forever in anticipation, when doubtless the wretched caravan would be forced to halt and wait out the storm in the valley below? Or seize opportunity by the forelock and risk going back to attack it when it was most vulnerable? A risk that entailed his own vulnerability, however, for to march into the head of a howling sandstorm, even as a tightly formed band, riding, as he had trained his men to do, flank against sweating flank, beast against beast, was no easy task. And to find the caravan in such conditions, even though it would be huddled in a circle to protect itself and would have no defence, would be a tall order when the visibility was so poor. The wise choice would have been to wait; the mountain could be as deceptive as the storm. He read that choice in the eyes of his men, like a mute appeal. For whether it came tonight or tomorrow, the caravan was bound to pass this way some time.

But the Chieftain was beginning to feel that this caravan was bewitched. It had eluded him too often. He had too many times assumed that it would come, and it did not. He had too frequently expected its appearance, and been tricked. Who knew what other delays might make it slip out of his grasp? The first time he had looked for it, three travellers had appeared who had been the cause of his first fatal digression, when he chased the Bedouin to his eagle's eyrie. The second time he had looked for it, he had been duped by the appearance of a eunuch, the loss of whose tongue had provided him with no pleasure at all, for the man had accepted his sufferings with a most unsatisfactory meekness. Why had he not killed the creature, crushed his soft brains against the rocks? Why had he let him escape with that elusive saddlebag? Now the caravan had been swallowed up in a sandstorm. Was he going to let it slip from his grasp again or go out and find it? Was he going to wait, meek as a eunuch himself, for his fortune to come to him, or go out like a man and make it?

He decided to return. Leaving his perfect ambush and security among the rocks, the Chieftain ordered his men to head back into the storm.

It was like walking into hell. To keep on the caravan route was both essential and dangerous. For if they wandered, they would be lost forever and tumble off the mountain without warning; if they stayed on it, with the visibility so poor, they might stumble upon the huddled caravan without any warning, and destroy their own chances of the raid. The Chieftain gave harsh orders. One guide, bound to the rest by a cord around his waist, would ride alone ahead and keep to the road, while the others should follow closely together, in formation, along the scrub to the sheer rock face on the right side of the path. There they might stumble on the rocks but at least hide themselves when they received a jerk from the guide to warn them of danger. Two jerks would tell them that the caravan was sighted and they could close the gap before attacking.

Normally the Chieftain would have sent the Bedouin, and would have stayed himself with the main body of the bandits to lead the attack. But the Bedouin was dead, curse him. Sensing his men's unease, their muffled fear and uncertainty at another change of plan, their doubts about the wisdom of turning round to track the caravan, he made one more foolhardy decision. Determined to show them he was not afraid of meeting fate, and tying the cord around his own waist, he rode up ahead himself as guide. Instead of the one he had cursed.

Within seconds he was isolated in cones of whirling sand. And centuries ensued. The mute and muffled sun gave him no sense of passing time. The particles of sand surged and coalesced in tidal waves around him and beat upon him like a gong. He was engulfed and hollowed out so that the sand seemed to sweep within and without him, both. Despite the *chaffiyeh* wound about his head, it entered his eyes, his nose, his throat so that he choked; he lost all notion of place as well as time. Straining to see ahead, he stumbled over and over again against the rocks on the roadside and had to readjust his direction. Groping like a blind man into the howling wind, he found himself several times on the verge of a precipice. He could only make progress in relation to himself; it was a valueless guideline. His mind became numb and he hardly remembered what it was he was looking for, in this eternity of sand.

Suddenly he felt a jerk. It was so strong it almost threw him off his steed. In his confusion and disoriented state he could hardly distinguish the difference at that moment between this physical jolt on his body and the memory it triggered of the tumbling Bedouin, somersaulting down upon the jagged rocks below the cliff. It took several jerks for him to realize that his men were pulling on the cord around his waist. They were pulling him instead of him sending the signal to them. Bewildered, he turned round and groped his way blindly back to the group of bandits. They were gathered in a close formation like a troop of ghosts, muffled in their headcloths, standing on the road. It was he who had wandered off it. And they had seen the caravan ahead and pointed silently, their eyes glinted within the folds of their *chaffiyehs*. He had been passing right beside it and had not even noticed. Only the severity of the storm had protected him and kept the caravan in ignorance of the bandits who had suddenly stumbled upon it, huddled in a circle against the wind.

It was another omen.

But the Chieftain did not linger to interpret this one. He could not gauge where, in this bewilderment of sand, they were: how far from Khulays, how close to Towal, how near the possibility of rescue or how vulnerable to a counter-attack by the tribesmen of Harb who controlled the region. They had to act fast. And grab all they could. Quickly.

At his signal, the bandits bore down on the terrified animals, whooping as was their usual custom, to frighten the pilgrims and, brandishing their open bayonets and swords, to kill or stun whoever or whatever they encountered. They had a skirmish with the armed escort surrounding the litter of the bride but despite the still whirling sands and their being on horseback, all the soldiers were dead within the hour and most of the Turks turned tail and fled. They had more trouble with the camel drivers, but the taste of blood and the slackening sands gave a certain zest and ruthlessness to the bandits' blows. The Chieftain had trained his men efficiently. And the excitement of the raid had begun to make amends for the previous hours of uncertainty and strain. At last, the edge of the blade could obliterate their sense of impotence.

Once he had seen all the camels and mules loaded with dowry goods herded together, the Chieftain began to feel the old confidence surge back, dulling the self-doubt that had goaded him all day. Several of the horses too, fine-blooded Arabs roped together with the pack animals, were seized and only the extra mules and camels were killed, and the litters and carts set on fire. The rest of the pilgrims and travellers were unceremoniously put to death with a single blow. If any escaped into the fading storm, there was no one of significance among them, as far as wealth was concerned. All the women were packed together with hardly any resistance and it was of considerable satisfaction to the Chieftain to hear their screams. They would be conducted to his camp in the hills and shared by the bandits later.

But he had kept the bride as his own privilege. The storm had died down to a whimper and the worst of the fighting was already over when the Chieftain approached the gaudy litter, with its tattered silk curtains and tinkling bells. His men had been ordered to make fast the wealth accompanying the corpse. Evening had fallen on that ill-fated day and a sick-looking moon was rising over the scene of devastation, an omen that he had at last wrested control from the hands of fate. Moans of the dying filled the air, some of the other litters were already burning, and the main treasure was being packed by bandits. This was the moment of a raid he liked best of all: his men at his command, the screams of women in his ears, the smell of burning in the air, and a virgin to be raped. He was in command again!

The Chieftain felt lust swell within him. How could he have imagined, hours before, that his luck had turned? How could he have doubted his good fortune? How right he had been to attack the caravan instead of waiting impotently for it to come into his hands. This way he had shown his men what kind of leader he was. He had shown them how he could turn the tide of events into his own favour. Why, he was at the height of his powers! Fumbling with bloody fingers to free himself, he ripped aside the curtain of the bridal litter and climbed in.

The sight awaiting him there, in the light of the glowing fires and the leaping tongues of torches, was not the one he had anticipated. There was a girl in there, all right. But she was expecting him. Not in dread, not pressed in fear against the corner of the litter, not screaming and whimpering and begging for his mercy with terrified eyes. She was waiting for him with a bright look of recognition. She knew him!

For a moment the Chieftain found himself hesitating, nonplussed. Who was this – a prostitute? he thought. For sure, she was no virgin bride! The fantastic extravagance of her garments reminded him of the tinselled frippery of brothels he had visited in the seedy corners of Jiddah. Where in the world had he met her before that she should know him here? And how in the devil –? As he paused, disconcerted, she lifted her arms towards him. 'You did not forget?' she whispered, in stilted Arabic. And smiled.

He was appalled. Was she a witch? He was sure that he had never set eyes on the creature before who was greeting him now like a long-lost lover! He did not know how to rape a girl in such a condition. Even if they were no longer technically virgins, the women he enjoyed were usually terrified, hysterical, and had to be cowed by his dagger into submission. That was a satisfying rape. Afterwards, if he kept them, they dissolved into a kind of dumb and frightened docility which had to be whipped up from time to time to the same fever pitch of fear to provide pleasure for him.

But this one? What kind of presumptuous lunatic was this? Her eyes were enlarged by more than antimony, her hennaed hands reaching towards him were trembling with something other than fear. In that timeless second of astonishment, when he was disarmed of intent and uncertain for a moment of his motives, he noticed in the dancing firelight a single, tiny bubble forming and then bursting on her lower lip. It was a miracle of ardour! Was such desire humanly possible? She seemed to be melting with love. Or was it just a trick? Did the little witch have a knife hidden in the folds of her silken petticoats? Was she teasing him because she thought to get the better of him? His heart thudding, he leaned forward with his dagger unsheathed, and then, just as he reached for her, he smelled the murmuring perfume of her body.

His dagger was caught as he bent closer to kill her and it tangled unpleasantly in the pearls about her throat; they spilled in blood-red seeds all over her silken clothes. Horrified, he could not touch a single coin among her rustling petticoats and stumbled out of the litter backwards, cursing his evil stars.

The bandits were still baiting the last of the footmen when the Chieftain arrived in a towering rage and scattered the fun. This was the usual game they played and one of the few distractions during a raid that their chief allowed them. They did not understand why he slashed the footman's throat without further ceremony and ordered them to head back to their camp immediately. He was in an ugly mood. He barked orders left and right and demanded to see the

treasure accompanying the corpse which had been travelling with the caravan. It was apparently not among the train
of goods belonging to the bride.

There was some confusion. Where was the corpse? But
when the bandits cast around to look for it, they found it
nowhere. No corpse and no bribes for heaven. No mule
train and no dead man's gold. In the mayhem of the
sandstorm, the carefully laid plans of attack had been
forgotten and no one had noticed the absence of a corpse!
Had the guards of the mule train escaped with the booty?
Impossible! All beasts on four legs, all men on two, had
been put to death instantly. There was nothing left but a
single mule standing motionless in the moonlight, with a
saddlebag sagging to one side.

The Chieftain sensed something had slipped between his
fingers again. He had lost half the value of the raid! He
stood with his sabre still dripping with blood and looked
slowly at the circle of bandits round him, at the haunting
absence of the Bedouin. Suddenly he seized one of his men
by the hair and compelled him to kneel at his feet, with his
face thrust in the face of the footman he had just killed.
Then he cut the bandit's throat too in one clean sweep.
This time, at least, there was nothing to catch on the blade
and spill at his feet in a harvest of ardour. 'Let no man
forget this!' he hissed.

He remembered. When he returned to camp and lay in his
tent waiting for dawn, he suddenly remembered. He had
been unable, that night, to avail himself of his women;
neither his regular concubines nor the new flesh that had
been brought in, squealing like stuck pigs. And he had
tossed from side to side unable to sleep. That was when he
remembered the solitary mule left in the moonlight.

Hadn't he seen that saddlebag somewhere before? And the mule? Where had he seen that mule?

He remembered. Wasn't that the eunuch's mule? Wasn't that the saddlebag stolen by the Bedouin? The likelihood of this conjunction seemed so remote and the coincidence so disturbing that sleep was banished that night and for many nights after. The mystery of the lost corpse, too, was the more disturbing because he also remembered having delivered a death blow, as he left the burning bridal litter, at the head of a man in his winding sheets. Could one kill a corpse? Is that what he had foolishly attempted? The gradual conviction of his having missed some chance, of his having lost control, of his having somehow found himself, or rather lost himself, in the position of the dice thrown in some game he did not comprehend, instead of being, as he had always claimed to be the master of the game – this uneasy conviction gradually worked on him. It worked on him.

There was nothing for it but to rise early the next morning before his men were up, to mount his horse and ride back to the valley of Khulays, alone. He picked his way thoughtfully through the mountain range of Dafdaf towards the well and then across the *wadi* towards the rocks and stones at the foot of the cliff. He wanted to look for that infernal saddlebag that had started all the trouble. And he did not find it.

What he saw long before he arrived was a column of smoke rising in the dawn sky. What he found was a heap of charred ash and a handful of burned bones where the Bedouin's body had been. It was curious. Nearby, half buried in the sand, he also found a folded paper, covered with delicate writing. He could hardly make it out because the writing was so fine, but he fancied he smelled perfume on it.

The Chieftain had reverence for writing though he could not read himself. He had learned that writing meant knowledge and knowledge gave power. He was not illiterate in the language of power. He could read it in the eyes of men and in the bodies of women. All his life he had wielded it, and now, was it wielding him?

He stood beside the charred heap for a while, in a deep reverie. Something there was in all of this – the burst bubble of desire on the lip of life, the explosion of pearls and pomegranates at the throat of death – something in these curious events that told him of his powerlessness. He had been an instrument only, but not the one who held it. He had encountered an omen which he could not interpret. He would always remember this because he was powerless to forget it. He lost all sense of time as he brooded on these matters and it was with shaking fingers that he refolded the piece of paper, reverently, and put it inside his shirt. He did not return immediately to camp but sat a long while beside the well near the ruined shrine on the other side of the *wadi*, struggling against the absurd desire to weep. For it seemed to him there was a lingering memory of perfume in the air about him. Later, he sewed the fragrant writing into a silk pouch and wore it round his neck like an amulet. He would wear it next to his skin for another nineteen years. He could not read but he knew what it had to say.

Not long after 'Amanih's Revenge', he abdicated. Leadership and lust for power had become distasteful to him. Before his fellow bandits could get over their surprise and murder him, he retired to another country too far for them to follow. There he bought a small plot of land and cultivated figs and apricots, which he sugared and sold to the fire-worshippers and their fellow community of Parsee merchants over the border.

Years after, whenever something happened to remind him of his powerlessness, whenever something happened to recall him to his impotence, whenever in his soul's bewilderment he found himself remembering the myriad mysteries which eluded him, the many enigmas he could never understand, he would finger the silken pouch around his neck and grow misty-eyed and distant. The unread words folded within it spoke to him, in a whispering calligraphy that touched the tendrils of his heart and clasped him close and murmured deep endearments. They spoke to him in whorls of perfume, scrolls of henna-coloured curls and subtle clinging silks that would not let him go. With infinite love they murmured to him to remember that all of creation across time and space had contained millions who paraded briefly with their powers as he had done. With tender compassion they reminded him that all these unnumbered millions had, like him, without exception, been utterly forgotten together with their petty lusts and powers. And with exquisite ardour they murmured to him never to forget that all those such as he, all these millions, and all of this creation, were less, far less than that which lay within the eye of a dead ant compared with the All he could not ever name, the All that he would not ever know.

THE MONEYCHANGER

T he Moneychanger had lived many lives. By the time he was forty years old he had been a *memsahib*'s lapdog, a carrion bird, a desert scorpion and a fly. But he had not yet been a man.

He had been locked in this cycle of *samsara*, or rebirths, as long as he could remember. It had begun when he was a young child, for his mother had been widowed when his father died and had been obliged to commit *suttee*, thus enabling him to understand at an early age how one could die in a variety of ways which might include the appearance of living. His mother's ashes were tossed in the river Ganges before he was old enough to know the difference between sky and heaven, and he was left at the mercy of his maternal uncles, who had little patience with this only son of a sister whose dead husband's relatives were of a lower caste. The uncles were cobblers and somewhat avaricious by nature. They were disgusted with the snivelling boy, who showed no aptitude at all for their profession and howled so loudly when he hammered on his thumbs that customers were dissuaded from entering the shop. They told him in no uncertain terms that until he made some reasonable money and a name for himself, they would not

86

help him find a wife, and unless he found a wife, he could not be accepted in the family. And furthermore, he would be disowned if he sullied the family name, for their caste was higher than that of the leather tanners, who were untouchables. And then they sent the orphan out to earn his living for himself.

This, then, was the extent of his uncles' powers of deductive reasoning as well as moral guidance, and it led the young boy, logically enough, to contemplate the need to change his name. He became a scavenger and learned to cheat in order to survive. For he quickly understood that the paths which the Gita exhorted him to follow – of wisdom and love, of knowledge and devotion, of *jñana* and *bhakti* – were the paths to perdition. He had no interest in perdition, but a great interest in knowing where his next meal might come from. This was the only certitude in his most doubtful life.

His first serious job, and the life that was its consequence, came when he was introduced to the East India Company in Calcutta through the parting charity of one of the uncles, who had earned the distinction of mending a pair of boots of a certain British *sahib* working there. The young boy had subsequently been employed as a flunky in the bureau of an English customs official in this establishment. There it had been his honoured task to sweep the floors, to pull the *punkah* on the hot, hot afternoons, and to wipe a wet cloth lovingly along the edge of the sahib's paper-laden desk. He was not to wipe it on the desk, that rather vile-smelling piece of sodden grey cloth, for this might disturb the *sahib*'s papers. But he could wipe the edge. He wiped the edge of the desk, therefore, the edge of the chair, the edge of the dusty windows and the door – and, when the *sahib* was not looking, the edge of his nose.

But the *sahib* did look. He looked frequently at the adolescent boy with his protruding eyes, his rather full lips and overdeveloped adenoids. Which of these attributes deserved the distinction of being so closely observed, he did not know, but one evening, in the monsoon season, this gentleman in charge of Her Majesty's Excise and Tax Control Department for the highly respected East India Company, located in prestigious buildings in the better quarter of Calcutta, lingered in his offices rather later than usual and took advantage of the occasion, and the dimming green light, to pass an experimental hand over the boy's trembling buttocks.

The hand had been reddened by the sun and was coarse and dry, but the Englishman was still young and at the beginning of a promising career. Shortly afterwards he had been promoted, and left the customs offices in Calcutta in order to assume the more distinguished post of a minor attaché in the British embassy of Constantinople. And he decided to take the adenoidal Indian youth with him.

Since alternatives were few, the uncles gave their permission and even held a farewell party for their promising nephew, after which short-lived fanfare of distinction he went off, leaving everyone's hopes high for a wedding when he came back. This was to be the first but certainly not the last of his voyages. By the time he passed the straits of the Bosphorus, he knew that his return to Calcutta in the future would be as doubtful as his past there.

In this new incarnation, Ashwin, as he was now called, was elevated to the rank of houseboy, where it was his task to clean the puddles and the messes left by *memsahib*'s lapdog. Whether it was because that animal died shortly afterwards, in rather mysterious circumstances, or because he now had to compete with a rosy-cheeked Turkish boy

for his master's attentions, this promising turn in his good
fortunes did not last long. He was abruptly dismissed after
some money went astray from the *memsahib*'s drawers and
the private garments in her clothes cupboard were found to
be distressingly dishevelled. The rosy-cheeked Turk vehemently denied all knowledge of the theft and although he
was revealed to be wearing a suspect amount of lace
beneath his burgundy silk trousers, the matter was hushed
up and the Indian was kicked unceremoniously into the
streets.

During this first winter of his life, he found himself
wandering and lost, penniless and frozen in Constantinople. It convinced him ever after that he would prefer to die
of heat than cold and that whatever other seasons he would
have to live again, none of them should be winter. Constantinople was a cruel city which changed its face each
night so as never to allow its inhabitants the complacence
of thinking they lived in it. For roads and alleys shifted,
buildings died and were reborn elsewhere, and nothing was
what it had been the day before in Constantinople. It was
one of those cities that take root and live in their inhabitants rather than the other way around, spreading laby-
rinthine alleys in the mind. Until such time as this sort of
city chooses to absorb a man into its meandering guts, until
such time as it is willing to take in and warm his body, to
chew and digest him and finally turn his spirit into offal, his
life is in jeopardy.

Constantinople did not like the taste of the young Hindu
from Calcutta and spat him out. He might have starved to
death one winter's day, as he leaned faintly and with blue
lips against the urine-splattered wall of the public baths,
had it not been for the appraising eye of a passing Turk and
his own quick decision, upon being asked his name, to

metamorphose into a young Sunni from Karachi, eager for service. Thereupon he became Abdullah, and entered the Turk's household.

The Turk was a devout Sunni himself, and a wealthy man. Since he was no longer young and had his needs, Abdullah was able to advance his fortunes fast, for he was becoming adept at the art of pleasing. But it was at a fateful cost. To his dismay and lasting discomfiture, it became apparent that his security in Constantinople required a certain abdication of virile pride. If he wished to be well fed, he would have to be unmanned, for the Turk trusted none of his own wives. If he wished to have access to the Turk's private apartments, to recline on the Turk's cushions, to eat the Turk's delicious food and smoke his water pipe and remain warm throughout the winter, he would have to give up all hope of returning to the bosom of his family and having his choice of tinkling Hindu brides. The Turk preferred him to be sorry and be safe.

This fourth incarnation then, rather than the previous episode among the British, was the period of life in which the Indian refined his philosophy of doubt. Here in the harems of the Turk, where he grew indolent and sly, where he was permanently overfed and pampered, where he embraced the pink rose of tattoo and other titillations, he gradually began to conceive of independent wealth and cultivate a lisp to hide his growing ruthlessness. Here, where he learned the art of flattery and guile, he began to plot how to escape the Turk and milk him still, how to act with treachery and still seem a friend.

And one fine spring day, he found his chance. A dealer in dried fruits, who had business connections with the Turk, came from Karachi with his daughter. The Turk, eyeing the daughter, offered the tradesman a deal he could not resist, but the last-minute condition set by the latter was that the wedding should take place back in Karachi. Some said that this was the wish of the girl's mother; others that it was the shrewdness of her father, who was interested in a better bargain. Only a few hazarded that the idea might have originated with the eunuch. In any event, although credit for the wedding conditions was ascribed to the dealer in dried fruits, and the Turk's agreement to them was attributed to his unbounded appetite, it was to prove obstructive to both parties and of great benefit to the Indian. Very cordially, the Karachi tradesman packed up his daughter, distributed his dried fruits as farewell gifts to the Turk's several wives, and departed. But after they left Constantinople, the business deal went back once more to the bargaining table and the wedding was postponed indefinitely.

The Turk became increasingly glum as the prospects of consummation dwindled into the uncertain distance. He was highly susceptible to the suggestion that the Indian might serve well as a go-between to speed up the wedding arrangements. That smooth young man assured him that he had valuable connections among the tradesmen of Karachi and would naturally be able to protect the Turk's interests much better if he were on the spot. Whereupon he was arrayed in finery, supplied with ample funds and sent as an emissary to the dealer in dried fruits to renegotiate for his daughter. He managed to extract full powers of attorney from the Turk to act on his behalf and delighted the old man with promises that he would not only gain a bride but also several useful business deals among the tradesmen of the town.

But when the Indian reached Karachi, he flaunted his wealth as his own and entered the town not as an emissary but as a successful trader in his own right. And then, as a special favour to the dealer in dried fruits and for a certain modest fee, with all expenses paid of course, he offered to serve as a go-between on the latter's behalf and try to press a better bargain with the Turk for the bride's dowry. When he returned to Constantinople some months later, his explanations included a few business deals, but to the Turk's disappointment the fruits proved drier than before and the dowry discussion demanded expenditure of further time and funds. Thus month followed month, delay followed delay, as the Indian became familiar with the pilgrim route and assumed his fifth life, as a carrion bird.

Now that he fed off the greed and need of others under the pretext of providing them with useful services, he decided to elevate his status by assuming a new name. Muhsin Aqa seemed better suited to his rise in status as a marriage-broker and middleman and disguised his doubts about himself under respectability. The Karachi affair stopped only when the dealer in dried fruits began eyeing this well-padded gentleman himself as a better bargain for his daughter. Thereafter, swearing loyalty to the Turk who had retired to his estate in Damascus, the Indian turned the game around and served as pander for the girl to other grooms, while he eased the Turk's attentions from Karachi to Kirman.

For he had lately found that he could play upon the nervousness of a certain merchant in the Zoroastrian community of this region who needed a husband for his daughter too. The man was a covert Zoroastrian beneath his social Muslim pieties, but since his daughter's currency had been tarnished by notoriety, a buyer had to be found further afield. The Turk was delighted with the rate of exchange offered, and ravished by the Indian's descriptions of the girl. He was particularly taken by the tiny miniature painting he was shown, couched in a case of porphyry, and the prophetic visions which the eunuch swore the child had about her wedding.

Although the Indian gradually wore out his favour among the merchants of Karachi and lost the confidence of the Zoroastrian community in Kirman as well, he managed to keep his relations with the Turk well oiled for years. By lying and manipulating those he claimed to serve, he gradually sucked off enough wealth for himself to begin his own business, in swindling, moneychanging and the sale of illegal alcohol along the pilgrim route to Mecca.

This then had been his sixth incarnation, the desert scorpion who made shifty deals with desperate pilgrims and swindled them out of goods and gold when they were far from home and helpless. At this stage of his existence, of the *ashrama* of his life, his name changed with the same fluidity as money crossed his palm. With Sunnis he was Muhsin Aqa, with Shi'ias he was Haji Abdullah, with Hindus – who were few and far between in these parts – he returned to his origins as Ashwin Munje, and claimed to have connections among the Brahmin of Bombay and Calcutta. He also developed the gift of tongues to offset his more doubtful occupations. Indeed, deprivations in one area of life proved to be richly compensated for by gains in another. His tongue became his greatest asset. He could speak Urdu, Hindi, Arabic, Persian, Gujarati and Turkish, as well as a smattering of English from his *sahib* days. Whatever the circumstance, his tongue was always equal to it, as far as wheedling, wangling, finagling and other forms of flattery were concerned. It served him well and often salvaged his pride. But it had not yet saved his life.

Once, however, his tongue had placed his life in serious

danger. It was during his carrion-bird period, when the affair between the Turk and the dried-fruit merchant was beginning to turn sour. His notoriety in Karachi was making it necessary for the Indian to turn his sights elsewhere but he had not yet found favour in Kirman. Since the Turk was engaged, at that time, in the purchase of lands and properties near Damascus, he could not proceed as planned to Constantinople either. So he found himself on the road from Jiddah unable to go forward or return. Stopping at a wayside inn one evening, in a particularly nasty mood of self-disgust, he began a desultory conversation with a young Bedouin lad who had appeared out of nowhere on the night of the new moon.

The boy had deep-set eyes and delicate bones, but although they had shared a *qualun* together, he had proven incorruptible. It was a pity. He was no more than a poor shepherd, a mere vagabond or worse, but the Indian suddenly found himself trusting him with his doubts. Late in the night, while the other pilgrims snored in the inn, he walked with the Bedouin boy into the desert and began to talk as he had never talked before. Whether it was the desert seeming so strangely pure under the new moon, or the *arak* he had drunk perhaps a little in excess that loosened his tongue, he did not know, but he began to tell the lad his story: all his hypocrisies, his lies, his subterfuge, his faithlessness; that he was actually a Hindu from Calcutta pretending to be a Sunni from Karachi; that he'd been castrated by a Turk and was now creaming off the pilgrim trade.

The boy listened in silence. 'So you do not believe in the Prophet?' he said.

'What prophet!' the Indian snorted. 'There are a thousand prophets.'

'But you pretend to believe, here with these pilgrims, you pretend to be a pilgrim?'

'Yes, I pretend,' answered the Indian dully. 'I pretend, I pretend and I'm sick to death of pretending. Would to God I could stop pretending!'

'But you don't believe in God,' the boy put in.

'There are a thousand gods,' said the Hindu sadly. 'And I suppose I believe in them all. Vishnu, Shiva, Indra, Kali. I believe in them all.'

And then he wept. Perhaps they were tears of self-pity; perhaps they were tears of relief, for it was the only time in his life he had spoken the truth without intending to gain something for it. It was the first time he had expressed his doubts and put his life at risk as a result. Seconds later he regretted his loquacity and could have bitten out his tongue for his foolishness. What if the Bedouin lad was untrustworthy? But the boy was looking at him with such a mixture of pity and disgust that it was plain he wished to have no more to do with him. Shortly afterwards he disappeared into the shadows from where he had come, and left the Indian to sleep off his *arak* and his gloom and be forever haunted by the spectre that someone, somewhere in this desert of a world, knew of his duplicity.

The Indian never saw the Bedouin again until he saw him dead, on his back, in the valley by the dried-out well. With a saddlebag beside him. And by then he had lost his tongue.

They were curious circumstances, those which led the Moneychanger to take that last fatal journey from Jiddah to Mecca, when he lost his tongue. He had been moving restlessly between Damascus and Duzdab Zahendan for a few years without the patronage of the old Turk, when he found himself in the small port of Langih, between Bushire and Bandar Abbas. Business was bad and he had decided to try his luck with the local *kad-khuda* who had been newly installed in office as the headman of the town and did not know him yet. His plan was to offer him a secret supply of *arak* in exchange for the monopoly to make money deals with the pilgrims. And there, in the courtyard before his house, he had a very strange encounter.

He met a 'holy man' from India, clothed in the simplest raiment, with a piece of green cloth wound about his head and carrying a staff in his hand. It appeared he was travelling all the way back home on foot. He was old and scrawny and his ribs protruded unpleasantly. He had been speaking to the *kad-khuda* and had just emerged from the house with a fierce light in his eye which disconcerted the Moneychanger. He was especially disconcerted when the 'holy man' asked for his family connections in Calcutta, and searched his face closely from under bushy brows when he spoke falteringly of Karachi. The Moneychanger was not accustomed to meeting his compatriots.

The 'holy man' then told him abruptly that he was returning to India from the city of Shiraz and asked him if he wanted to know why. It was an odd question and pronounced with a certitude that made all answers immaterial. Since he was clearly not a tradesman and Shiraz was not a place of pilgrimage, the Moneychanger was at a loss about the point of this remark when, without warning or excuse, his interlocutor suddenly announced that he was coming from Shiraz because the last *avatar* had appeared and the new age of Krta Yuga had begun.

The lack of logic in this remark caused the Moneychanger to stare blankly for some seconds at the bright-eyed man before him. What *avatar*? Was he a mad millennium-monger? There were many about these days among the Muslims of his acquaintance, but this was the first time he had encountered an evangelist of the Vedic scriptures. The 'holy man' smiled. 'Are you not proof yourself that the end of Kali Yuga is at hand?' he said. 'For do not the Vedas tell us that "Petty-minded people will conduct business transactions and merchants will be dishonest" at that time? Why, look at yourself; you are the living proof!'

The Moneychanger was startled. Was it madness or some less innocent faculty that permitted the 'holy man' to construct logic from abuse? He began to doubt his motives, but despite his cynicism, the deep-seated reverence that a dead mother had taught him to have towards those who turn to *Sanatana Dharma*, or the universal laws, made him bite back his words. Mad or sane, he was after all a 'holy man'. Long absence from the scriptures of his old religion had made them strange and unfamiliar to the Money-changer; he only dimly remembered that the Kali Yuga was the present iron age of darkness and Krta Yuga was to be the new golden age of enlightened peace. But even though he had been more interested in profit than in prophecy from his earliest days, he still respected those who sought the path of *jñana*, or enlightenment, whoever they were. A 'holy man' should be honoured, even if he seemed slightly mad, even if he watched too intently and approached too closely and smelled of garlic.

'You are the living proof!' the old man repeated in a low voice. 'For does it not say that when Vedic religion and the *dharma* of the law books have really ceased, then the Kali Yuga is almost at an end? When people are ignorant of religion, when men like you, "corrupted by unbelievers, will refrain from adoring Vishnu", then, we are told, "the blessed Lord Vasudeva will become incarnate here in the universe" and a new age will begin!' His eyes never blinked as he contemplated the shocked features of cosmic moral degradation before him.

At this point the Moneychanger was so uneasy that he tried to distance himself from his persistent interlocutor, but the half-naked man simply followed him as he stepped away. He leaned forward and hissed in his face, 'I tell you, he has come!'

No question but that he was mad. Perhaps it was just as well. Had he been sane, the Moneychanger would have had to worry about whether he might trace his family connections and cause a scandal in Calcutta. He turned away rapidly and walked out of the courtyard. After so much garlic and lunacy, he really had no appetite to try and make a deal with the *kad-khuda*. Disturbed, he turned his steps towards the stinking pier to distract himself a little with the newcomers to town, to see who was waiting to board the pilgrim boats for Arabia.

And there, to his astonishment, he had a second unexpected encounter. He saw the Parsee merchant he had swindled in Kirman some years ago. The man was accompanying his daughter and her bridal train. At a glance the Indian saw that it was a substantial one too. Was it possible that his patron, the old goat, had finally come round over the dowry? And without his personal services? Was it feasible that they had made a deal that deprived the middleman of his part of the bargain? Or had the marriage of the mad girl been arranged with someone other than the Turk? What were they doing now, masquerading as Muslims among the other pilgrims on their way to Arabia, when they were Zoroastrians? There was some cream, some fat, some oil to be skimmed off here. And he wasn't going to let it slip through his fingers.

But the Indian hung back for some moments, hiding behind the rank fishing boats near the old sea gate. How could he present himself now without a careful introduction? His last encounter with the Parsee merchant had not been felicitous, to say the least, and as the Indian well remembered, the daughter had a penchant for dreams and portents that always wrecked his best-laid plans. He tried to avoid being seen by them and cast about how he should best proceed. It was the first time for many years that he had needed the services of a go-between, some neutral third party to serve as his advocate. And he struck upon the plan to go back to the local *kad-khuda* and ask for an introduction. The man did not know him yet and if he could wheedle this favour from him on the basis of some small return of *arak*, he could reinvent himself rapidly. And find the means to line his own purse while appearing to do a favour to others. With renewed zest, he turned back from the pier towards the house of the *kad-khuda*.

But he did not get far. To his dismay, he saw he had been followed by the 'holy man' accompanied by the *kad-khuda* himself. Worse still, they were approaching the pier! They were heading directly towards the Parsee party! Confounded, the Moneychanger saw the Zoroastrian greet the 'holy man' with deep reverence and some familiarity as though he were a long-standing friend. And then he watched dismayed as the 'holy man' introduced the Zoroastrian to the *kad-khuda*. All his hopes evaporated. He was engulfed in the gloomy odours of garlic and rotten fish. Why was his *karma* working against him? He had lost his chance.

But the worst was not over. Minutes later he saw the 'holy man' pointing him out – he could not escape! He was unmasked by this millennial lunatic! He had to prepare himself for humiliating shame and public exposure. The Parsee merchant would certainly see to that, and his opinion would destroy all further chance of striking any deals with the *kad-khuda*. The Indian was in half a mind to duck from view and flee the pier. But precisely at that moment, when the Parsee was looking upon him with dawning recognition as the party of three men approached, the 'holy man' suddenly took matters in his own hands.

'Allow me to introduce a compatriot,' he announced, and then, turning courteously to the Parsee merchant beside him, he added, 'a gentleman I think you may have met before. But he is my friend now too, and I can vouch for him.' Then, after resting his eager eyes briefly upon the *kad-khuda*, he concluded, 'You can surely trust him. For does it not tell us, when the new age of Krta Yuga comes, "the minds of people will be awakened and become pure as crystal"? This man will be your living proof!' With that final enigmatic utterance, he pressed his palms together, looked hard at all three men in turn and then gave each of them a reverent bow.

Thus it was that the Moneychanger had the go-between he least expected. It was because of a mad 'holy man' that the Parsee merchant reluctantly accepted to renew the Indian's services as a spy. It was because of this curious encounter that he embarked on what proved to be his seventh life and his most recent career, as a fly. When he boarded the boat for Jiddah, the thin old 'holy man' had stood on the pier, gazing intently at him, for the longest time.

Initially, the situation could not have been more propitious. On board the boat, the Moneychanger had ample opportunity to consider what strategy to follow, and when they arrived in Jiddah, it looked as if the dowry might fall plumb into his hands. The Turk who had been expected to send his escort to accompany the bride towards Damascus had not yet arrived. There was even a possibility that he and his escort had been massacred along the way, since rumours were rife that the savage sheikh of the Harb tribe had been attacking Ottoman officials in that region in a bid for independence. But the chances were also that the Turkish escort would simply arrive late. If they could leave Jiddah quickly, they would miss them.

The Moneychanger knew he had to act fast. He started negotiating with the caravan leaders so that they could continue towards Mecca in the company of the other pilgrims. Once on the road, he intended to drop a few timely hints about the bridal party's Zoroastrian inclinations and then take advantage of the consequences of this knowledge becoming public. Nothing could be simpler than disposing of non-Muslims in the sacred precincts of Hijaz while keeping one's own hands clean. A little skirmish, in the name of religious orthodoxy, could result in a few slit throats and a considerable amount of wealth. The Indian knew well how to play the mourner. He had to act swiftly, and at the appropriate moment.

But the appropriate moment came and went several times without his being able to take advantage of it, and he had difficulty keeping his patience with the caravan leaders, who proved much greedier than he expected. To his intense frustration, just as the deals were finally made and they braced themselves for a departure, the Turkish escort arrived and foiled the Indian's plans. Worse still, they delivered a signed letter from the Turk with instructions that the bride should avoid the holy city at all costs and proceed immediately in a wide detour round Mecca by the trade route to Osfan. When the Indian protested against the discomfort of this deserted camel route and suggested the more sensible solution of continuing with the pilgrims as far as Hedda before cutting across on the shorter detour round the holy city to Al Jamum, the caravan leaders then raised their prices and the bargaining had to begin anew. Although the cowardice of the Turkish escort served him well (for they were mortally afraid of crossing the desert alone), their clumsiness in negotiating proved a stumbling block, and the appropriate moment was lost once more when the Indian woke up one morning to discover that the pilgrim caravan had finally left before dawn, without them.

He was intensely irritated. He had lost the perfect opportunity of goading the pilgrims' religious fanaticism against the bridal party, although he wondered, in retrospect, whether one of the most fanatical among them, an overwrought Shi'ia priest, had not actually been responsible for the caravan's hasty departure. For this young man had been horrified to hear that his *hajj* might have been sullied by the presence of Parsee women. There was no choice now but to try and meet up with this or some other pilgrim caravan on the far side of the holy city, either at Al Jamum or Osfan, and to face the initial desert crossing alone.

It was the least appealing way of relieving himself of the bride. Travelling in the company of an escort of uniformed Turkish soldiers in a region rife with hatred against them was hardly his idea of an appropriate occasion to dispose of Zoroastrians. Unfortunately, wild rebel tribesmen waiting in the dunes ahead would not discriminate between him and them, nor be inclined to share the spoils. He would be hard-pressed to save his life in such circumstances and the bridal goods would fall plumb into other hands than his own.

As much to reassure himself as to try to make some money in the process, he offered to find bodyguards for the Turks, who wanted protection against the threat of marauding tribesmen. His prices were several times higher than those suggested by the bodyguards themselves, a pathetic troop of beggars scraped off the streets of Jiddah and supplied with borrowed clubs and daggers for the occasion. But despite all his efforts to cheat the Turks, they finally proved more parsimonious than pusillanimous. After two more weeks of delay, when a small trade caravan left Jiddah to cut across the desert route through Bariman to Osfan, they decided to leave with it. And without the bodyguards.

The Indian was sure they took this decision because of the interference of the Falasha woman who was the young bride's slave. He did not trust the colour of her skin or her religion. He was sure that she had been working on the soldiers' anxieties, telling them that the towering rage of the Turk should be feared more than wrath of the Harb tribesmen, that the Turk's impatience was more guaranteed than the risk of any attack. She had a way about her that filled one with foreboding. And she must have worked on the Turks' fears. Thus the Indian found himself still waiting for what he called the appropriate moment all along the tedious and unfrequented trade route from Jiddah to Osfan, during which three days' journey there was not even a hint of the excuse he was looking for. Or the threat he dreaded.

Finally, on the fourth leg of the journey after their departure from Jiddah, some hours after sunrise, the moment came. The day before, the Indian and the Turkish escort had, for quite different reasons, been gratified to meet up with the pilgrim caravan again, at the caravanserai of Osfan. The Turks had no difficulty in negotiating a deal

103

with the caravan leaders this time for the bridal entourage to continue under their additional protection, and the Indian noted with satisfaction that by a stroke of luck, the fanatical Shi'ia priest was still among the travelling pilgrims. He began dropping hints and suggestive innuendoes, and since the young man seemed particularly repulsed by the presence of the Falasha slave, the Indian took advantage of this to stir the priest's scruples and disturb him with doubts.

He himself was disturbed, however, by the addition of a dervish to the caravan. The fellow had obviously joined the pilgrims in Mecca and his *hajj* seemed to have increased rather than clarified the hotchpotch of Sufi mysticism in his head. He was a walking travesty of superstitions. The Indian was particularly irritated by his habit of chanting songs about ghouls and jinn which frequently provoked the pilgrims' laughter and detracted from his own efforts to play on their more orthodox sensibilities. But when the caravan was obliged to halt on the road between Mecca and Medina just outside the fourth caravanserai of Khulays, he realized that nothing he might have hinted nor anything implied by the dervish could have been half as provocative as the shrieks coming from the bridal *takhteravan* itself.

The bride's hysterics played right into his hands. What could be better than this? The entire caravan had been forced to halt because of a woman! Now was the time to expose the infidels. Here was the opportunity to goad the young priest into action. The heat was deadening. The caravan leaders were upset about the unscheduled stop. The stench of the corpse which was travelling from Mecca to Medina was unbearably foul, and all the pilgrims were complaining. It would not take much to allocate blame where it would serve his purposes and then, with swift arrangements and some well-placed bribes, he did not doubt that he could absorb the greater part of the wealth and the Turk need never know he was even involved. For he had lied, of course, about still being in the former's trust. The caravan was in an uproar. Everyone was shouting and complaining. The guards surrounding the corpse, who seemed ready for the least provocation, were demanding explanations. All the pilgrims were disgruntled, except a wizened man with one tooth who had attached himself to the Moneychanger at the previous caravanserai of Osfan. This old pilgrim spoke a cracked kind of Persian no one could understand and had apparently adopted the Indian for reasons of interpretation, but he could not be aroused to any form of irritation whatsoever, even against the flies. His odd habits and uncertain origins had excited a flood of accusations on the part of the overwrought dervish, who claimed he was a jinni in disguise. The charge did indeed exacerbate some suspicion among the pilgrims, for no one was sure of the old man's faith. It seemed he had been travelling for some years along the Silk Route, which had wrinkled him to skin and bones. But the Indian had managed to deflect the dervish's absurd allegations, to answer the pilgrims' questions and to protect the harmless fellow because he wanted to direct antagonism instead towards the bridal party, for reasons of his own. Now the moment had come at last.

He took out his bottle of *arak* and congratulated himself on his patience, for it was much more satisfying to see the Zoroastrian bride and her entourage beaten to pulp and put to death through no special effort of his own. At that moment he noticed that the Falasha slave was calling to him. She had stepped out of the *takhteravan* and was walking towards him. An unprecedented honour, he smirked. He knew she loathed him. Suspicion and rivalry between them was mutual. He had been frustrated as long as she was there, guarding the girl like a hawk. She had been responsible for his irritation in Jiddah and had even presumed to issue ultimatums to him. She had dared to threaten the Turkish escort with a scandal if they did not leave Jiddah quickly. And now he was sure she would try to undermine his plans again. Though she was no more than a freed slave, this woman had considerable powers. You witch! he thought. What's your game this time?

He glanced over his shoulder to see if the nervous priest was near enough to overhear them. He wanted to arouse the anxiety of this cleric whose breath smelled as sour as the corpse. In the past he had always been afraid that one fine day his own duplicity would be found out by such a one as this young man, with his pale, twitching hands and three days' beard. Now he was as eager to excite the attentions of the fanatic as he had previously wished to avoid being butchered by them, and he was glad the dervish, with his superstitious nonsense about ghouls, was not around to distract the man.

As the Falasha woman started to talk, as she began to tell him something about how he should ride on and retrieve some other thing from someone somewhere, the Money-changer asked her to repeat herself, in the priest's hearing. She did. And he smelled suspicions stronger than a corpse or the breath of a priest in the strange instructions she gave him.

He narrowed his eyes, knowing very well what she was pointing to, with her bone-thin black finger. There was an old well in a ruined shrine a mere *farsang* ahead, an hour away from the slow caravan. They called the place Abwa'. A man on horseback, even on a mule, could reach it within half an hour. It shimmered in the distance like a mirage. He had passed it before on previous journeys. It was an old grave, a place inhabited, according to the dervish, by ghosts and jinn; he had never lingered by it in the past and cared even less to do so now. Why was she sending him there, the African witch? How did she know about it? Had she arranged for him to be murdered?

It was some fool's errand, evidently. Squinting between the embroidered slats of her veil he saw something that unnerved him in her eyes. He understood by it that she had lost control of the bride. Fine, he thought. So the mad girl is finally more than even you can handle, is she? Well, if I do you a favour, you'll have to do me one, *khanum*! But what he said sounded accommodating enough. With a glance over his plump shoulder, he sighed deferentially and shrugged, giving her to believe that he was the servant of her mistress and would do all that was required of him. He assured her, in the hearing of the priest, that he would do his utmost to fulfil her wishes. He would exert himself, he said plaintively, to satisfy her desires.

When the woman left, it was not difficult to arouse the priest. He was already furious. What business was it of these infidels to stop at the sacred well of Abwa'? The Indian agreed with all his heart that the request was nothing short of blasphemous. How dare they defile the grave of the Prophet's mother? asked the priest. The Indian stressed how burdensome were his obligations to these infidels at each step of this sacred route and how he wished some pure and more righteous hand than his would wreak the vengeance on them that he was certain God intended. For (and here he whispered certain obscenities in the priest's ear about the relationship between the slave and the bride, to say nothing of the perversions practised by the other Zoroastrian women attending the girl, which made the young man flush to the roots of his hair and turn aside vehemently to spit at the burning sand) – for, he whined, they certainly deserved that vengeance!

After that, he set off towards the well on his reluctant mule. He intended to take his bottle of *arak* and rest in the cool shadows of the cliff on the opposite side of the valley until the caravan arrived. Afterwards he could present his excuses or look for his rewards, but he was not about to put himself to any further discomfort. Ideally, by the time he rejoined them, the priest's anger would have already erupted and caused mayhem among the pilgrims, and he would have little left to do but suck off the sweets. The Moneychanger was not a fly for nothing. He knew how to irritate and frustrate and stay clear of all trouble; he knew how to feed off the living and the dead. While the bride and her entourage were being disposed of, he had no intention of lingering among jinn and ghouls by a dry well.

Although the arguments with the caravan leaders were still in full swing when he left, and the priest was already loud in his accusations against the Zoroastrian party, the shrivelled old pilgrim, who had stayed aloof from all these matters, noticed the Moneychanger's departure. He ran some way after the eunuch's mule, waving his arms and calling out in a strange, high-pitched voice. It was curious. The Moneychanger turned and waved back, nodding and smiling and assuring him that he was not going away forever, but the old fellow would not give up. His behaviour was all the more strange since he had so rarely been ruffled before. He remained for a long time on the road, in the crushing heat, gesticulating and calling out in high falsetto notes, like a bird. It was as though he were trying to tell the eunuch something. Or warn him. The ominous sound of his urgent, fluting cries echoed across the dunes and made the Indian shiver slightly in the sun. He began to imagine the jinn and the ghouls.

When the bandits seized the Moneychanger and dragged him howling to their chief, his worst fears were confirmed. These ghouls were real enough and their hands and feet were violent. These were jinn with a purpose! And he knew well that it was more concrete than anything envisaged by the babbling of the dervish. Fleetingly, in the intensity of his pain – for the bandits pinned his arms brutally behind his back and kicked the air out of his chest – he even imagined that the wretched Falasha woman had conspired with the dervish to summon these devils to attack him. In his terror, he was convinced the African witch had planned for this to happen, had known these brutes were waiting to throttle him for his misdeeds, had sent him to his doom. How did she know? Who had told her? He even began to imagine that she had taken a Bedouin to be her lover, the very lad to whom he had confessed his crimes. His imaginings were wild; his thoughts were whirling.

But as the men began to question him, as – for fear of his very life – he had to steady his mind in order to reply to them, he realized they were desert bandits, no more. They were cheap and vicious thieves. They were not even the tribesmen of Harb with political fury in their hearts but just robbers governed by blind greed.

He had been robbed before; he had been attacked by bandits in the past, but had always managed to wangle his way with bribes and booty, with promises of more and hints of unless. Even when he had been most uneasy about the possibility of attack by the tribes of Harb along the lonely desert road from Jiddah, he had not imagined anything like this. For he was entirely alone, now that the dread had finally struck; he had nothing with which to negotiate either, except his twisted tongue, his empty words. He had no one left to betray, nobody to hide behind, and no doubts on which to build. The certitude that threatened left him breathless.

He tried all his old ploys, he offered all his old tricks, he used all his old charms to provide service as a guise for self-preservation. But after the questions, after the answers, after the facts about the caravan were ascertained, after the numbers of guards and the relative value of the wealth in the dowry train had been assessed, he realized with growing terror that the old games would no longer work. With rising panic he saw that another life was coming to an end. The bandits had squeezed him dry and it was not *arak* they were after. They had taken from him whatever was of value to them, and they had no need of him any more.

The lust for blood was in their eyes, their smiles were ruthless. These were savages, not men. They were animals. They would stop at nothing. If he came to the end of this life, would there be another for him? The 'holy man' had been right when he said that the age of Kali was upon them, when countries would be laid waste by robbers and vagabonds. Here was the Kali Yuga indeed! He was at the brink of ruin and certain death. It was all over! He was so sure they would kill him, so sure they would disembowel him before his own eyes, that when the chief presented him with the choice of giving up his tongue or his life, it seemed like pure mercy.

His tongue saved his life then, as he entered upon his eighth incarnation.

*   *   *

The saddlebag was the first thing he stumbled on as he staggered away from the bandits towards the cliff side of the valley. The cool shade of the cliff had been his last coherent thought as he had wandered into the noonday heat and now he had no more coherent thoughts. So he allowed this last, like the patient mule, to carry him on. His own being was concentrated in a howling mouth of agony. The sun beat molten light against the rocks and the sand rose and fell like a burning sea. Had the 'holy man' standing and watching him from the pier of Langih seen his voyage to Jiddah across this sea of fire?

Then he saw the saddlebag. It had burst open and some of its contents lay scattered about the low rocks. He stared uncomprehendingly. The blood was pouring down his chest and he was dizzy. Unable to bend, he slipped off the mule and sat down abruptly on a rock, like a leaking sack. Half dazed, he leaned forward tentatively and touched one of the packages near him. The twine had unravelled and the pieces of paper rolled open into his bloody hands. With the sweat pouring over his eyelids and his mouth a hideous O, he pulled the roll of paper onto his lap and began to read. It was in Arabic, written with exquisite penmanship.

'The Day of Resurrection,' he read. And paused. The words released a piercing sound that shook a flock of carrion birds from the rocks ahead of him. They rose, clamouring, cawing, and wheeled like dark arrows round him. The Indian started again. 'The Day of Resurrection is a day on which the sun riseth and setteth like unto any other day.' It was like a clap of thunder out of the clear blue sky. 'How oft hath the Day of Resurrection dawned, and the people of the land where it occurred did not learn of the event.' His head spun with flies and the shadows of birds.

'Had they heard,' he read on, 'they would not have believed, and thus they were not told!'

The logic was of a circular perfection that defied denial. Who had done this to him? Who was telling him such perfidious certitudes on this day, which had begun, appropriately, like any other ordinary day? He began to whimper like a lost child, moaning with pain, turning to the left and the right, looking behind, and everywhere around him, as the birds settled slowly down. He was alone under the implacable sky. Where could he go? Quickly! He did not know where he wanted to go, but he must run somewhere, quickly. And hide himself.

And that was when he noticed a black cloud hovering over some formless thing among the rocks. It was flies. And many were already humming round him, attracted by the blood.

The Indian recognized the Bedouin immediately. Ten years had passed, at least, since he had seen that face, now thrown back on a broken neck and the bleeding eyes wide open, but he would have recognized him anywhere. The desert boy on the night of the new moon! The only human being to whom he had told his tale of insincerity and subterfuge! The only human soul who knew his secret! And – suddenly the Indian was certain of it – his only true friend. He kneeled down, bleeding profusely, with the paper he had been reading pressed against his sodden front. He slumped down among the rocks, mindless now of his own pain, beside the body where the flies buzzed furiously. He bowed his head, alone under the high cliff and the faceless skies where carrion birds flew low, and he began to weep, deep racking sobs as though his heart would break. His friend was dead! And he would never speak again to any living soul!

Time stopped still for the Indian. He had no idea how long he kneeled there. The full flood of his life's futility came upon him, the wretchedness of being locked within the rebirth cycle of *samsara*, the prison of misery, of *duhkha* and suffering in the world. Oh! for escape! To achieve the release of *moksha* and move beyond the doubts of material existence! To be free of these rebirths ever more mean-spirited and meaningless. He could not bear these endless resurrections. Vishnu, lord of sacrifice, he prayed in his heart, release me! Rama, Krishna, Buddha! Help me! Why did the *avatars* of old not come to his assistance? Why did they not speak the words of release?

But why should they? And how could they? And had he ever listened to their words before? Why, even when the 'holy man' had told him it was the new age of Krta Yuga, when the last *avatar* Kalki was at hand, he had not listened. And then he remembered the words he had just read: 'Had they heard they would not have believed, and thus they were not told!'

Even as he recalled the words, distant shouts and cries of the camel drivers could be heard across the valley. The caravan had arrived at the well. There was a certain inevitability about this event which echoed the appalling logic he had begun to recognize around him. Since he had not listened to the words of the *avatars*, perhaps he should prepare himself to hear the meaning of their deeds. They had placed the rocks all where they should be. The body of the Bedouin had fallen here for him to find. He had been sent to look for a message, and here it was before him. The caravan had arrived so he had to deliver the saddlebag. The lucidity of it all throbbed like an open wound in his head. This, he realized, was the moment he had been waiting for, for all these days, for all this time, his whole life long.

The Indian knew that he had to play his part or he would never be free of playing a part. If he wished to deserve the words of release, he had to put them into action so that he might hear them when they were uttered. He scrambled to his feet and began to snatch up the packages scattered among the rocks and stuff them into the saddlebag. The flies festered about the dead boy's eyes, and he beat them off with furious hands. He had to take the saddlebag to the slave and return immediately to keep the flies away. The carrion birds were gathering too, their ugly necks stretched out as he shooed them off with mounting rage. He had to deliver the saddlebag back quickly and then keep vigil over the bones of the Bedouin boy. He had to deliver this message from gods and angels and return to burn the body on a fitting funeral pyre in order that this one at least might be released. He had to do all this to free the Bedouin from the cycle of *samsara*. For the first time in his many lives he felt no doubt, but since belief was valueless unless it was expressed through deeds, he mounted the mule and rode hard across the valley.

Later, as the Indian was staggering back to the dead body with a sack of charcoal on his back, he heard the cries of the camel drivers once more and the whips of the muleteers. By the time he had returned from his mission, the caravan had left the well and was on its way again. He had stolen the coals set aside for the bride's bath, watched by the astonished pilgrim, whose old eyes had widened beyond the limits of the wrinkles round them. He had filled his bottle with water from the newly dug well there, which to his own dim astonishment flowed abundantly. He had also stolen a tinder box from the slave's baggage in the bridal train. The old man had seen him do all these things and approached him murmuring syllables of uncertainty. But he had brushed the fellow away, mutely. When the pilgrim made those same high-pitched sounds, he had quickly placed the reins of his mule in the fellow's wrinkled hands, to quieten him, for he did not want to attract anyone's attention. He knew he would have no need of the mule any more.

The only person he had seen when he delivered the saddlebag, other than the old pilgrim with the wrinkled eyes from who knows where, had been the Falasha slave who despised him. But it was a brief encounter. He had managed to avoid the priest.

Evidently, the priest's attempts to stir up public anger against the Zoroastrians had been diverted by more pressing matters. Ideological outrage had given way to olfactory indignation. Besides, the fragrant preparations for the bride's bath provided momentary relief, so it was no longer appropriate to blame the Zoroastrians. The corpse stank so badly that a row had broken out between its guards and the caravan leaders about where they should carry this objectionable load, and this issue had overridden all others. Everyone was complaining that the guards should stay at the back of the train. But they argued that this was dangerous and if they trailed behind the rest they might be vulnerable to bandits. The Indian thought of the bandits up ahead and hurried past the shouting footmen and gesticulating guards, his head bowed under the bag of coals. A great weight had dropped from his shoulders.

He had decided not to travel any further with the caravan. No more pretence. He had only one thought in his mind: to achieve one good deed and perform one act of loving devotion, by building up a funeral pyre and burning the body of the Bedouin. If he could do this, perhaps the

Lord Vishnu would have pity on him. If he could fulfil his pledge, perhaps he too might be released by death. As the caravan straggled slowly across the valley and passed out of sight between the dunes, he worked feverishly, piling up the coals around the body below the cliff. He was so absorbed in his task that he did not notice the sandstorm till it came upon him.

The sandstorm came like a great balm on the wounded spirit of the Indian. It came like a cleansing wave that took him in and swept him up and purged him through and through. It came like a confirmation of release, from the burning Lord Vishnu, that his previous lives were being purified. The wind blew all the flies and carrion birds away. It also swept the sand like a winding sheet about the broken bones and the heap of dark congealed blood. It obliterated all his doubts with its undiscriminating disrespect for evidence. It forgave.

The Indian took refuge against the cliff face, near the body, till it was over. He closed his weeping eyes and his bleeding mouth against the sand and hid his head in his arms against the kindly rocks, and felt blessed. He no longer moved his blackened lips, but listened, listened for the words of release.

By the time the storm was over, his mouth had stopped bleeding. He drank some water he had brought back from the well, and despite his pain, he washed out his mouth. Then, as the sun was setting, he kindled the fire.

The body of the Bedouin burned gently all night and the Indian kept vigil by it, sitting on his haunches and swaying gently to and fro. His head was thick with sounds and syllables. They pounded in his ears: the harsh cry of the carrion crow and the rustle of the deadly scorpion, the buzz of the flies and yap of lapdogs. He had to listen to them all. Sometimes they were so clamorous that he howled. He bellowed without words and the echoes came back to him from the faceless black rocks, like the voices of jinn and ghouls. And then, when all the syllables and sounds were hushed, in the last hours before dawn, he heard another murmur deep inside him.

'When the blessed Lord Vasudeva will become incarnate here in the universe in the form of Kalki, the minds of the people will be awakened and become pure as crystal.'

He recognized the tones of the 'holy man' immediately but the sound came from within himself. Had he too gone mad then? He considered the possibility calmly, with a quiet resignation. A tongueless eunuch in the middle of the desert. The likelihood was high. If he had not already gone mad, perhaps he was on his way there. In fact, perhaps that was where he was going now. Mad. Because where, otherwise, should he go? And what, otherwise, should he do? Or why?

With that why, he remembered how the 'holy man' had said, 'You are the living proof!' His last doubts evaporated. He understood he had to be the living proof that, through *bhakti* or devotion, a man could find his way to nirvana in this life. He had to live in such a way that he was proof of crystal purity. He was certain there was no other way out of this why. And if this way was what the sane called mad, he did not care; for to do otherwise would be true madness. His life would prove that this was pure reason.

The sun rose that day as it rose on any other day, but the Indian who had been born a Hindu knew it was the day of his resurrection. He turned his steps back then, and for the first time after all those years, to Calcutta. Renouncing his fears of foes and family, of shame and shamming, he struggled to find the meaning of 'return' and set himself upon the long journey home. He went on foot, carrying a staff. When they called him a 'holy man' along the way, he laughed silently and shook his head, and pointed to the tattoo of a shrivelled rose on his now shrunken belly. Since he had lost his words, he sought release through deeds.

It was not easy. Whether he succumbed at times to stealing as was his wont, whether he dramatized his abject misery for sensational effect as was his instinct, whether he was tempted by his speechlessness to open wide his mouth to shock or to compel charity as would have been his daily temptation, is unknown. It is probable that he did all these things; it is possible he did not. Who can be sure of anything? Old habits die hard and he was, after all, only human. But if he could believe in more than his own doubts just long enough for action, then one thing is certain: this was the last of his lives in this contingent world. He died a man.

THE SLAVE

The Slave was a Jew from Abyssinia, a Falasha, who had been sold to the Arabs when she was no more than a child. She had laughed only twice in her life. The first time had been when she lost her virginity; the last when she lost her child. Raised in the harems of a ruthless sheikh, she had been raped young before being sent across the Gulf in her early teens in exchange for cargo rights. The sheikh was murdered shortly afterwards. Later she was sold to a converted Zoroastrian living in the eastern provinces of Persia. And his wife died shortly after that. Perhaps her laughter carried a curse.

She was a slender, willowy young woman of twenty when she was compelled, against her religious customs, to submit to the attentions of the Zoroastrian. She had odd habits, never eating with the other members of the household, and insisting on preparing her own food, apart. There were certain days of the month, too, when she took refuge in a small room above the stables, reached by a rickety ladder, and at these times, despite threat of punishment, she quietly refused to perform any of her regular duties. She had soft, dusky skin, large almond eyes and angular limbs, and her heart-shaped face was very beautiful before it was marred by the smallpox at the time of the plague. They called her Sheba but it was not her original name.

The prejudice of race and religion in the Middle East combined to make the Jews a people whose laughter was often dangerous. Abyssinia had provided Arabs and Persians with slaves for centuries, but not many of these sons and daughters of Ham were of the Falasha people. Most were Coptic Christians and many were Muslims, both Sunni and Shi'ia, but the Jews among these dark-skinned servants were few. They bore themselves too haughtily to serve with satisfaction, as if ancestral links with Solomon were still too close, as if their possible conversion among Egyptian oppressors was still too raw a memory. And though it was the custom among Arabs and Persians to treat slaves as members of the family and to free them after some time, a Falasha slave was rarely trusted with this privilege and often persecuted with lingering humiliations, many self-imposed.

The woman called Sheba was no exception. She had been born with the shackles of Mosaic law as well as slavery around her ankles; she carried the heavy yoke of superstition as well as prejudice about her long, black throat. But to all she had inherited from her forebears she added a dark, brooding intelligence of her own that dwelled on doom and famished devotion; the negative anatomy of her severe gnostic beliefs had evolved from a capacity for self-punishing obedience. It was these that had embittered her laugh.

When her baby died of the smallpox that also claimed her mistress, Sheba the Slave laughed for three days and nights. They heard her terrible laughter in the little room above the stables where she had placed herself in quarantine. She knew she had been punished by God. She knew that by submitting to the trembling, wet-lipped embraces of her master, who was divided between his guilt and his desires, she had committed a grave sin. The fact that she had no choice in the matter made her laugh the more. So did the irony of her motives, for she had broken one of the divine commandments in order to have a child. To lose the child therefore was perfect punishment.

But while the fault of her defilement may have been to some degree her own, she also calculated that her master's infidelity had in certain measure exonerated her fault. For she had felt nothing for the Zoroastrian herself. So, she reasoned, since her motives were not strictly adulterous, her life had been saved during the plague, though her beauty had not. According to the same logic, she believed that though her baby had died, she had been recompensed for this loss by being given the Zoroastrian child to raise as if she were her own. The Falasha woman had her personal theology, in effect. She doted on the child and protected her fiercely, like a she-panther. And with the same annihilating lack of humour.

It therefore meant nothing to her whether she was a slave or free. When her master granted her the latter privilege, after having taken advantage of her former condition, the Falasha shrugged her fine shoulders and adjusted her veil so that he would not see the expression on her ugly face. It was an enigmatic one and would have troubled him, not because of the pockmarks but because it told him there was nothing he could give her that she would more readily give up again, to his child. There was nothing he could take from her either that would have mattered so long as she still had his child. Had he enough imagination or intelligence to have surmised the significance of that shrug, he might even have feared its implications for the girl. As it was, he remained mercifully free of imagination and intelligence, and the Jew enslaved herself to her idolatry without impediment.

Thus the Zoroastrian did not try to dissuade her when she determined to remain the girl's maid after her marriage. In fact, he was secretly relieved, for the presence of the Slave had been a problem in the household and a shadow on his heart for many years. She was still exquisite, bone-thin with a lithe body and a high instep, but her beautiful face was riddled with craters and her baby had died of the pox. She was a constant reminder of both aching losses and forbidden gains. Now, though he had to send his child away, he hoped to be liberated of his guilty conscience too. Besides, he had taken another wife with even wealthier connections, and although her pregnancies had not produced more than terminal morning sickness so far, he was a man who chewed long on his food, sucking the juice out of his choices. His appetites inclined towards optimism, or at least that variety of it which, once achieved, resisted re-evaluation and required no mental effort or spiritual expense to maintain. For he did not believe in overexpenditure of any kind. Except for the sake of his daughter.

The endless negotiations for the marriage intensified the Slave's preoccupation with the girl and, if possible, increased her possessiveness and jealousy. During the months before their departure, she refused to allow the worldly midwives and salacious old women who customarily prepared a bride for her wedding night to pollute the girl's mind. The Slave claimed this right herself and brought to bear upon the task a combination of Judaic severity and superstitious asceticism which endowed it with deep seriousness. She tried to impress upon the girl the sacredness of the subject. It was a holy task when she taught her how to use the cloths to staunch her monthly blood, and how to learn her cycles by the moon. She spoke in tones of hushed awe, as if in the presence of deep mysteries, when she explained to her the expectations of her husband in the marriage bed. But all this only served to make the little bride ever more light-hearted. She was incorrigible.

Her mercurial spirits seemed immune to all influence. Her expectations were startling and could not be gainsaid and her ardours were embarrassing. As for her fits and trances, no epilepsy could have been so lucid and no madness so endearing. Among the Falasha, they used to excise a girl's genitals at the onset of puberty to avoid such disturbances, but though the Slave had herself endured this and other brutalities, and had suffered the consequences of gnawing pains in the womb for long years since, she would have died rather than mutilate her darling to make her the more docile for a husband. She would rather have died too than lessen the intensity of the girl's dreams and visions. The dark side of these angels found their counterpart in her own superstitions.

And her superstitions were legion. She was trapped within antitheses of her own construction, superstitious contradictions that cancelled each other out, like fever accompanied by chills. Throughout the protracted preparations for the wedding, the Slave brooded on the likelihood that they might also be for a death. Although she had permission to accompany the little bride and would remain with her in her new life among the Syrian hills, she feared she would experience some fatal separation from the girl. This going, she sensed, might have no return. This return implied no resurrection. The fluctuations became ever more intense until the Slave felt sick with apprehension. By the time she boarded the fragile *dhow* crammed with its pilgrim cargo in Langih and set her face towards the coast of Arabia, where her own misery had begun, she began to suspect that the fever and the chills were not imaginary. A sickness was swelling within her like some monstrous pregnancy. It had settled into that part of her body she had so long denied and had begun to gnaw at her with rats' teeth. Her fatalism whispered that some hideous beast was threatening birth within her.

At first she attributed her disease to a dearth in the bride's visions over the past few weeks. Ever since she had become the sole object of her father's attentions on this journey, the sterility of the girl's imagination was unbearable. There were no dreams and without them the Falasha woman was left to her own nightmares. But gradually, as the weeks passed, she had to recognize that there might be other reasons that were responsible for her discomfort. Sea voyages had painful associations for her; they encouraged memories. They reminded her of the lingering grasp of a mother's hand torn from hers, the early horrors of the harem. They reminded her of the pure waters of Abyssinian mountain streams which they were not. The first time she had crossed these waves, she had tried to throw herself into the becalmed waters, and had wept her eyes dry in the sea. The sting of the salt broke open the old wounds and the rough voices of the sailors, the harsh orders of the captain, the sight of a tall, dark, unshackled man, another Abyssinian, whose eyes searched deep into the slit of her veil at the port of Mocha, filled her with sickening memories and mounting dread. Mits'iwa and Djibouti and Aseb were just across the fatal straits of Bab el Mandeb, those waters that had witnessed the calamitous beginnings of her slavery.

But such habits run deeper than even these waters. She hardened herself to hold the rats at bay. She concentrated on fanning the languid salt-laden air with palm fronds to relieve the petulant bride. She fixed her attention on peeling sweet lemons for the seasick girl and pressed the faint spray of lingering acid in their thin skins against her nostrils to ward off the nausea. She was relieved that the weather was now rough, that her duties were constant, that she had not time to remember when she had been on such a boat as this before, and where she had been coming from and going to.

But even when the voyage was over, the gnawing of rats did not cease. Now it was she, on land, who felt the waves of nausea. Perhaps it was due to the sultry atmosphere of Jiddah. The port was stagnant with humidity; it was teeming with pilgrims and ordure and flies and thieves; it was rank with the corpses of dogs and the odours of defiled cooking and decay. When she entered the bazaar and walked the narrow streets and winding passages of the town in search of delicacies and necessities for her young charge, she stumbled into tall Africans stalking the shadows like exiled kings. There were too many of them; Abyssinia was too close. It sickened her to see them and yet she yearned for it; their features were familiar, their haunted eyes were beautiful. Once, she met the same slave who had looked so searchingly at her in Mocha, with a pearl in his ear, and what she saw reflected in his eyes disturbed her even more than most. Had she known what to call it she might have named it the knowledge of freedom, but she fled from its gaze for it reminded her of something she did not wish to admit.

Perhaps her nausea was the result of anxiety, for despite his promise to come and perform his *hajj*, the Turk broke his word. He was not in Jiddah to receive them. The Indian insisted on making alternative arrangements for the bridal train to proceed to Mecca, which resulted in changes of plans and costly negotiations. Perhaps, in fact, her nausea was due to the suffocating presence of the moneychanger himself, for ever since he had wormed his way into the confidence of her foolish master in Langih, he had been inventing new lies every day. He seemed determined to put their lives at risk. She distrusted him with all her heart but she was a mere woman in the shadow of her slavery and her opinion was not even consulted. When the Turk's soldiers finally did arrive at the eleventh hour to escort them around the sacred city towards Medina, she was gratified that the Indian's arrangements had foundered, for none of them were Muslims and according to legend they should have been turned to stone if they had stepped within the *haram*. She was certain the moneychanger was plotting their deaths.

The Turkish escort, however, were more neurotic than the women in the bridal train and provided little protection. The Falasha woman knew that if the wild Arab tribesmen attacked, as they were everywhere rumoured to be doing, the Turkish soldiers would save their own lives first and leave everyone else to the mercy of the bandits. Perhaps it was because she felt so ill with nervous stress that she finally sought an audience with the captain of the escort. She chose a moment when the Indian was otherwise occupied and the mercenary was well-tempered by his water pipe and coffee. Heavily veiled, she approached him as he sat sprawling among his men. She stood nearby, head bowed, and waited for his attention, shifting from foot to foot in order to ride the waves of sickness that gripped her. When the soldiers' ribald comments roused the leader and he finally asked her for her business, she requested to remind him that his employer, the Turk, had already been kept waiting in Mecca too long for his bride to be kept

THE SLAVE

waiting in Medina as well. There were roars of laughter as
he waved her away, but her wit worked and won her the
reprieve she had been waiting for.

When they finally crossed the desert safely to the
caravanserai of Osfan, the Slave's nausea was worsened
by the stench of the corpse that joined them on the road
to Medina. At the third caravanserai from Mecca, they
met up with the regular pilgrim caravan and learned that
the decaying body of a Shi'ia merchant, who had died
during his *hajj*, would now be their travelling companion.
They were lucky not to be accompanied by more than
one corpse, in the circumstances, for this route was
frequented by many pilgrims in their decrepitude who
aspired for burial in the holy city of Medina. It was of no
advantage that this one had been a man of means, for
decomposition has no respect for wealth. The sickly sweet
stink was unbearable and it would worsen all the way to
Medina. And anyway, could they trust the Turk to be
waiting for them when they arrived there? With these
fears and her sickness growing upon her, she could not
sleep at night but lay at the child's feet, like a waiting
panther.

But for all her fierceness, she could not guard the girl
against the angel or herself against the rats. On the fourth
day of their journey out of Jiddah, when the little bride
gave a piercing scream an fell into a faint, saying that an
angel had fallen from the sky ahead of them, Sheba the
Abyssinian Slave felt an unspeakable stab in her groin, and
knew it to be mortal. There was only one thing to do, and
she did it. She placed a sliver of opium syrup under the
girl's tongue and in her own mouth too. And then for the
first time in many years, she smiled.

*   *   *

The camel drivers cursed, the donkeys brayed for water, the corpse stank worse than ever before, and the Slave, emerging veiled from the *takhteravan*, had to cover her mouth with a second cloth to stop the impulse to vomit. She was bleeding heavily, as if some dam had broken within her, but she summoned all her strength to look for the angel's message.

Where did one look for angel's messages in the middle of the desert? She shuddered at the sight of the young priest approaching the *takhteravan*; he seemed always to be watching her and he was certainly no angel. He was a Shi'ia scholar, so they said, and puritanical in the extreme. He had been in Jiddah when they disembarked from the boat and was among pilgrims in the caravan they met again on the road to Medina. From their first encounter he had shown intolerance towards the women in the bridal train, and his *hajj* seemed to have intensified rather than lessened his fanaticism. One of the bride's Zoroastrian attendants, a buxom, red-cheeked girl with a roving eye, complained that he had threatened to stone her because she walked near him during his noonday prayer. If he had really been saying his noonday prayer, protested the girl hotly, how come he noticed her? This interchange provoked a state of war between the priest and the women of the bridal train. The Slave had counselled the bride's attendants at all costs to maintain silence and the veil, for she feared that if he was aroused they would surely find their throats cut. But the journey was long, the heat dull and the silly maids were stimulated by the entertainment of attention; the idea of this nervous and scrofulous young man approaching their throats for any reason at all made them giggle to be near him and caused them to talk louder than ever.

No matter how much she maintained a discreet distance

and ignored his interjections, however, the priest seemed unusually provoked by and had a special antipathy towards the Falasha Slave. Now at the first glimpse of her emerging from behind the curtain, he drew near again. She pulled her veil lower over her face and hovered, head bowed, in the heat.

'And why must we be subject to your whims?' he spat harshly. 'Why have you women stopped the caravan and forced us to conform to your demands?'

She said nothing then but turned from him as quickly as she could, picking her way delicately across the islands of dung. This inability to respond afforded her a sense of freedom that was refreshing. She knew that whatever she said would be wrong and therefore there was nothing to say. Her veil clung to her bone-thin body in the desert wind. She hoped the bleeding would not show, for the ravage of the rats was proving unstaunchable. But here too she felt a kind of release; here too there was nothing she could do and whatever she tried to do would be wrong. Not for the first time in her life she tasted that delirious and paradoxical sensation of freedom which accompanies all loss of choice. She recognized it. It was dangerous. It had heralded her bouts of manic laughter in the past. With a perilous lightness of heart, she beckoned to the Indian moneychanger, who was riding nearby on his mule, and solicited his help. He had probably been eavesdropping. So much the better. Since it was her child's fantasy, let the eunuch go and look for messages of angels in the madness of the noonday sun.

'Please, Muhsin Aqua,' she said, 'I beg you, ride up ahead and wait for us beyond the well up there. There's someone waiting for you.'

The Indian squinted at her deferentially and rubbed his

nose. He had such vulgar gestures. 'Willingly, *khanum*,' he murmured smoothly. 'But why does the respected *khanum* send this servant to a dry well? There are others,' and he licked his lips odiously, 'that offer more relief than this. The shrine has been disused for many years.'

'There's a message for you there,' she answered curtly. 'Wait till we come and give the message to my mistress.' It was an absurd request and she knew it; she bit her lips to stop the dangerous ripple of levity that threatened to spill from them. Secretly she hoped there really was an avenging angel waiting for the eunuch in the shadows of the well. She prayed that his destructive flames would turn this oily man into a heap of ash by the time the caravan arrived. Let him rot and never return! May the angel strike him dead! That would be the best. The worst would be that the Indian would simply refuse to go, or merely pretend to, or that by the time they reached the place, he would be waiting for them, smug and empty-handed, in revenge. Then she remembered the realities of expectation and groped inside her girdle. Ignoring the burning eyes of the priest on her, she gauged the Indian's greed through the slit of her veil and drew out a palm of silver, quickly, from inside her belt.

'Take this and do as my mistress asks, if you know what's good for you!' she hissed, thrusting the coins into his sweating palm. But she was not quick enough for the mullah. He had seized a fistful of hot sand to throw at her.

'Whore!' he cried hoarsely. 'Devil's prostitute! Do you pay a eunuch for your pleasure?' The sand blew back into his face, caught in his throat and he doubled up, coughing.

As the Slave ran back towards her *takhteravan*, she found herself smiling again. With the narcotic mercifully dulling her senses and blood streaming down her legs, she wondered idly how it was that she shared exactly the opinion of that vile-mouthed priest with regard to the emasculated spirit she had just sent on a mission to an angel.

When the Indian returned, some two hours later, she was so weakened by the loss of blood and dazed by the drug that she did not easily grasp what he was saying. She shook off the lethargy of opium with difficulty and drew back the swaying curtain. She had been roused by a violent shaking of the *takhteravan* and loud noises on the other side. The camel drivers were arguing with their bad-tempered animals, the caravan leader was shouting instructions that everyone ignored, she did not know where she was or why they were stopping. It seemed the caravan had reached the well. Perhaps the moneychanger was telling her what she would later learn with some surprise, that there was unexpected water near the ruined shrine. Perhaps he was saying nothing at all. She could not remember afterwards. Only when he thrust the saddlebag at her did she understand, with a stab, that by some miracle he had indeed encountered an angel and had brought back a terrible confirmation from this holy presence.

Where had he found a saddlebag in the middle of the wilderness? And what had happened to him to make him sweat so profusely and turn so pale, with his robes dishevelled? What was the dark stain across his chest and belly? Was that blood about his mouth? The man said nothing but stared at her with such a sudden lack of guile that the remaining veils of torpor were instantly scattered from her senses and she drew a coverlet over herself, ashamed of the stains in her own lap. Having handed her the saddlebag, mutely, he turned and left before she could say anything. That was the last she ever saw of him.

She stared dumbfounded at the dusty bag, with its torn

clasps and leather straps, which her young charge had seized from her and now embraced in her thin arms. Was this really a message from an angel? Inconceivable as it seemed, it apparently was. The angel had indeed sent a message. Several in fact. The saddlebag was full. And their import was terrible, for the calm that settled on the girl when she began to read was more disturbing to the Slave than her hysterics had been before. So was her secrecy.

As the daughter of a wealthy man, the little bride had been instructed in the rudiments of reading and writing so that, as the popular saying went, she need have no go-between to communicate with her lovers. But she was a histrionic creature. Whatever she read of poetry or song was shared with her Slave; whenever she wrote, she read her words aloud. Privately the African woman was suspicious of these magic marks, afraid of paper that could carry human voices. But as long as her darling voiced the words, she felt safe; as long as she made music of the marks on the paper, the Slave was content. Now, for the first time, she was excluded. The angel's message had brought a barrier of writing between them.

When the girl insisted on being left alone to read in the stifling heat of her *takhteravan*, the Slave, dreading that she would open all the bundles, pulled the straps of the saddlebag after her as she left and brought it and its deadly load out into the sun. It looked like an ordinary enough saddlebag, but she did not trust it. The bundles inside were many, and of varying shapes and sizes; they were all wrapped in silk and twine and all equally capable of coming between her and the child. She had no desire to open them. In fact, she had a strong revulsion against them and was tempted to throw them away. Only her strict obedience stopped her, for had the bride required to see the rest, she would have had to produce them all. But the girl seemed not to notice that the saddlebag had disappeared and was absorbed in her solitude for the next hour.

The Falasha woman did not know what to do with the saddlebag. Her head was whirling with loss of blood and her body was breaking apart. Dimly she was aware of shouting voices. Most of the travellers and pilgrims had gathered round the leader in the front of the caravan and were engaged in a vociferous debate on some matter, so there were few people and only animals around her. She was relieved that the priest was nowhere to be seen. Near the well stood a mule, which she vaguely recognized as being the moneychanger's. It seemed to be in the charge of a poor old man, for he was holding its reins as it drank water from the well. She envied the animal. She thought she might possibly strap the saddlebag to its side and leave it to the Indian. Let him take charge of the wretched thing he had found from God knows where. She could not cope with it. But as she stumbled forward with her load, she half fainted. And fell.

The old pilgrim knelt beside her making curious clicking noises and crooning sounds. His eyes were kindly and he placed a shrivelled old hand on her belly. She winced. Then he clucked more and crooned again and rested his hand on her head instead. It had a gentle, fatherly touch. She felt an absurd desire to weep. But something was washing the taste of tears from her mouth and she realized she was drinking water from a cup he held to her lips. It was sweet and cool. She noticed then that he was trying to tell her something in an alien tongue and had brought out from under his robes a curious little black ball which he held towards her in the palm of his hand. He mimed how she

133

should break it with her fingers and place the paste of it in her mouth. She obeyed him, wonderingly, feeling no shame when she lifted her veil in front of him. They were hidden by the mule and no one was near. The paste was entirely tasteless. She mumbled it under her tongue and allowed him to place the rest in her mouth. He made soft encouraging noises, faint fluting birdlike sounds, as she swallowed the strange substance. She was too weak to question what she was doing and thought in a hazy sort of way that he was perhaps some kind of healer, this shrivelled old pilgrim, that he was a shaman or witchdoctor, maybe. No one knew where he came from, though some murmured that he was not a Muslim.

She stayed quietly with the saddlebag beside her, next to the old pilgrim, on the sand. She sat quietly in the shadow of the mule, leaning against the cool stone of the well, as the last of the paste dissolved on her tongue. Time was suspended for her. This black ball seemed to cement the widening breach within her. At least for a while. Her strength was returning. Had the old man healed her? Was it possible? She mumbled her thanks to him, in Amharic. He understood nothing but nodded and smiled, quite unperturbed. He offered her a second ball of paste, but this she refused. Her command of herself was restored sufficiently to warn her against the subtle strangleholds of debt. She owed him something.

Impetuously, for she knew too well that nothing was free, she gave him the saddlebag. She picked up the heavy load and pressed it upon him. When he shook his head and backed away, she became insistent. You must take it, she said, please! And she struggled back to her feet. You must keep it, she urged in Amharic. And in order to show her determination, she placed it on the back of the moneychanger's mule whose reins lay in the old man's hand.

From that moment on, her hands were full. She had no time to think. She had to work and to forget. It was a blessing. For the time being, the breach was dammed again and she had strength to return to her task. For the bride was calling.

The girl had acquired a crazy whim to be dressed in her wedding robes in the middle of this desert. As soon as she had read the message from the angel, she insisted that her Slave heat water, that she prepare a bath. She refused all food and asked only to drink quantities of water from the well, instructing that for every cup she drank they should add nine cups to the water for her bath. Nothing the Abyssinian could say had any effect. No gentle admonishment, no wise counsel, no cajoling, no appeals: she was adamant. She had, of course, always had a weakness for baths and on this journey, perhaps as a result of the revolting odours and oppressive heat, the predisposition had developed into something of an obsession. Her fastidiousness had become troublesome. She had even turned vegetarian and refused to eat dried fish or anything tasting of heavy oils and garlic. Nor was this any ordinary bath she was demanding, now, instantly, in the middle of the desert. It was a full-scale bath of purification, with all its accompanying rituals and ceremonies. It did not seem to occur to her that such a procedure was almost impossible to accomplish in the present circumstances. Let alone in such deteriorating conditions.

Given the girl's heightened sense of the impure, it was all the more remarkable that she seemed not even to notice the Slave's heavy bleeding. She seemed blind to everything except her preparations for the angel. She noticed nothing, saw nothing around her, heard nothing that was said to her, remained unaware of the uproar that surrounded them for the remainder of that terrible day. When she spoke it was only to reiterate that they should hurry, hurry, so she would be bathed and dressed and prepared for the angel. It was the only time in all these years that her Slave lost her patience with the child.

'There is no angel!' she shouted, at the limit of her endurance.

But the bride ignored her and continued to pare her nails with a little knife she always kept about her whose carved silver handle was graced by a semiprecious stone. 'His eyes were amethyst!' she said.

The poor woman stared at the knife with horror, fearing the worst. She thought that her beloved girl was finally mad and believed she had been the one to cause her wits to turn. Had she not sent the Indian into the wilderness, he would not have returned with this accursed saddlebag. Had she been less weak, she might have better protected her child against the epilepsy, the opium and the angel. Whatever terrible catastrophe was bound to occur next would surely be her own fault. So to expiate the deadly deed, she worked even harder.

A bath of ritual purification in the middle of the desert is not easy to arrange at short notice. The only advantage at this precise time and place was that the well provided a plentiful supply of water. They emptied the skins hanging under the *takhteravan* and replenished them immediately, for the girl refused the old water in her bath; it had to be fresh and new. The Abyssinian Slave did most of the heavy work, ransacking the ruin for old straw and blowing on the coals beneath the warming copper basins. And then they discovered there was a bag of charcoal missing from the mule train; it had been stolen. The Turkish armed escort immediately took the matter up with the leaders of the caravan and demanded recompense. The guards of the corpse were suspected and accused, for they had already made themselves notorious as thieves, among the pilgrims. Subsequently, since one argument evolved into another, a huge row ensued regarding where exactly the corpse should travel in the caravan. It was as if the pilgrims had nothing better to do.

Fewer corpses travelled this route than was habitual between Najaf and Karbila where traffic of the dead among the Shi'ia pilgrims was often congested and always taken for granted. This corpse belonged to a very wealthy pilgrim, a Persian merchant from Bushire, who had died, they said, while actually circumambulating the sacred Kaabih. This was a consummation devoutly to be wished, of course, by those who took their 'last pilgrimage' in the evening of their lives. Some people even became *mojavers* in order to earn the sanction of burial in the famous graveyard of al Baqr in Medina. But the old merchant from Bushire had clearly no intention of dying for he had been on his way to conduct business transactions in Damascus. He had been travelling with the intention of trade, his muletrain packed with cottons and indigo. Should he, therefore, have the right of burial in al Baqr?

The theological, political and economic aspects of this subject provoked much difference of opinion and stimulated opposing theories among the pilgrims. The only consideration that united them was that the corpse should be kept as far back as possible, in the rear of the caravan, for the stench of it was most objectionable. The footmen who were guarding the dead man's wealth, however, and who doubtless had an eye on their own financial benefits in the process, refused to travel so far behind the others for reasons of security, they said. This provoked an uproar in which voices were raised on every side. The Slave, struggling to heat the water with insufficient fuel, had to shout repeatedly for help from the three women of the bridal train, who had been drawn to watch the spectacle and listen to the row. These brainless Zoroastrian maids did not seem to have the least idea of the inappropriate nature as well as the dangers of their involvement in this debate, even as members of an audience.

Had she been less overwhelmed, the Slave might have wondered what had become of the Indian then, for in normal circumstances he would have hovered nearby like a fly above a plate of sherbert and *baklava*. He would have turned the turmoil into some advantage for himself, and into an excuse to foment trouble for the bridal entourage. She assumed he was at the centre of the argument about the corpse; the wealth of the dead man was considerable after all. In the opinion of many the quality of his indigo alone would guarantee him an easy place in paradise and its quantity was worth more than mere prayers.

Wherever the Indian might have been, her squalling at the other women did draw the attention of the obstreperous young mullah to the Slave once more. As if drawn by the smell of blood he approached again, his skin livid under the coarse beard, his eyes fixed on her bare ankles where she squatted near the disused well, blowing on the coals beneath the warming copper pans. She was pouring orange blossom essence into the warm water as he drew near and the fragrance was heady and fresh, banishing the sickly odours of the corpse that clung to the heavy heat around them. It cleared her head. She noticed he was scratching his scabby hands furiously.

'Vanity of women!' he breathed, 'who caress your lascivious bodies with waters and oils and perfumes and balms to prepare them to entrap the unwary soul of man!'

She laughed briefly, harshly. And he stumbled back, appalled.

The water had barely been heated before the caravan started up again. The Slave had to place the hot and cold basins in the rocking *takhteravan*, with water and oils and perfume spilling everywhere, and had to concentrate all her strength in order to rub the girl's body with the rough cloth and her feet with the pumice stone as they were jolted to and fro. She felt herself swaying with vertigo. The mysterious black paste which had shored up her broken dykes, gnawed by the teeth of innumerable rats, was strong but not impregnable. How long would it last?

She did not know how much time passed but was aware only that the bride was still in the midst of her bathing when another crisis occurred. More calls of the camel drivers; more shouts from the guards. The corpse was missing, they said. It had been left behind at the well. The Abyssinian had not even noticed that the sickening smell was no longer with them, for the *takhteravan* was heady with the perfumed balms and she was working doggedly. Now, when she heard that the corpse was lost, she wanted to laugh again, wildly and irreverently.

In fact there was a mutiny, of sorts, in the caravan. The guards turned their beasts round and started to head back to retrieve the corpse. They refused to send one man back alone, claiming it was not safe to do so. They insisted instead on going all together, with the accompanying goods, which they said they could not trust to the caravan leader. The latter cursed them roundly and refused to be responsible for the consequences: there was a sandstorm brewing and their safety was their problem. Everyone began shouting different instructions and airing conflicting opinions and in the midst of the chaos the priest decided it was the moment to give the call for prayer. He had a thin, nasal voice that rose and fell with mounting desperation above the arguments. The Slave began to wonder whether the devils of laughter were not threatening to attack. Could she resist them?

But they did not attack immediately. They sent their emissaries of sand ahead of them. Shortly after the mutiny of the guards, the sandstorm engulfed them. It penetrated all the cracks and human crevices of the caravan and found its way into each individual weakness, each private flaw. The pilgrims had to follow the semblances of unity now, they had no choice. Even though it was only forced by circumstances, they had to act as one. Everyone had to obey the caravan leader and all the beasts and their burdens, both men and their material goods, gathered round to form a circle. The armed escort created a protective barricade around the bridal *takhteravan*. But as far as the Slave was concerned, there could be no protection against the whirlwind and dissolution raging inside her, and none against the terrible laughter rising, rising. The brief resistance afforded by the old pilgrim's ball of paste was crumbling rapidly.

The storm was at its height when the bride bundled up all the soaking silken cloths which she had soiled and ruined by her bath and told her Slave to throw them out. 'Just throw them out', she said shrilly, thrusting the priceless silks into the woman's arms. Precious satins that had taken months to embroider with fruit and flowers, exquisite cushions beaded and braided with gold by countless seamstresses who had worked their fingers to the bone, all sodden with soap and water now, all stained with oil and perfume, and ripe to be tossed into the howling storm. The Falasha woman clung to the costly materials for a brief moment of resistance. She came from a people of weavers, of spinners, of cloth makers; to throw all this human effort into the sand and wind was a form of blasphemy to her. But the girl would brook no opposition. Her sudden rage broke the last remaining barriers of resistance in the Slave, and though she was doubled up with pain, she obeyed. Leaning against the *takhteravan* in the howling storm, she watched in wonder as the silks were instantly whipped up like departing ghouls and sent whirling like missives from hell into the outer world. Messages came from angels to her child, but when the Abyssinian sent back replies, see what devils came out of the hell she carried in herself! She gasped with the pain now, barely able to breathe.

For two hours the sand surged about them, rising in ever wilder crescendos. For two long hours they were surrounded by the shrieks of unhappy ghosts, the howl of unhouselled souls. The Slave knew these were vomited from the pits of Tophet within her and became as cold as ice. Her darling girl sat like a princess at the still heart of the screaming storm, submitting calmly to the complicated ritual of her hair. But the Slave could hardly feel her fingers now, they were so chill. For after all the delicate designs of henna had been retraced on the palms of her hands and the soles of her feet, the little bride had demanded not the ordinary oiling and braiding of her hair, but the full regalia of a bridal headdress. Now. This instant. Without delay.

What a strange wedding preparation that was! What a

beautiful bride the little one became! By the time the storm was beginning to abate in its fury, she was completely ready. Transfixed, her Slave looked at her as if from a great distance, and knew she was quite perfect. The devils of laughter might do their worst, she thought; they could not harm this beauty now.

When the devils struck, they came from within. The floodgates fell; the dam was irretrievably broken. The Abyssinian heard the thunder of the devils' hooves and the sickening thud of the camels falling on their knees, the whooping of the devils' wild voices and the death screams of the mules. She saw the greedy flames of the torches and heard the donkeys bucking and braying with pain beneath the devils' spears. And as the blood flowed, she began to laugh and laugh and laugh until she was knocked senseless.

Sheba the Slave woman did not die during the raid or because of the brutality of the bandits; the wound they inflicted on her was nothing to the one she had already borne for years before. When she came to consciousness and recognized it was her own blood that had soaked into the sand beneath her, she knew, with clinical detachment, that she had not been raped either. She knew that the rats had been born, however, and that she was dying. And she noticed that there was a man nearby who would die soon if he did not drink.

It was the priest, the mullah. He lay some distance from her, delirious with thirst, tangled in a bloody shroud, as though fighting against burial. His turban had fallen, exposing dark hair that was ashen with sand, and his head was bleeding. He was so young. The moon was young too and glimmered softly on the tufts of desert grass among the dunes. A mule of indeterminate age stood nearby in the mottled darkness. There was an acrid smell of burning in the air and Sheba the Slave felt immensely old.

The priest was begging for water. With infinite pain, with her last ounce of strength and impulse to obey, she untied one of the steaming water skins slung beneath the still-smouldering *takhteravan* and brought it to the parched lips of the priest. She raised his head with great difficulty and gave him water.

'Drink,' she commanded. But her compassion was harsh. She was careful to let him drink only a little at a time. When he began to retch she pulled the water skin away and waited. In such cases, one should restrain desire to tiny sips or the body would revolt against the very thing it needed. She had learned this long ago, when she was young, when she had seen the consequences of great thirst, when she had become drunk on love and crazed herself with drinking. Now she was old and it was time to use her wisdom. He drank a little at a time of the revolting warm water she held to his lips, at one point even kissing her hands in his delirium. She had no energy left to marvel at this.

He fell asleep then, and even snored. She lay beside him and considered why she was not already dead. It must have been an avenging devil, she concluded, who decided this. It must have been the fatal devil of the damned who loosed the gates of *Sheol* and summoned the spirits of despair and laughter to inhabit the earth and who kept her alive just long enough to save the life of a man who hated her, although she had been unable to save the girl she loved. It must have been a dark and terrible devil whose scourge had fallen on her and punished her for some nameless evil she had not known she had committed. What deed had she done? What evil deserved such a punishment? She searched to find its name in the complex labyrinth of her personal theology. But she could only think a certain human perfection, whose green eyes were lined with dark antimony and whose henna head lolled like a lily on a broken stem. A human perfection that could not be named and the mystery of her brutal destruction. Beyond that event there could be no further thought. And there she came to rest, concluding that she no longer believed in God. This, she thought with a certain satisfaction, was her sin.

Sheba the dying Slave ceased to think then, until she saw the priest staring at her. He was on his knees. He had woken and found himself lying beside a half-naked woman on the sand. He stared at her without recognizing her at first. Her veil had fallen, and her ravaged face was exposed in the moonlight. She was soaked in her own blood. Then he broke down and wept. That was when she gave him the carnelian ring which she had been given by a certain human perfection, for pity's sake. For he seemed to have lost faith in God too.

He took her back to the well for pity's sake, for there was nowhere else to go. She was dying of a wasting disease and could not take one step further. Forward or backward was the same to her. The well was where hell had begun so she was content that it should end there too. With infinite delicacy, he lifted her and placed her on the mule, walking beside her so that she might lean against him, for she was too weak otherwise. In solicitous silence he walked beside her past the burning carcasses of the camels and disembowelled bodies of the hapless pilgrims scattered round about the dunes. Quietly he guided the mule through the remaining hours of that night. One hour before dawn, they finally reached the ruined shrine and the well. But it was only when they arrived that she saw what was strapped on the mule.

It was the angel's saddlebag.

The Slave became afraid. How had the saddlebag survived when all else had been destroyed? How had she come to inherit the saddlebag when she had lost all else? She lay in the ruin and leaned against the side of the well with the saddlebag beside her. Confused in her mind now, and weak with fear as well as pain, she asked the priest to give her one of the silken bundles within. It took long to open it. When she succeeded, she found that it contained a thin scroll, bearing a single invocation. Shuddering from head to foot, she asked him to read it for her. And he did so in his nasal voice that rose in the dawn air.

It was an invocation to a hidden mystery, a blessed beauty, a remembrance of compassion and joy through which the whole of creation would be stirred up and renewed. What remembrance, she pondered? What beauty? What compassion and joy? There were none of these left, surely?

The question occupied her for the short remainder of her life. She remembered the compassion of her mother, the joy of her newborn baby and the beauty of the little bride. And then she remembered the mystery of brutal destruction which had wiped human perfection from the world. Brutal destruction beyond which there was no thought. And just as that threatened to unravel all other thoughts, she remembered too her pity for the priest. Pure pity for the all too human priest. And in the remembrance of pity, her soul began to speak to her like a trickle of water running through the dry rocks. Her soul sang a little song of fresh water that washed over her in waves, rising out of the well.

It reminded her of the voice of her mother singing songs to her when she was still a free child and her own voice singing the same songs to her dead baby. It was full of simplicity. And it came upon her unawares, between these waves, that while she might not have been an adulteress, she had committed the far graver sin of idolatry.

Was that it after all? Was belief in a certain human perfection more vast a sin than disbelief? And if so, who, she thought, was immense enough to forgive her for this vast sin? What pity was there great enough to understand and have compassion on this too human weakness? Where, in the absence of a God, under a ruthless moon, amid the carnage of ambush and death of perfection, when beauty was dead and could not be thought of any more before the hundred lunar years of the old prophets were fulfilled, where and in what or whom could such unbounded forgiveness be found?

Herself?

The mystery within her was vast and so was her surprise at finding it. It was not thinking, exactly, that brought her to this realization. It was something other than thought that made her suddenly limpid with the truth of this immensity standing within her. Lofty with forgiveness, ancient with knowing, imperishable and everlasting.

When a wandering dervish who was passing by asked the priest for the price of the saddlebag, she let him have it gratis. Afterwards, they did as she had requested: they threw her wasted body into the dry well in the ruined shrine, and covered her up with stones.

THE PILGRIM

T he Pilgrim was an old man who had transcended many fears. But he still had one which overcame him every time he was caught in a sandstorm. It was the fear of being buried alive, of being choked with sand and covered up with earth and stones. This riddle of fear had accompanied him all the way from the Gobi Desert to the Najd and he still had not resolved it.

The Pilgrim had searched for and found a thousand keys to this riddle. Sandstorms were like the palms of hands and not one was alike. Each palmful of fear had a different name. There were certain general principles, however, which were always the same in looking for the key and naming the fear. If the sandstorm indicated movement, one had to be still; if it indicated stillness, like that which hit the pilgrim caravan on the road between Mecca and Medina, then onc had to move. But the stillness and the movement had to be of the right kind; the pull inward must match the outward thrust. If the sandstorm indicated darkness and cold, the Pilgrim had to search for the right position of light and heat; if it was a male sandstorm, he had to respond to it with the appropriate female powers. The riddle of each sandstorm was resolved by balance. And in balance lay the Buddha's secret.

'There is, O monks,' the Buddha had said, 'a state where there is neither earth, nor water, nor heat, nor air; neither infinity of space nor infinity of consciousness, nor nothing-ness, nor perception nor non-perception; neither this world nor that world, neither sun nor moon. It is the uncreate.' The Pilgrim was seeking the uncreate in order to decipher the sandstorms of his life's riddle.

In this case, when the sandstorm struck some *farsangs* away from the fifth evening oasis on the road to Medina, the old Pilgrim knew immediately that in order to uncreate the sandstorm, he had to move in the direction of the well which the caravan had passed at noon. He had to uncreate his way back there and trust the sandstorm, which he feared so much, to guide him. He sensed this in the force of the wind and deciphered it in the sting of the sand particles against his skin. He recognized that this was a male sandstorm and knew he had to resolve it with female instincts. Its riddle, in the howl of the parched wind, corresponded with the hollow he sensed within his heart. He could feel the wards of its key turning through his whole being, from the top of his head down to his bare and horny feet. So, instead of obeying the leader and encircling himself among the others, he obeyed the sandstorm. Some minutes after it struck, he abandoned the Indian's mule with its load and, clutching his flapping robes about him, turned back in the direction from which they had just come. Towards the well.

Few knew this elderly Pilgrim or had bothered to make any acquaintance with him. He was among the poorer class, and had walked in the rear of the caravan along with the pack animals. He owned no camel, and this mule he had recently acquired was not his own. He had trudged along beside it all that afternoon, one hand resting on the saddlebag it carried, but he had not ridden it; he did not wish to burden the poor animal. Besides, he was accustomed to the sensation and texture of sand beneath his callused feet; he needed to feel the earth beneath him in order to remain alert to the purposes of his pilgrimage. Now he patted the mule and gave it a parting slap of affection on the rump, causing the beast to bray in a mournful accolade as if bidding him farewell. The sad sound was soon covered by the howl of the storm.

Nobody noticed him going. They were all huddled against their animals, their bowed heads and faces cowled inside swathes of protective cloth. The Indian, his only friend, had met another destiny earlier that day and was no longer with them. There was also a dervish who had shared some bread and oil with him from time to time, but he too had disappeared since noon and no one else paid the old fellow much attention. Only the young priest, who had goaded him about his prayers when they first left Mecca, was conscious of a slight, bow-legged figure turning aside from the protective circle of the caravan and stumbling into the storm. But he was otherwise occupied and soon forgot, for the Pilgrim disappeared from sight.

The Pilgrim was an Uigur from northwestern China and spoke a curious mixture of Turkish and Persian which not many could understand. He had been travelling for several years before he reached the deserts of Arabia and had anyone thought to question him about it, he could have proved he had lived for more than seven decades by the number of teeth that he had lost. In fact, he had lost so many that he now only had one left. No one had showed any interest in him or in his teeth, however, since he had joined the pilgrim caravan in Mecca, not even the Indian who had bequeathed the mule to him. Once it had been ascertained that he never carried any money, the Indian had been gentle with him but incurious. Since the money-changer was the only person on the caravan who understood his mixture of languages, the Pilgrim had attempted to tell him of his philosophy of life and how one had to set one's heart upon learning at fifteen so that by seventy one might follow the dictates of the heart. But whether it was because the Indian knew nothing of Confucius or because the old man's speech was garbled by the loss of teeth, he had stopped listening by the time this philosophical chronology arrived at the age of forty. The Uigur was as shrivelled as a walnut when he went on his pilgrimage and as bald as a shiny brown egg, but he still had one tooth in his head with which he could bite incisively into life. And his eyes, when they could be seen within the folded wrinkles of his face, were as sharp as pins and equally bright.

Since he rarely spoke and used his eyes instead, he noticed many things that others did not. One of the things he noticed was that the dervish, who sometimes lagged along beside him in the wake of the caravan, had dyed his beard and hair black with antimony. There was a shimmer at the roots that betrayed an alien blond. The fellow was a charlatan. He was very good at being a dervish, had learned all the gestures and the incantations and spoke Arabic as well as Persian, but the old man, who had seen many things, suspected him. He had met others with icy eyes like his in the high passes of Kashgar and the hills of western Persia, among the Bakhtiari. He diagnosed the fellow to be a political monkey under his mask of piety. And of all the other pilgrims, including the priest who wanted him disembowelled, he was most wary of the dervish.

The Pilgrim had been born in the province of Xinjiang of northwestern China, in the Tarim basin above the old salt lake of Lop Nur. It was a barren, arid country that held its past as closely hidden as its future secrets. His people were farmers from the lowland oasis of Turfan, at the origins of the ancient Silk Route, and his Manichaean ancestors had been converted by the Turkomen many centuries before. Although he was originally a Sunni and lived in later years on the Mongolian steppes, his Muslim beliefs had been tempered by Buddhist philosophies, for as a young man he had chosen to be a monk and had studied in northern Tibet. Thus, by practice and patience, by discipline and determination, he had overcome all fears but one: he had adapted himself to many riddles of change but not yet that wrought by annihilation.

This Uigur had dreamed a dream when he was young that the land of his fathers would one day become a poisonous wilderness as blasted as the moon. In his dream he realized that it was his destiny to lead his people from this deadly place before it was too late. In fact it was this dream that had initially drawn him to become a monk. When an old Chinese teacher in his monastery had told him of the saying of Confucius, 'In the morning hear the Way; in the evening die content', he thought at first that he had found the answer to his dream. He believed that contentment was the way his people should live as well as die for nothing was more blasted nor more poisonous than the moon of discontent. It seemed simple enough, but the solution to his people's fate appeared to be more complex than this sort of simplicity; it seemed as enigmatic as the problem itself. For in his dream he had been made to understand that the 'Way' out of the wilderness lay through a desert; it was waiting like a rivulet of quicksilver in a circle of sand. It was a solution that was directly linked to the problem itself. Since there seemed little difference to him between a desert and a wilderness, between the resolution in the one and the annihilation in the other, the Uigur had been somewhat nonplussed by his dream and did not at first know how to proceed.

He was of a literal turn of mind in his youth. For several years he raked through the Gobi Desert in a rather desultory fashion, looking for rivulets, but the only 'Way' he found lay in the quicksilver arms of a Mongolian milkmaid whom he saw among her father's herd of goats one day and instantly desired. That was when he abandoned the monastery and gave up his search without a qualm; that was when he decided to ignore the poisonous aspect of future prophecies in favour of a more fertile present. He was not afraid of living and spent many years seeding sons, raising horses and herding sheep in the Mongolian steppes. He even forgot his dream until his wife died. But by then he had already begun to lose his teeth and name his fear.

His wife had borne him nine strong children who had all survived, but after her death the Uigur tasted the salt of a lifeless desert on his lips. He felt his days as arid as the moon. And then, for the first time in many years, he remembered his dream. He remembered the poisonous annihilation awaiting his people and found himself driven by a sense of urgency he had not felt before. He gathered his sons together, gave them his blessing, divided his goats, sheep and horses among them, and took up the search he had abandoned in his youth. If the 'Way' was to be found in a desert, he determined to search through every desert known to man, despite his fear. He turned back, then, to search among the Gobi dunes, but he was less literal-minded now and found it had become the desert of his mourning.

After two years of fruitless grief in the Gobi wilderness, the Uigur travelled back to Turfan and began to follow in the footsteps of his forefathers. He travelled for whole nights and days without water in the Taklamakan and heard the strains of spirit voices and stringed instruments calling plaintively across the sands. He was pursued by the grasping fingers and brutal hands of buried warriors and heard their drum rolls in the rumbling dunes. He walked along the ancient Silk Route through the Yarkand towards Tashkent. He searched among the Altai mountains of Kazakhstan and lived with nomad peoples of the Turan lowlands. He encountered many sandstorms, and gathered innumerable keys to as many riddles. But all these paths led him further into loneliness and doubt. Through all of them he fled his fear. By the time he had reached the salt and sand basins of the Dasht-i-Kavir and Dasht-i-Lut in north-eastern Persia, he had arrived at the borders of the desert of cynicism and was not certain that he would ever find the 'Way' to lead his people from this blasted wilderness.

It was with a sinking heart that he turned his steps towards the Arabian Peninsula. He decided to don his monk's robes once more to be a pilgrim on the road to Mecca, for although he had lost almost all his teeth he still had faith. Although fear caught at his throat in the sandstorm, his eyes were still bright with looking for quicksilver. The Silk Route still lay before him, all the way to the Sahara. But he knew that if the deserts of Arabia did not show him the 'Way', he would have nothing but the desert of despair to explore before he died. And his heart was heavy for the future of his people.

*   *   *

The Pilgrim had kept his own counsel ever since he left the city of Mecca. His presence in the caravan was as unobtrusive as an absence. Some, when they had heard him mumbling his prayers, had whispered that he was an infidel, for he performed his devotions in a manner that was wholly unrecognizable. It was ironic that he had excited the suspicion of the pious, while the dervish did not. The young priest was ready to have him stoned to death but the moneychanger had intervened and had assured the pilgrims that the harmless old man was as devout a Muslim as he was himself. Those who had been with him in Mecca vouched for his having performed his *hajj* with scrupulous accuracy in all respects, except for the final day of sacrifice, when he had not been seen. It was noted that he did not eat meat. In fact he hardly ate at all: just a little bread dipped in oil, a few dates and goat's cheese. He spoke rarely and only to barter for his daily needs, which were few. Indeed most people offered him food free in exchange for the remedies he prepared, for the Pilgrim was able to cure many ills. Among the skills he had acquired in the course of his life was the science of healing and he employed this instinct to relieve his fellow travellers. He was as unobtrusive in his healing as in his other activities and always offered remedies as though embarrassed at their need. And so he was pronounced to be one of the faithful and escaped the wrath of the overzealous priest.

He kept a stock of remedies with him on his journeys and had learned, in all the deserts he had passed, to find substitutes and adapt his skills to the sicknesses endemic to each region. In fact, this skill of his may have accounted for the survival of his sons for he protected them from death by the accuracy of his diagnoses and healed their diseases with remedies he prepared from the herbs of the Mongolian steppes. They were rarely ill. When his wife died it was not from sickness either. She just looked at him in bed one early morning, her cheeks as ruddy as the hour when he first kissed them, and said, 'I'm tired.' Whereupon she turned her back to him, as if in sleep, and died. The soft breeze of spring winnowing through her hair was like human breath, but it came from *T'ien*, the Mandate of Heaven. He never forgave himself for not having recognized the proximity of her immortality and realized then that it was not enough to have mastered the art of diagnosing death.

When he left the Middle Kingdom and turned his steps towards the nine districts of the Divine Continent of the Red Region which were the world, the Pilgrim knew that he would have to search all the deserts to heal himself from the death of his wife. He knew too that until he could find the prescription of his own immortality he could not hope to heal other people's ills. And as he searched the riddles of a thousand sandstorms, he also realized that he would never be able to save his people from the poison of his dream unless he overcame his fear. Fear's antidote lay somewhere in the region of trust. But where was that?

His keen eyes searched for the signs of trust he had missed before and made them his principal cares. For the Superior Man, the Pilgrim knew, had nine cares. In seeing he was careful to see clearly. In hearing he was careful to hear distinctly. In his looks he would be careful to be kindly. In his manners he would be respectful, in his words loyal, in his work diligent. When in doubt he would enquire for information and when angry he would have a care for the consequences. And finally, he should first ascertain whether the pursuit of gain would be consonant with the Right. If he could heal in such a 'Way' as this, he thought, perhaps he might protect his people from the poison and find a prescription for his fear.

But from the outset of this journey, the Pilgrim felt that he had failed. He had not only failed to be superior but had become *xiao ren*, an ignoble and inferior being, for in all his journeys he had not yet crossed a desert worse than that of his pilgrimage. The abyss he had encountered in Mecca had almost defeated him. Although he had been obliged to perform all the rites and rituals, he had been inclined to undo all his efforts by turning and fleeing from the holy of holies. The resulting paralysis caused by this failure, with its sense of bottomless vacancy, filled him with the nadir of all his sandstorm fears. He diagnosed his spiritual death in his *hajj*.

Worst of all, he had made three attempts to heal others during the subsequent journey to Medina and had failed in doing this too. He had failed to diagnose the condition of three others rightly. In fact, these three attempts had all occurred on one day: this very day that the sandstorm had struck. Part of the riddle of this sandstorm, he was certain, lay in his triple failure. And its key, apparently, lay within the well.

It was a sudden realization of this fact, as the sandstorm struck, that made him turn back and retrace his steps towards the well. Now, as he faced his fear with the wind stinging his eyes, he thought back to the beginning of that day and determined to uncreate his failures one by one. 'The uncreate,' according to the Buddha, is 'neither coming nor going nor standing . . .'

It had begun well enough. He had woken at dawn with the voice of his wife calling his name. And there was dew hidden in the folds of his skin. He took it as a blessing. Then the routine of living intervened. The priest had raised his battalion of morning prayers, as usual, to attack the rising sun, and despite the grumbling camels and mournful mules reluctant to resume their burdens, the caravan was soon on its way. They had journeyed three days out of Mecca already, and this was the fourth. They had been joined by a bridal train with its entourage of Turkish soldiers and the dervish had become even more elusive than usual. In nine more days they should have arrived in Medina and the corpse, the Pilgrim thought, would doubtless be relieved by then, for it was in sore need of burial in the cemetery of that city.

The Pilgrim pitied the corpse; it had become the butt of everyone's complaints. Instead of praying for the soul of the departed, the pilgrims cursed the stink he left behind. The Uigur had his own methods of protecting himself from the offensive stench. He had a pungent balm, made from eucalyptus and ginger unguents, a pinch of which inside the nostrils banished every other smell. Enveloped in his own odours, therefore, he could afford to send a few whispers of peace towards the miserable corpse whose poorly constructed coffin was collapsing on the jolting back of a mule. He prayed for its efficient decomposition and rapid release in the sweltering heat.

He had not failed the corpse, for it was beyond the reach of healing, but he had failed three other living souls. The Great Tao said, 'Be good to the not good for virtue is what is good, and be faithful to the unfaithful for virtue itself is faithful', so he felt these failures keenly. The Indian, who was a member of the escort accompanying the bride to Damascus, had been the first of the pilgrims to befriend the Uigur since they had left the holy city. Ironically, he was also the first of those he failed. And although the Indian was neither good nor faithful, he had been the old man's advocate when stones were threatening. The Uigur had nothing to offer in exchange for his advocacy but ointments for a headache and powders for a stomach pain, but he was grateful to the moneychanger and was looking for an occasion to show it. In the course of that fourth morning, a bare hour after the caravan had left the little caravanserai, a crisis occurred that caused the entire train of camels and mules and pack animals and pilgrims to halt in the middle of the desert. Shortly after this unscheduled stop something terrible happened to the moneychanger. It was an accident which the Pilgrim was not only powerless to deflect but, worse still, one for which he felt entirely responsible.

They were nowhere and had reached no place the caravan leader would normally have paused when the crisis occurred. Up ahead of them, the Pilgrim's sharp eyes could see a high cliff rising to the north of the road. Down below, to the right, in the watery distance, he thought he could see an outcrop of rocks or perhaps some ruin, but it was still a good *farsang* away. As he shielded his eyes against the brightness of the sky he thought he could see figures of men standing high on the clifftop. A fair number of them. Bandits or robbers probably. The Pilgrim had been beaten by so many bandits on his travels that he no longer feared them. The reason he carried no money and only bartered with balms and ointments for his bread was to give bandits no cause to kill him. But the presence of bandits was a matter of concern for the rest of his fellow travellers, especially the wealthy members of the caravan. He decided to seek out the Indian and tell him of what lay ahead. He would surely warn the leader and alert the camel drivers to proceed with caution.

The reason for the caravan's abrupt halt was not clear.
Some said there was a crisis among the women of the bridal
train. Others said it was due to the corpse, whose stench
was so infernal that it was to be relegated to the rear. By the
time the Pilgrim fought his way up through shouting
guards and angry muleteers to the front of the caravan,
he found the Indian in conversation with the tall, thin
Abyssinian woman who was the young bride's slave. The
Pilgrim had rarely seen her. She was extremely discreet and
did not mix with the pilgrims. She kept close inside the
bridal litter most of the time, but here she was suddenly,
standing among the complaining mules and camels with
the Indian, pointing up ahead. Towards the cliffs to the
north.

The coincidence seemed strange. The Pilgrim wondered
if she too had seen the silhouette of robbers against the
skyline on the top of the cliff. He strained his eyes and saw
nothing now. If there had been any there a few minutes
ago, they had dispersed, unless he dreamed them. But the
slave, from her pointing, seemed to be sending the Indian in
the same direction. Why was she doing this? He scrutinized
the two of them closely. There was something about this
dialogue that seized upon his susceptibilities. What was it?

And then it came to him, like a gulf yawning at his feet. It
came to him with the smell of his own fear. He snuffed the
odours of death here. He diagnosed it to be the Indian's.

When the old Pilgrim saw the moneychanger mounting
his mule and riding away towards the cliff, he began to run
after him, shouting in his own tongue. 'Stop!' he called
urgently. 'You are riding to your death! I have seen bandits
up ahead and wherever you are going, they will see you.
They will kill you! Do not trust this road! Come back!'

But the moneychanger did not listen to him. He

continued, impervious to the old man's desperate calls, turning once only to wave, as if to some mentally defective child who needed assurance of return. The Pilgrim felt a terrible sinking within him of despair. He followed the mule for several hundred yards, calling out again, begging the Indian to return, telling him it was death, death that was up ahead, death waiting to seize on him. But to no avail. The lopsided mule bearing its rather heavy load proceeded irrevocably, dwindling away in the horizon's heat. The Pilgrim stood in the desert and called till he was hoarse and the figure of the moneychanger disappeared altogether. Then he bowed his head to the sand.

That was his first failure. But the second was even worse, for it involved a greater loss of trust. As he remembered it now in the sandstorm, he shivered at its recollection, despite the hot wind. Fear clasped him in its burning arms on every side and throttled him and choked him and suffocated him. His eyes were caked with its fury and its fingers were tight about his throat but he still sensed he was heading in the right direction to uncreate his day. He forced himself to think of his second failure and kept moving as the storm dictated.

By the time he had retraced his steps to the caravan, he found that the debate about the corpse and the women had been suspended. The leader of the caravan had given orders to resume the journey and had promised that matters would be resolved on both these subjects in a while. As a special concession to all the pilgrims who were offended by the stench of death the caravan leader promised he would address the corpse question at the ruined shrine one *farsang* further up the road. There was no water in the well, apparently, but as a further concession to the bridal entourage, the leader had agreed that the caravan would pause there while the ladies were arranging their affairs. The priest was furious and was trying to provoke general protest against this decision.

The Pilgrim did not know how to warn the leader about the bandits up ahead, for the man was distracted and had refused to listen to any more protestations or requests. It would take diplomacy as well as the right language to approach him. Whom should he turn to, now that he had lost his advocate? Whatever his original language, the dervish clearly did not wish to acknowledge the Uigur's tongue; bread and oil he might supply, at a pinch, but he was more miserly with his words. In any case the Pilgrim had noticed him skulking into the dunes and he had vanished shortly after the caravan's unscheduled stop. The man would disappear on nameless errands and uncertain missions and reappear later, further along the route, slipping in at the rear of the caravan, like an afterthought. If questioned, he would claim to have been meditating. Who else could help him warn the leader of the caravan? He had to give up.

The priest did not want to give up his crusade against the women in the bridal entourage, however. He spent the remainder of the morning's journey trying to rouse the pilgrims, as they drew near the ruined shrine, to protest against the forced delay imposed on the whole caravan by these godless infidels, and to demand their immediate separation from the rest of the caravan. He gave a long dissertation on purity and graves; he protested against the blasphemous presence of unclean women on this holy route. They had their own escort, he said hotly. Let them be gone! Let them not sully the company of the pure with their filthy appetites! The burden of his argument seemed to rest on some sacred association up ahead which was about to be irredeemably violated by the presence of the bridal train.

The Pilgrim noticed that this young, unhappy man was suffering from a skin disease that had left angry scabs and itchy scales across his face and hands. He also noticed, from the odour of his stale breath and the colour of the whites of his eyes, that the youth was dehydrated in the extreme. He seemed almost inflammable, he was so angry and so dry. The old healer did not diagnose his imminent demise as yet in this discomfort but he determined that when they stopped, he would try to offer the poor young man some modicum of relief. If he had failed to warn the Indian of his death, he might at least make the life of this fellow pilgrim less miserable. What harm was there in that?

But once they reached the well, about an hour later, everyone's life took a turn for the better without his intervention. Except for the priest. For it was discovered that a new well had been dug recently next to the dry one in the ruined shrine and there was general jubilation. Everyone seized on the excuse provided by the women to celebrate the water. The priest's arguments were totally invalidated. Water skins were replenished, containers over-flowed, people doused themselves from head to foot, and only the mules and camels complained, for the caravan leader had insisted that they could not stay long enough to allow all the animals to be watered. The priest kept stiffly apart, however, and refused to drink anything from the well. His reasons were evidently unrelated to sympathy for animals.

The Pilgrim approached the miserable young man hes-itantly. He was pacing to and fro, muttering to himself. He was biting his lips, which were already cracked and bleed-ing. The flies were plaguing him, festering on the open sores of his face and hands. The Pilgrim thought of his clear-browed sons and his heart twisted with pity for the lad.

He held out both hands towards the young priest. He had learned from his experience with sandstorms that the open palm presented the clearest message; this gesture, in the absence of language, required the least interpretation. In each open palm, therefore, he offered the young priest his healing. In the right, he held a cup of cool water drawn directly from the well; in the left he held a small box in which he had a special white cream of zinc powder mixed with oils and essences of his own extraction. Gently he spoke in his own language and told the young man that his body needed water and his soul calm before he could pray properly. Quietly he advised him to drink and use this salve.

But he had misjudged the priest's unfortunate temper and his lack of trust. With an ugly oath that ill-beseemed his dignity, the young man dashed the cup to the sand and spat in the old Pilgrim's face. Then he stalked away like a furious cormorant, his black robes stiff with sand, the flies pursuing him in an orgy of delight. His misery was more rank than that of the corpse. Soon afterwards his loud, nasal voice could be heard high above the rest as he added his complaints to the caravan leader against the guards, the corpse, the suspect Pilgrim and above all the women, though no one cared. It was clear that he needed to rant and rage, whatever the subject. And he certainly did not want help.

The old Pilgrim had barely overcome his sense of shame over his second failure when the first came back to life again. He was wiping his face when he was confronted by the Indian's sudden re-appearance. But was the money-

changer alive? Blood was pouring from his mouth and had
soaked into his shirt and run over his belly. His eyes looked
glazed and wild. He was carrying a saddlebag in his arms
and looked straight through the Uigur. The old Pilgrim
realized with awe that he had somehow escaped death.

He watched with fascinated concern as the Indian delivered his load to the Abyssinian slave who lifted the
curtain of the litter. He watched in deepening astonishment as he turned away from her, with his face set and
expressionless, and rifled among the mules of the bridal
train. He watched in shock as the Indian loaded a large bag
of charcoal on his back – he who had never deigned to carry
even the slightest load and demanded assistance from the
flotilla of the bride's footmen for everything he needed –
and was appalled when he staggered off again towards the
fatal cliffs.

That was when the Pilgrim saw the birds of death circling
above the cliffs and understood his mistake. It was not the
Indian's death he had sensed but some other's. In fact, it
was not death he had diagnosed in this man at all, but the
proximity of immortality! For it seemed he had walked into
death and out of it again; he had discovered something
more terrible and wonderful than death beneath those
cliffs. For he was heading back there.

When he ran after him, the Indian had pushed the Uigur
away, roughly but kindly. He had turned and picked up the
reins of the mule he usually rode and thrust them unceremoniously into the old man's hands. The Pilgrim saw then
that the Indian's tongue had been cut out, and he began to
keen, as he had done before. He understood that the Indian
had become a son of Heaven and that *T'ien* alone knew him
now.

As the Pilgrim remembered his sense of failure at that

moment, he bowed under the weight of the sandstorm, which emptied its load of fearful enigmas upon his bare old head. How bitterly he had failed to protect his only spokesman from the desert of perpetual silence! How blind he had been to the Indian's 'Way'! How fatally he had confounded the difference between death and immortality, again! But the worst was yet to come.

For even as the Uigur had stood there by the well, with the reins of the mule in one hand and his small cup in another, with the argument still raging over the corpse and the poor animals all around still craving water, a figure stepped out of the litter of the bride. A slight figure, thin, delicately boned, wrapped in a veil that could not hide the sickening stain that was spreading down her legs. It was the slave, and the Pilgrim smelled the odour of death undeniably upon her.

So this was his third failure. He had diagnosed death in their dialogue all right, but it had been the slave's and not the moneychanger's. And he had sensed the proximity of immortality too, which had belonged in some strange way to the moneychanger and not to the slave. And he had made the fatal error of approaching the priest, who was neither ready for death nor prepared for immortality, and so he had wasted his chance of trust with three human souls. Of all the deserts he had known, the sense of shame he felt at these failures was the worst. And there was no glimmer of quicksilver to lead him out of it.

The only thing he could think to do in the circumstances was to offer temporary relief to the woman who collapsed by the well, for it did not take him long to know that he had no cure for her illness. He laid her against the cool stone and dipped his small cup in the bubbling waters. She

revived when she drank. And then he gave her the only
medicine he had for one in her condition: the traditional
female medicine. It was used for all the ailments, except
this ultimate one, from which women were known to
suffer. It was often used for barren women and for those
who would never bear children again. He had prepared his
own version of the healing paste and he offered it to the
slave in his usual fashion: like a black kernel in the open
palm of his hand.

She had received it with entire simplicity. After she had
drunk the water, she had stretched out her narrow hand,
tattooed with blue markings, and lifted the paste to her
lips. She had raised her veil quite simply too, revealing to
him the ravages of smallpox on her face. Why had she
done this? As he remembered her condition and reas-
sessed her disease, as he realized what kind of life she
must have led to bring her to such a pass, he found
himself bewildered by her simple trust at that moment.
What could have caused it? Not his gesture, surely, for he
had evidence enough from the episode with the priest that
his own gestures could not guarantee trust. Besides, death
was corroding her vitals and it was a death that was caused
precisely by a tortured complexity of doubt and self-
disgust, by the loss of love for the simple life. This he
diagnosed swiftly and surely. She was dying from broken
faith. So how did it happen that she so simply accepted
his medicine then? How could she trust him, despite her
condition?

Groping through the whipping winds of the lashing
sandstorm, the Pilgrim pondered this question anew and
realized he was lost.

What had enabled her to accept his help?

He could not understand it; he was lost.

How could his paste be any use without the simplicity of her acceptance of it?

He was bewilderingly and irreversibly lost.

Where had she found what she was dying for the lack of?

He did not know whether the well was ahead or behind him. He did not believe there was a beginning or an end to this sandstorm, which lashed at him with a sudden fury of triumph. Its hands gripped him, throttled him. His fear engulfed him. He was lost within and without.

And why had she given him the saddlebag?

As soon as he remembered the saddlebag, the Pilgrim realized that it was because he had received the saddlebag from the woman at the well that he now had to return there. Could it be that the saddlebag contained the key to this sandstorm? It was the same saddlebag that the Indian had carried in his arms; of this he was sure. It was the saddlebag that had guided him on the back of the mule all morning. After she had eaten the black medicine for women, in all simplicity, the slave had given him this saddlebag.

He knew she would have three or four hours at most before the pains and haemorrhaging would return. And as her strength slowly returned, she groped at her feet and struggled to lift up the saddlebag. It had fallen from her arms when she had fainted and now she held it out to him and urged him to take it. She begged him to keep it. He understood what she was saying in a distorted fashion, because he had learned the Amharic script in the monastery of Labrang. But although the meaning of the sounds survived the passage, he had pulled back in horror when he saw the Indian's blood on the saddlebag.

She had been insistent, however. She had staggered to her feet and put the saddlebag on the Indian's mule. And then she had left him with this strange legacy and gone about her business. Which was to build a fire and warm some water for her mistress.

The old man found himself the inheritor of a mule he would never ride and a saddlebag he would never use. But it seemed that the saddlebag was not for use after all, because it was already full. It was crammed with packages. When he opened it, he found bundles and rolls, all wrapped in silk and parchment, and bound in twine. He strapped the saddlebag on the mule, extracted one of the bundles from it, and there, beside the well, as the preparations for the bridal bath were being made and the priest protested against violations at the grave of the mother of the Prophet, he opened the roll of parchment and found onion-skin paper inside, all covered with Persian calligraphy.

The Uigur's eyes were bright and keen, but he had difficulty reading the fine script on that delicate paper. The noonday sun was beating down on the page and it blazed before him, blinding him momentarily. He could hardly make it out. It was written as if at a great speed, without the dots. And yet it seemed to be one enigmatic dot. The words ran into one another, equivocal. They told him that the path is strait and the way is narrow even while it is more spacious than the heavens and the earth and all that lies between them. It told him that the primal point was the beginning and end, the centre and the circumference of the heavens and the earth and all that lies between them. He did not understand.

The Pilgrim could not conceive of primal points. He could not see how paths could be strait and spacious, how a dot could contain a circle. He was puzzled by this legacy of all that lay between the heavens and the earth. If there was

168

a meaning in this message, he had to trust it would ripen, for he did not understand it now. His three failures had darkened his mind.

So when the call came for the caravan to continue, he folded the pieces of paper and placed them among his other medicines in the pouch he carried round his waist, and bowed his head under the burning sun. They had to start up again. Towards Medina. He walked behind the grumbling camels and the braying donkeys alongside the mule, which was one of the few animals to have been refreshed by the waters of the well. And he kept his hand resting on the saddlebag all the way.

One hour later they noticed that the corpse had been left behind. There was a hue and cry of protestation and counter-accusation. The Pilgrim smiled to himself at the constructed surprise of it all. He knew it already; he had seen it happen. He had watched the guards leaving the corpse behind against the north wall of the ruin by the well. They did it on purpose, he was sure of it. For it had been decided that they should follow in the rear of the caravan with their unpleasant load and the Pilgrim, who was walking among the pack animals, saw everything. They waited till the caravan started up and then, as everyone was finally in motion, two of the guards slipped behind the shrine with the sagging coffin and emerged on the northern side of the ruin without it.

As the mutiny ripened, it became quite clear from the noisy protest of the guards, who insisted on taking the dead man's wealth with them back to the well to retrieve the corpse, that they were absconding with the barrels of oil and bags of rice, the bales of silk and cotton and spice. It was obvious that they were returning to the coast with their booty of fine indigo and had no intention of taking one step further towards Medina. He realized that the dead man's soul was no more likely to receive the prayers of priests than his body to receive a proper burial.

But there was nothing the Pilgrim could do about this knowing. Like the knowledge of the bandits somewhere up ahead, the knowledge that the corpse was left behind remained rolled up in his wrinkled skull, waiting to be deciphered by time. Like the meaning of his youthful dream, like the message in his medicine pouch, knowing needed ripeness to be understood. The riddles of sand-storms too could be deciphered only when the key was found and his fear was faced. He sighed, patted the mule. Trust, he realized, had to be first exercised on himself.

After all, when the sandstorm struck, he had had to trust it too. He had sensed that if he wanted to solve its riddle he must go backwards also – to the well – where the guards had unceremoniously dumped the corpse to rot into un-perceived innocence. He knew he could find the female balance of this male sandstorm only if he returned to the well. He had to abandon the Indian's mule and uncreate his day step by step in order to arrive at the stillness at the heart of this sandstorm's riddle. This knowledge had come to him, too, without any fanfare or fuss. It had come like a quiet ripeness and needed no drama of surprise to shake him, although his heart was seized by the familiar shudder of his fear as the particles of sand imprinted this knowledge on his skin.

And then in the midst of this howling gale, when he had lost his way at the heart of this stinging desert storm, he had suddenly remembered the saddlebag which he had left behind with the caravan. He had thought at first the secret of the slave's simplicity lay in it and had been eager to unravel its mystery, but on closer scrutiny the saddlebag had rendered him whirling words, as bewildering as the sandstorm itself. It had offered him a message that he could not understand. But in spite of being tested by the worst of his fears, in spite of being lost, he had to trust this enigmatic message too, and go on.

By now, he had been wandering for several hours. The sand had found its way into every orifice and its howling was loud in his ears. He sensed from the blurred light about him that there was still an hour left to sunset. He was so buffeted and beaten by the wind at this moment that he stumbled against some rocks at his feet and fell, cutting his lip. As he felt the blood on his gnarled fingers, he realized that he had just lost his last tooth.

So! Suddenly, then, it came to him, lucidly, calmly, like the turning of a well-oiled key. He need not bite life any longer so long as he could drink immortality. He understood everything! *The source of the slave's simplicity was the water from the well.* He had given her water to drink before he offered her his medicine and that was the source of her trust. That was what prepared her for immortality though she could not escape the ills he diagnosed. And the saddlebag had been filled from the same source: just as a stream of letters flowed out from a single dot of ink. He had not recognized the simple remedy it offered through its seeming enigmas, just as he had not seen the Indian's proximity to immortality in his daring death. He was no better than the poor young priest who had refused his cup of water! This final ripeness came upon his heart like a physical blow. Why had he not understood before?

As soon as the Pilgrim realized the reason why the slave had accepted his medicine, the riddle of the sandstorm began to unravel. The whole point of it began to dawn on him. It seemed, as he groped his way forward, that all enigmas had begun to converge, and he wanted to shout, to sing, to call out and embrace his wife. His joy almost equalled his fear.

He kept his mouth shut, however, and drank his blood gratefully, for the storm was still at its height and the sand was thick. It had settled into the creases of his clothes, the folds of his skin, the wrinkles round his eyes, the crevices of his ears, everywhere. It was a struggle for him to rise to his feet and stagger on in the solid wind. He had a great yearning to lay down the heavy load of the heavens and the earth and all that lay between them, to uncreate himself. 'There is, O monks, a state where there is neither earth, nor water, nor heat, nor air; neither infinity of space nor infinity of consciousness, nor nothingness, nor perception nor non-perception; neither this world nor that world, neither sun nor moon. It is the uncreate.' Remembering the words of the Buddha, he took one more step.

Blindly, with wind and sand full in his face, he felt his feet sinking. And deep beneath him came the rolling drums of embattled armies buried in the dunes, waiting to engulf him. 'The uncreate,' he remembered, is 'neither coming nor going nor standing. It is without stability, without change; the eternal which never originates and never passes.'

Both his feet were sinking rapidly into the sand. His fear shuddered to his throat as he heard the clash of arms, the thunder of war within him. He had stepped into a quicksand. In seconds, it had reached his knees. He was locked fast. And now the time had come to hold still and face the great inward encounter. He could not flee from his fear now. But the joy was mounting. 'There,' says the Buddha, 'is the end of sorrow.' He had reached the balance. And he began to sink into the quicksand with a sensation of simple astonishment.

So this was the centre of the heavens and the earth and all that lay between them! Here was his 'Way', the primal point of his circle. The path was strait, most certainly, and yet how wide he had wandered to reach it. All his journeyings had brought him to this spot and to no other. All his search had come to this end and he could have gone no further. The Book of Changes told him there are many different roads in the world, but the destination is the same. There are a hundred deliberations but the result is one. The names are different, but the source is the primal point! Lucidly, he diagnosed his death and prescribed the antidote of immortality.

He was being pulled inward and his heart surged outward. He was caught between this vice at the solar plexus and drawn into the vast of the uncreate. Sinking fast, he fumbled with his robes and managed to pull the roll of writing free from his medicine pouch. The words from the saddlebag were the key to the sandstorm, like water and air. They affirmed that the riddle of fear was unlocked by simple trust. He held his arms high as the sand reached his armpits and covered his face with the parchment, held it to his nostrils, as if it were breath. The heavens and the earth and all that lay between them rose from this primal point in which he was sinking, and to it would return, like him. He could no longer read, but he remembered.

He repeated the words then in a strong voice, with his last remaining breath. He shouted them aloud in his own language, letting them ripple through his lips like water, like the love of his wife, like the joy of living. And then, as his life ran through his veins like quicksilver and out of his lungs, the Pilgrim sang the words with the sand at his throat: *The primal point!*

As he sank deeper, his heart's seed simply cracked with joy. He opened his mouth as the sand reached it, and drank it in eagerly, with his blood, for the healing of his people, for the protection of his fertile lands, for the strength and beauty of his sons and his sons' sons. And when the sand swallowed him entirely, toothless but content, he had already died, free of fear.

The quicksand which swallowed the Pilgrim lay in the gully just below the ruined shrine of Abwa' on the road between Mecca and Medina. It lay within five paces of the heap of rubble which led from the bottom of the dry well where the body of the slave was thrown within the shrine. But the corpse leaning against the north wall of the ruin had been laid too far away from the edge of the gully to be engulfed by the mercy of the quicksand, and still stank, bitterly.

THE PRIEST

The Priest flung the body of the dead woman into the old well and covered it up with stones. Then he drew up buckets of water from the new well and threw them over himself. He was afraid he had been contaminated. He knew she had not died of any communicable disease despite the ravages of her face, but she was a woman and he had been obliged to touch her.

The Priest was scrupulous about his religious obligations. He had been born the youngest son in a God-fearing family who were all scrupulous about their religious obligations. All his uncles and older brothers before him had completed their studies in theology and jurisprudence in Karbila and were among the most notable Shi'ia *mujtahids* and scholars in Persia. All the women in his family were known for their impeccable virtue and had long pedigrees of equal distinction. It was said by certain of the envious in their town that each of these embodiments of modesty must surely be the equal of the Virgin Mary whom the Christians worshipped, for how else was it possible for them to have conceived any children at all? The Priest was the last with the privilege of being born of such a chaste conjunction, and was rather ill-favoured, with a tendency to itchy patches of eczema. He had also inherited, so they told him, the uneasy temper of his mother, God rest her soul, who had died of respectability before he reached the age of thirteen and left him orphaned among mournful aunts. From this time he was sent to the *madrasihs* of Karbila, where he was educated by some of the most distinguished *'ulama* of the age. When he decided to go on his pilgrimage to Mecca, he was barely twenty and a terminal virgin.

Of course he had been married. The first time, when he was seventeen, was to a young girl who had developed a virulent dysentery on the eve of the wedding and died shortly afterwards. Needless to say, the marriage had not been consummated. Then there had also been a temporary wife, but she had not proved satisfactory either and the marriage had been annulled after three days. Finally, after much debate, his father arranged for him to be betrothed to a third maiden, whose parentage was so distinguished that it was hardly possible for her physical appearance to be its equal, despite all assurances to the contrary. Naturally, he had not yet seen the girl but had asked for the wedding to be postponed until after his pilgrimage.

He was frightened of women. The only females he had known, other than these unsatisfactory brides, were dim-featured cousins who had teased him mercilessly in childhood and vague, mothlike aunts dressed in perpetual black, with aubergine shadows under their eyes. There had also been a simple nurse from the provinces who smelled rank with mutton fat and who had engulfed him against her capacious bosom when his mother died, causing unforgettable sensations of suffocation which haunted him still from time to time. The reason he went on pilgrimage that year was because of a woman too. And she was the most frightening of all.

She had arrived in Karbila some nine months before while he was still a student. It was just after the death of one of the well-known teachers in the Shaykhi schools and this woman had assumed the authority to conduct his classes from behind a curtain. Certainly she had impeccable credentials from a family of *'ulama*. Certainly she was a poet and a scholar of distinction. But she was a woman! All hell had broken loose in the Shi'ia community of Iraq because of her.

They said she had rejected the veil. They whispered that she had deserted her husband and her children. They began to accuse her of heresy for she had ideas that were shockingly nonconformist. And she defied them all. She taught classes for women as well as men and dazzled her audiences with proofs from the Quran. She claimed the laws of the past should be annulled and undertook to put this outrageous theory into practice. Theological debate was rife and had heightened the political tensions between the Shi'ia community in Iraq and their Ottoman governors, causing the Persian consul to appeal to the British powers to intervene. Many of the clergy in Karbila were willing to forgo their ideological differences in order to have this dangerous woman banished from the Shi'ia community. She had raised a high scandal.

The young Priest had attended some of this woman's classes. They had caused him nights of feverish sleeplessness and furious mental strife. She sat hidden behind a curtain and held sway over a room full of men by the power of her oratory alone. She always listened to her critics and let them talk for as long as they desired, but when it was her turn to speak, she demolished their arguments in a single sweep. She reduced their protestations to pulp. No one could equal her Quranic knowledge. He had seen, with his own eyes, men twice his age trembling with impotence before her logic. He had seen one mullah break down and weep.

A young colleague of his had been provoked to challenge this woman to a verbal tournament. He had claimed that the only way to get the better of her was by flat contradiction, by refusing to let her speak at all. To prove his point, he had interrupted her again and again in order to deflect the argument, and had finally resorted to hurling petty curses in an attempt to undermine the force of her proofs. He had not followed the correct procedures of *mubahala* but simply tried to silence her by shouting. At that point she had lifted the curtain and had suddenly entered the room, unveiled, before all those men.

When the young Priest remembered it, he still flushed to the roots of his scurfy hair and felt his limbs tremble beneath him, even though months had passed since the event. For he had abandoned his studies from that very hour and day and had decided to go on pilgrimage because of what ensued. She had entered the room, unveiled, this woman, and had looked his dumbfounded colleague full in the face for a few moments. Her cheek bore the imprint of a black curl. Her eyebrow was raised, like the curve of a crescent moon. She had observed him coldly, from the top of his turban to the toe of his foot under the soiled hem of his robes, and then, before the company of his peers, she had quietly told him he was not worthy of speaking on such sacred subjects till he had learned the rudiments of proper decorum for religious debate.

The Priest had been so shaken by the experience (far more shaken in fact than his colleague) that he broke out in a violent rash which nothing could assuage. What troubled him was not the sight of her face, the astonishment of her beauty or the shock conveyed by her actions. What disturbed him most was that he found himself agreeing with her. He doubted the opinions of those who condemned her. He began to lose respect for his teachers because they disagreed with her. When she reprimanded his colleague, he was appalled to find her words entirely justified. And when this colleague spread rumours that she received lovers in her chamber and fed them with pomegranates from her mouth, he could not bear to listen to these lies, despite the outrage she had committed. His pulse had stopped at the sight of her face, the sound of her words, and even now it shuddered when he remembered them, but if he was honest with himself he knew this had nothing to do with pomegranates. It was because she had caused him to question his motives and deepest convictions. It was because he found himself losing all sense of purpose, all confidence in his studies, all point in his future profession. As a result of listening to her, he began to doubt that he should be a priest.

The lines of demarcation between sexuality and spirituality were unclear to him, however. And it was therefore in considerable mental confusion and physical arousal that he fled from Karbila. He turned towards Mecca as his salvation, seeking to purify himself from this woman's seductive powers. He determined that his pilgrimage would dispel his doubts, restore the true temper of his blood so he might take up his profession anew. He wanted to purge his tongue, his heart, his mind from her pernicious influence. He had ardent hopes that he would be so confirmed in his faith that he would never, never in his life, be vulnerable to such a woman or submit to such heretical ideas again. The earnest young man felt that he had to fulfil every last ritual and obligation of the pilgrimage to ensure his salvation.

His was an uncompromising faith, sustained by dreams of martyrdom and self immolation. His lacklustre life was made vivid by the ardent fancies associated with the suffering and death of the Imams during the special ceremonies of the Shi'ia calendar. Since his rather spotty adolescence, fed by a fervour that verged at times on fanaticism, he had fasted for days and prayed to die to prove his faith. But although he allowed his imagination to dwell on these passionate scenes, he governed his actions by a strict obedience to the laws of his religion, bordering even on obsessiveness when it came to matters of ritual and dogma.

He was particularly meticulous about traditions related to the *hajj*. He had read everything on the subject and learned it off by heart. He knew what invocations he should repeat and how many times and where; what historical events he should meditate upon and why; which robes to wear, what animals to sacrifice and how to walk between which places during the ten days of his pilgrimage in the most sacred city of Mecca. He knew every significant rock and stone and shrine and ruin between the sacred cities. He had even practised his stone-throwing so as to be able to fling righteous scorn with accuracy at the satanic images in the valley of Mona. He was determined to attend the *Hajj-i-Akbar* this very year when the Festival of Sacrifices, the *'Id al-Qurban*, coincided with the sacred Friday during the month of *Dhu'l-Hijja*. This was a most auspicious time according to the Islamic calendar, to be a pilgrim. His expectations, like those of many round him, were intense; the fever of millennial zeal was contagious. Some enthusiasts even said that the fulfilment of all the Shi'ia prophecies was imminent, that the Twelfth Imam might appear at the Kaabih at this very time. Although he did not, of course, admit to such excesses, the young Priest did harbour secret hopes. He prayed that if his pilgrimage was acceptable he might be given proof of it. He ardently desired, as a reward for his virtuousness, to be among the chosen first to witness the appearance of the long-awaited *Qa'im*.

He left Karbila in late spring, therefore, in order to ensure that he would reach Arabia in good time to perform his *hajj*. He spent some weeks in his family home, dissuading relatives from marriage plans until his return and submitting to the doleful attention of his aunts. These ladies insisted that the condition of his skin required a daily change of shirts and strict avoidance of all dried fruits. When he protested faintly at this last instruction, since he had a particular weakness for dried fruits, they also loaded him with useless salves and tinctures for his eczema. His family were hard bargainers. His father and elder brothers, too, initially judged his decision to go on pilgrimage to be overzealous. They also argued with him about leaving his studies incomplete and tried to point out the presumption of his going on his *hajj* before them. But they finally gave in to his wishes and did not stint to provide him with supplies, for they felt, in the long run, that this journey might help him mature, settle down and marry. After a brief period of preparatory fasting, therefore, he set off on his long journey with a secret store of dried fruits, a vast quantity of shirts and a heightened sense of destiny. He managed to leave all the salves and balms behind.

But his triumphal exit was short-lived. Long before he even reached Shiraz, he was waylaid by robbers who stripped him to the skin and left him wandering the wilderness without so much as a single shirt. Only his handful of dried fruits saved him from starvation, and he pondered then over the prescience of his aunts. Had it not been for the kindness of a passing merchant who knew a distant uncle of his with ecclesiastical connections in Shiraz, he would have been forced to return home in ignominy. This clerical relative replenished his supplies with modest comforts, however, and scolded him severely for his lack of practicality. He brushed aside the young man's enthusiasms regarding God's protection as well as his expectations of spiritual honour and gave him strict instructions about safety measures on the pilgrim route. The ways were long and hard, advised that worthy; one's head could stay in the clouds only if one's feet remained firmly on the ground. Although he was never again to enjoy the same luxury of shirts, the young priest set off for Bushire, therefore, in the company of a trade caravan that promised much better protection.

However, sensible advice did not entirely satisfy the Priest's voracious appetite for spiritual improvement. Suffering endured in the course of pilgrimage, he had learned, was at least double the value of difficulties sustained at any other time, besides providing accreditation among the ranks of the pious. He had become a shrewd calculator when it came to the debit and credit system of religion. He added all his meritorious actions together in order to ensure that the obligatory and desirable ones outnumbered those that were undesirable and forbidden. He also tried to limit the number of neutral actions, because they were a waste of spiritual energy. And he kept a sharp eye open for the bonus of accompanying the righteous. There was nothing so efficacious, in his opinion, as the company and example of God's righteous, for this offered one instant spiritual improvement at a relatively low cost.

*   *   *

The boat was crammed with God's righteous. There were dozens of notables and commoners, all drawn to their *hajj* at this auspicious period, like himself. And the young Priest was satisfied to note that he could count on suitable company, though it was more abundant than he would have liked. The flimsy *dhow* was teeming with passengers only a few of whom were provided with seats. The rest were massed at the stern and in the bow where they had to shift for themselves on coils of salt-drenched rope, subject to the curses of sailors and the worst of the sea. When he saw their miserable conditions and considered the interminable length of the trip, the young man gathered his robes about him and used all his arts of persuasion to insist on his rights to sit in distinguished company.

There were not only personages of high social rank aboard his boat but also dignitaries of the ecclesiastic world. His heart thrilled at the privilege. He strove to sit as close as possible to these distinguished passengers in order to have their spiritual gloss rub off on him, as it were. It was highly gratifying, as a result of his avuncular connections, to be found worthy of an introduction to several of them early in the voyage. He felt sure this distinction anticipated later spiritual honours at the height of the *hajj*.

The corresponding tests were severe, however. The weather was rough and the rations were low. He suffered from seasickness and there was not enough water to go around. Tempers rose with the swell of the waves, but he redoubled his prayers and hoped his devotions would not go unnoticed. Surely these miseries would add to his spiritual credit in the end?

While he managed to sublimate his seasickness to the advantage of his soul, the Priest was less successful in handling the ill-humour and discourtesy among his fellow pilgrims, particularly those from whom he had hoped to benefit. This was very troubling to him. One of these gentlemen had connections with the royal family of the Qajars, and was responsible for public order in the capital; another was a mullah like himself and was related to the *Imam-Jumih* of Shiraz. Both, he discovered in the course of the voyage, were insufferably rude. The reverential relative found occasion to argue even with the mildest of passengers on board and became so objectionable on one occasion that the captain threatened to throw him into the sea. Had it not been for the earnest advocacy of a young merchant who came from his city, the *Imam-Jumih* might have lost a brother in the Gulf of Oman.

The Priest was shocked. Was it possible that men with high ecclesiastical rank could lack spiritual qualities? The brother of the *Imam-Jumih*, who was the only person to have water in excess, saw fit to ignore his extreme thirst when the supplies were low and remained impervious to his evident need, despite his clerical connections and the fact that he had placed himself close enough to have all his prayers overheard. Could this distinguished gentleman be more governed by greed than God? Was it possible that religious study did not necessarily ensure spiritual refinement? The very thought filled the young man with a misery that was more desperate than thirst and more familiar. It was from thoughts such as these that he had fled Karbila.

He tried to find some way of interpreting the circumstances to fit the framework of his faith. Since he must not criticize the actions of his spiritual betters, he found relief in placing the blame on his inferiors instead. He decided that his fellow passenger, the young man who had been so quick to defend the brother of the *Imam-Jumih* of Shiraz, had been overpresumptuous in showing up the behaviour of a mullah. The fellow was a mere tradesman, after all, despite the irritating presumption of his green turban; to be of the lineage of Mohammed did not give him any theological superiority. He decided this pious *sayyid* with his delicate features and mild manners had profligate aspirations to virtue and determined to despise him.

After this purgatorial sea journey, they finally arrived in Jiddah. The city was agog with pilgrims. And, to the young Priest's dismay, crawling with pickpockets and panders too. He was cheated of a full purse within half a day of his arrival, and lost one of his uncle's carpets, the replacement of which cost almost as much as the price of his voyage from Bushire. He found the task of arranging the journey towards the sacred city of Mecca dogged at every step by unscrupulous caravan leaders, dishonest merchants and a host of other middlemen and thieves who made it their business to earn money off the gullible and cheat the wise.

Pilgrimage, he discovered, was something to bargain and haggle for. He was revolted by the large variety of charlatans who roved through the bazaars, hawking their so-called charms and trinkets made sacred by association with the holy shrines: amulets and beads which had been carried round the Kaabih seven times and were guaranteed to ward off the evil eye; fermented vinegars brewed in sacred sunshine which carried promises of eternal youth; pastes and ointments and putrid-smelling salves mixed with dust from the holy of holies which claimed to be elixirs against all kinds of diseases. One day he was accosted by a ragtag troop of sophisticated street urchins who negotiated with him for alms. When he told them to be off, they raised shrill voices and accused him of being a hypocrite. It was in one of the busiest *maydans* in Jiddah near the public baths, at the entrance of Bab al Mecca, and many people turned round to see what the uproar was about. Mortified, the Priest found himself thrusting pennies at his pursuers just to shut their mouths, but he felt ashamed of himself and sullied by the action. He fasted the next day to purge his distaste and grew impatient to be on his way.

There were interminable delays. A large caravan, due to leave shortly, would absorb the majority of the pilgrims heading for Mecca, but its departure was being put off from day to day. A wealthy bridal train, stranded in Jiddah since the previous week, was the apparent cause. Some said the bride was heading for Syria through the Gulf of Aqaba; others said that the entourage was looking for an escort to go by land towards Rabigh. Greed had induced the leader of the caravan to consider a detour in order to conduct the lady and her innumerable train of mules and donkeys at least part of the way before cutting east to Mecca. The pilgrims were outraged. Some of the more impatient among them were making alternative plans that required last-minute loans of money and men. A few had decided to risk travelling towards Mecca alone, despite the danger of brigands along the road. Most were becoming embroiled in haggling with the caravan leaders. The conflict had raised religious hackles which the young Priest felt keenly. Fulminating against women, he swelled the complaints and joined in the vociferous rows that took place daily at the city gates.

In the process he found himself frequently in conversation with an Indian, a Sunni moneychanger from Karachi, who appeared not only to be serving as the go-between for the bride but was active in arranging alternative transportation for some of the pilgrims who wanted to proceed directly and without delay to Mecca. The Priest suspected him of also trafficking in illegal alcohol, but since the fellow was on friendly terms with several of the most distinguished ecclesiastics, there was no one with whom the young mullah could share his doubts on this particular score. The moneychanger seemed familiar with the route and offered to provide quick service for ready cash to the wealthier members of the caravan. He had convinced one old man from Bushire that he could arrange a private escort of bodyguards for a very modest fee. The rich old merchant was going on the *hajj* to ensure his benefits in the next world but had been unable to resist earning a few extra in this one at the same time. His baggage consisted of innumerable bolts of silk and bales of cotton, sacks of wheat and barrels of oil, bundles of myrrh and casks of pomegranate essence, and he wanted the consignment of indigo, in particular, to be as well protected as his soul. He accepted the Indian's offer to hire the guards at a sum which turned out to be three times as much as the regular amount charged by the caravan leaders. And in the end he decided to join the regular caravan anyway, for reasons of additional security, he confessed, because he was rather afraid of the bodyguards he had hired. The indigo, he said, was priceless.

The Indian cultivated the friendship of the Priest assiduously. He was deeply distressed about the delay and wished there might be some solution, because it was anathema to him, he said, it was *haram*, to bring these defiled women one step nearer the sacred city. But what could he do? His hands were tied; he could not say all that he knew. The Priest felt himself begin to itch all over as he listened to the fellow's innuendoes. The Sunni dropped hints on several occasions regarding the dubious religious affiliations of the young bride and her immediate entourage of female servants. Although they pretended to be followers of the Prophet, in reality they were fire-worshippers, sun-worshippers, idolaters, he breathed. They were unfit to approach the sacred precincts of the city of Mecca. They were the scum of the earth. And the black slave – here he dropped his voice low enough to suggest a whole hell of possibilities – was a Jew! Imagine! He had been among these disbelievers since they left the southern coast of Persia, he complained. He had been forced, as a result of obligations to the girl's father, to undertake this task. This was the price he had to pay to duty. Such sacrifices! Such deprivations! It was a hard life.

Hard as he tried to shrug off the Indian, the Priest found he could not. The man clamped onto his conscience like a leech. And from that time on, during the interminable days of delay, the young Priest became obsessed with the Falasha woman who attended the bride, hidden in her *takhteravan*. He watched her closely for any sign of disrespect at the times of prayer. He scrutinized her like a hawk for any hint of blasphemous behaviour. He even found himself hovering near the bridal *takhteravan*, watching for her to appear on her errands to the market or her interminable preparations for baths, to which the bride appeared to be addicted. She rarely spoke. She wore a veil which stirred his senses. Her feet were bare and bone-thin. Her skin was dust-coloured, not black like the skin of Nubian slaves but subtly dark, that dusky darkness of the slaves of Abyssinia. Her ankles were delicate and her instep high. She wore a string of blue beads against the evil eye that circled the ankle bone to perfection and had painted henna on her toes. They gleamed with a burnish that stung his eyes.

When plans were finalized for the bridal train to accompany the caravan, the Priest became increasingly restless and imposed a fast on himself. He redoubled his prayers and earnestly begged for release from tests. The moment of pilgrimage was drawing nearer and with every day that passed he felt himself drawing further from the proper condition of the pilgrim. He had left the '*Atabat* because of a woman and had turned his steps towards the Kaabih in order to be purified of all desires, and now he found himself dogged once more by a woman and consumed by desires. He yearned for a miracle.

It was a huge relief to him, therefore, when God and a Turkish escort came to his rescue. The escort, which had instructions to take the bridal train directly to Medina, arrived at the last minute, just as the caravan was preparing to leave for the holy city in the unendurable presence of women. He was sure he had been blessed because the pilgrims could now proceed without them. But to his horror, the Indian tried to reopen negotiations with the caravan leaders. He bargained with them to take the bridal train at least as far as Hedda, at the outskirts of the holy city, where they could take the shorter detour round to the caravanserai of Al Jamum in the north. The caravan leaders raised their prices, the departure was put off for one more day and the Priest's skin itched all night and did not let him sleep.

The Turks, however, did not want to pay the additional cost. And in their dithering, the Priest saw the hand of God once more. Summoning all his uncle's resources and his own feeble powers of bargaining to his aid, he made his way to the city gates at dusk the following day and astonished the caravan leaders by offering to pay them the same sum as the one being negotiated with the Turks. In return for this, he said grimly, they should agree to leave immediately, at dawn the next morning, and without the bridal entourage. He had come with the money in his purse, he added.

The camel leader stopped chewing his evening meal and stared incredulously at the young man who had sought him out with this irrational proposal in the caravanserai at the eastern gates of Jiddah. It was a well-appointed *khan*, unlike those in the desert, with a fine pool in the central courtyard and ample quarters for the camels under the high vaulted arches that enclosed the square. The camel leader was well known here and courted by the camel drivers who had competed for their contract with him by providing a large meal that evening, which was being interrupted now by the untimely arrival of this would-be passenger. He was a student, evidently, and of the Shi'ia variety, from across the Gulf. One avoided arguments with fellows of his type, but if the poor fool was so eager to lose his money, it would be no more than charity to accept. He wiped the grease from his mouth with the back of his hand, emptied the purse, and shrugged his assent. The Priest immediately raised his hands in a loud prayer of thanksgiving. The violence of his gratitude quite took the caravan leader's appetite away, but it was worth losing a meal to get such a good deal out of the will of God.

They left, therefore, the following dawn, and had already placed several *farsangs* between themselves and the gates of Bab el Mecca by the time the Indian discovered they had gone. The young Priest was in a state of exultation. He determined to consecrate himself to his task and forget all other distractions. He continued to purge himself of any lingering memories of the Falasha woman by fasting from sunrise till sunset, and he dressed in the white robe of pilgrimage, the *ihram*, to purify his outward self as a reflection of his inward dedication. Since the weather was unseasonably warm, the robe felt hot and made his body itch all over, but he did not care. He increased the number of his devotions and was scrupulous in saying his prayers at the right time and place. He kept his spiritual balance sheets assiduously and was on the lookout for any signs of divine approbation. If God were in debt to him, he would feel all the more secure.

By the time they had drawn near the sacred city, the Priest was light-headed with expectation. The Kaabih was thick with important people, high-ranking *'ulama* from the caliphate as well as Karbila, all of whom were influential and many of whom, from Persia, knew his uncles and his brothers. He felt gratified that several of their reverences were walking near him when he circumambulated the house of God and he was pleased to recite the special verses in their hearing. He felt himself lifted on waves of spiritual energy as the crowd surged and swelled and carried him in a sweep of emotion around the sacred black stone. Surely here he would see, he would hear the confirmations he was so eager for! Surely God would bless his pilgrimage with a sign from His holy presence!

But these emotions soon evaporated as the days of the *hajj* passed by and his expectations were unfulfilled. The only signs he witnessed were those of human frailty. To his dismay he noticed that several distinguished pilgrims were bending the sacred regulations to suit their own conveniences. Some did not participate at all in the more difficult rites. Many seemed to be on their *hajj* for reasons of curiosity and cupidity only. He was oppressed by his old doubts, by the discrepancy he saw between religious rank and moral integrity, by his own reactions to these. In Mona, on the second day of his *hajj*, someone threw a stone from behind and hit him so hard on the back of the head during the *rajim* that he turned round in a rage and cursed the man before he could control himself. The shame of doing so was as painful as the stone. Was he himself any different from those he judged so harshly? He interpreted the act as a reprimand from God for having negative thoughts and tried to make up for it by buying twice the prescribed number of lambs for the sacred day of *'Id al-Qurban*.

On the last day of the *hajj* he slaughtered his lambs with a desperate sense of urgency. He begged God for a sign. But all that was forthcoming was an overpowering stench of rotting meat. This he had not anticipated. The air was rank with the putrid and noisome smell, for hundreds of other pilgrims had performed the rites of *zibh* with him. Many of them distributed their offerings among the poor, who were more than willing to receive these, but an equal number, who wished to benefit from their own sacrifices, laid slabs of meat in the sun to dry. The stink was insupportable. He endured it with mounting impatience. Surely if he had done his part, God would send him a sign? Surely if he had performed his pilgrimage properly, God would not let him down? Surely he deserved that the *Qa'im* would appear to bless his efforts –?

But nothing happened. There was no caller who called out from heaven. The sun did not rise in the west nor did any bright star appear in the east. There was no fire in the sky and no redness covered the faces of the people, except that which was due to the excessive heat of the season. The young Priest saw none of the expected signs. He fixed his eyes on the Corner of the Kaabih and the Station of Abraham, where the *Qa'im* was expected to announce himself, but was crestfallen to see that nothing occurred of any significance. In deepening gloom he listened as the *'ulama* around him confirmed his disillusionment: the *Qa'im* had not chosen to appear that year. He was deeply disappointed by the indeterminate nature of his *hajj*.

Only once, when the place was packed with teeming pilgrims, did he catch sight of something strange, as if in a dream. But it was probably his intense expectations that had made him so susceptible. It seemed to him that there was someone standing near the Kaabih holding the ring of the stone in his hand. It was curious because fleetingly he half recognized the slight figure. But then the crowd swept on and he thought no more about it.

Shortly afterwards, one of the pilgrims collapsed nearby and there were some moments of disturbance while the old man was carried away. He appeared to have had a heart attack. The Priest, surrounded by the press of curious pilgrims, craned his neck with the others to watch while people struggled to lift the dying man from underfoot. He was fat. He was flaying his arms about and shouting, 'Indigo! Indigo!' It was very disturbing. They managed to remove him through the chanting crowd as it surged around the Kaabih, but the young Priest found it impossible to concentrate his thoughts on his own performance after that. For he had recognized the dying man: it was the rich old merchant from Bushire in their caravan who had been so keen to employ the guards from Luristan to protect his goods. Only afterwards, considering his will in the light of God's, was he relieved to think that the *Qa'im* had not appeared at such a time and place, when his attention had been on the rasping gasps, on the livid blue lips of the dying merchant. It would have been embarrassing to have to choose where to place his attention at that moment.

The only other unusual episode which occurred on the

last day of the young Priest's *hajj* was a brief glimpse he caught, through the tumult of the crowd, of a curious interaction between two men standing close to the sacred black stone. At first he was not sure whether he recognized the one with delicate features, wearing a green turban, but when he saw him speaking with great intensity to one of the well-known Shaykhi leaders, he remembered the over-virtuous young merchant in the pilgrim boat, his fellow passenger who had remonstrated with the captain to save the brother of the *Imam-Jumih* of Shiraz from the stormy sea. There he was again. He was holding the hand of the respected cleric in his own. It was evident that whatever he was saying had embarrassed the Shaykhi to a remarkable degree. The Priest felt a tremor of disturbance, a stab of alarm, for there was something familiar about the discon-certed air of the mullah that reminded him of his own deepest misgivings, his own unsettled purposes. There was something presumptuous about the very mildness of the *sayyid*'s gesture because it seemed to question the author-ity of the *'ulama*. He flushed with jealousy too: what did this merchant have to discuss with a mullah of such high rank? Was there some event, some theological debate he had missed? What religious questions could make a Shay-khi leader turn so pale that he had not already thought about? But he concluded it must have been a personal appeal merely, or further evidence of that young *sayyid*'s brazen zeal and exaggerated piety, for there were no repercussions in the ecclesiastic community.

He thought no more of this occurrence until some days later, when he learned that the Shaykhi leader had left Mecca. Suddenly and without warning left, without com-pleting his pilgrimage. Had changed his plans and gone with all speed to Medina, leaving no explanations.

Although there was no suggestion that the Shaykhi leader's abrupt departure had anything to do with the mild-faced young merchant whom the Priest had seen accosting him, he found this an odd coincidence all the more irritating for its lack of significance. The cleric's departure was interpreted as pressure of work, of course. Some murmured about a problem in Baghdad related to heresy which required his immediate presence. Others mentioned the heightened political tensions and the interference of foreign powers. The young Priest could not calm his agitation at these rumours and would almost have preferred the cause to be related to the presumption of the *sayyid*, whom he never saw again. He recalled the troubles from which he himself had fled the '*Atabat*; he felt his old doubts rise up within again. Had the repercussions of the terrible woman followed him from Karbila and reached the sacred precincts of the House of God? Was her influence hounding him here at the very heart of his faith? But his questions remained unanswered and indeterminate, like his pilgrimage.

The Priest concluded his *hajj* in a state of dejection. The great spiritual theatre was over and the sacred event had come and gone, leaving him with a sense of its irrelevance. He felt embittered by the anticlimax, the lack of meaning in the moment. Despite his vigilance and all his preparation, he had not been graced by any signs, had not encountered any symbolic occurrences. The only satisfaction was that, with the exception of the deplorable incident at the stone-throwing, he had conducted himself with scrupulous propriety and in a manner that would have brought credit to his family. Even if God had not shown him any outward gesture of approval, he could not reproach himself for failure. Curiously enough, this fact did not leave him with a sense of victory or clear purpose either, but with a feeling of deepening disappointment as he turned his steps to Medina.

The desert is a place where motives can be seen from a great distance and where they can also be rendered meaningless. As he began the last part of his journey, the vast immensity was waiting to engulf the young Priest. He had ample time, in the days that followed, to measure his life's goals on the relentless scales of sky and land. His resolves rose nobly before him, only to dwindle to pebbles and stones. His ideals shimmered like cities of light on the far horizon, only to fade into stale deceptions as he drew near. Each step brought him closer to that fatal crossroads where faith became futility and took him further from certitude. The Priest felt himself shrinking as he left Mecca, and dwindling into the desert, which mocked him pitilessly.

The pilgrims in whose company he now found himself were of a much lower caste than those with whom he had performed his *hajj* in Mecca, and afforded him no spiritual gloss. The more significant ecclesiastics appeared to have travelled on to Medina in a separate caravan and he felt excluded from the circle of the elite, and forgotten. He found himself particularly irritated by the presence of a shrivelled old priest or *faqir* from the Far East whose prayers bore little or no resemblance to his own. He was annoyed too by the laconic dervish of dubious quality who had joined them outside Mecca and who had a habit of disappearing and reappearing like a mirage as they toiled through the dull dunes. The Priest concluded that the old *faqir* with wrinkled eyes was either mentally defective, for he seemed incapable of grasping any argument, or a pernicious infidel rather than a holy man. And he suspected the dervish of being a thief.

The ranks of the caravan had also been unpleasantly swelled by guards and mules from Luristan accompanying the corpse of the wealthy old merchant to Medina. Since he had died during his last pilgrimage while circumambulating the Kaabih, he had the privilege of burial in the sacred cemetery of 'al Baqr, where so many of the holy Imams and great saints of Islam were also buried. All his goods and chattels were being taken as dying bequests to the priests in Medina so that prayers might be said for the continued progress of his soul. And his continuing stench was unbearable.

But what soured the temper of the young man even more, what almost annulled the validity of his whole pilgrimage, was the appearance of the same wretched bridal train they had left behind in Jiddah. When the caravan was joined at the *khan* of Osfan, some *farsangs* beyond the city boundaries, by the bridal entourage, the Indian and the escort of Turks, he became almost hysterical. He caught a glimpse of the same black slave, the same Zoroastrian attendants. What injustice was this? Would these infidels and idolaters, these – women! – be galling his steps all the way to Medina? It was unthinkable! Why was he being dogged by them when he had done all he should have done, when he had surpassed himself in obedience, when surely he deserved more from God? Where were His blessings? And what of all the money he had spent to acquire these blessings? He had a strong sense of debts unpaid.

But the caravan leader shrugged his shoulders. There was nothing he could do. Yes, the Priest had paid for them to go to Mecca without the Turks, but now the Turks had paid extra to join them on the road to Medina. His job was to serve everyone's best interests. And he spat fruitfully at the sand between them and squinted back at the horizon.

Desperately, the young man resumed his fast. He reduced his intake of water to a minimum. His face became swollen with red scabs in the relentless heat. He was tormented by oozing sores. His fevered dreams returned and nothing could calm his agitation. Encouraged by the Sunni from Karachi, who had once more resumed his company, he fumed and fretted and finally began to foment anger among the other pilgrims. He began to speak of the sacredness of the path on which they were treading. He began to rant about the blasphemy of having these heathens tread it with them. He even began to feel he had a just cause on his hands. For they were approaching Abwa', the shrine of the mother of the Prophet. How was it possible that in this holy spot, at the sacred burial place of the holy Amanih herself, the resting place of the daughter of Vahab, the mother of Mohammed, the grandmother of the mystic Fatimih, at this place where she had died on her way to visit the grave of her husband 'Abdu'llah, on this path made sacred with her virtuous dust, how was it possible that they should have whores and prostitutes among them? How could it be that the pilgrims could allow such a blasphemy? The long-suffering mother of the Prophet had already been humiliated by the centuries, her grave had been covered in the dust of ignominy, her dignity and virtue had only just been re-established by the devotion of a pilgrim who had restored and renovated her shrine, she had only just been raised to her rightful place and honoured once more as she deserved, and now would they stand by and allow a bunch of silly women, filthy women, worldly and contaminated women – infidel women! – to desecrate her holy shrine? He demanded that the caravan be stopped and the women of the bridal train told to separate and travel alone with their Turkish escort, apart from the rest. The Indian said he thought it a very proper suggestion.

But on the fourth day out of Mecca, just one hour after they had left the *khan* of Khulays and one hour before they reached the shrine of Abwa', the caravan was stopped by a shriek louder than any protest he could have raised. It was the bride. She had fainted, they said. Everyone had to come to a halt. What was going on? Why was she screaming if she had fainted? What had made her faint that she should shriek like that?

The young Priest found himself drawn closer and closer to the Zoroastrians. He hovered beside the bridal *takhteravan* and could not tear himself away. The girl seemed hysterical, all right. But was all this shrieking due to the stink of the corpse, as some of the pilgrims seemed to suggest? Or was there an orgy going on in there? The caravan leaders pressed around the *takhteravan* too, demanding explanations. But when the black slave emerged, chiselled from stone and implacable, the Priest forgot all about the shrieks of the bride. There was a ringing in his ears and, had he known what to call it, the taste of lust in his mouth.

He watched the Abyssinian woman sway past. Her hand, which brushed her narrow hips, sheathed by her veil, was exquisite, with long, elegant fingers. She was a slave but she had the fingers of a queen. There were marks of an indigo-blue tattoo on the backs and the palms of her hands. Her wrist, he noticed, was of the same perfection as her ankle. He fixed his eyes on her feet. A rivulet traced a dark, serpentine course around her delicate ankle and disappeared under her heel when she trod on the sand. It was not blue. It was not a tattoo. He stared at the stain it left on the beads she wore. Blood.

Caught up in paroxysms of desire and disgust, and dizzy with dehydration, the young Priest turned his camel round with a jerk which caused it to protest violently but gave it no other recourse than to obey. Within minutes he placed the greatest possible distance between himself and the bridal train. For the rest of the journey, until they reached the well of Abwa', he remained in the company of the corpse, whose rank stench, he felt, caused less contamination to his body and soul.

When the caravan resumed its journey, the Priest still trailed in its wake, more like a corpse himself than a living man. He hardly noticed that he rode beside the old *faqir*, who was leading the Indian's mule. He was dazed with disappointment and disgust. The shrine of Amanih had been desecrated. The information he had been given, that it was renovated and restored, had proven to be untrue. The place was wrecked. Either it had never been repaired or else the forces of negation were stronger than the forces of affirmation, and it had been reduced to rubble in a few short years. His uncle in Shiraz had told him he had seen the place repaired when he had come on pilgrimage, but here were crumbling walls, a roof that had collapsed, signs of pillage and robbery, a ruin around a dried-up well. What had happened? Certainly, someone must have dug the new well, but he had refused to drink there, in protest against the desecration, in outrage against the women who were using it for their own purposes. He was burning with thirst but had been furious when the presumptuous old *faqir* had offered him water, like an absolution. He felt choked by temptations and the memory of his sycophantic aunts. When the bridal bath was being prepared, the sickly odours of oils and balms filled his head with intoxicating fumes. He thought he would go mad.

After he had watched her squatting before the coals to heat the bathwater, he had not seen the Falasha woman for a long time. She had been preoccupied inside the *takhter-avan*. At one point, when the curtains swayed, he fancied he saw someone naked inside. But he might have been hallucinating. His lips were blackening from lack of water and he was almost delirious. The flies would not leave him in peace. They followed him everywhere.

Where, he wondered feverishly, does a fly come from in the middle of a desert? How can a fly survive amid all this sand and stone? We carry them with us, surely, into this emptiness, he thought. We carry them round the drooling corners of our mouths, clustered like gorged sequins at the edge of our blinded eyes, drunk on our dung, drugged on our droppings, sucking on the slack water skins of memory where mere moisture is all that is left of yesterday. We create the filth of flies in all this purity of sand, he thought. We spawn them out of our own corruption in this holy air, then feed them on our own thin juices. If we did not exist, there would be no flies, the Priest concluded. He wished he could die but the thought of the flies feeding off him impelled him forward. Still he did not drink.

Besides his meditation on flies, the other insignificant mystery that concerned him was the whereabouts of the Indian. At one point he thought perhaps he should inform the leader of the caravan that the Sunni from Karachi was missing, for after they stopped at the well, the Indian had disappeared. But there were other crises for the leader to attend to and far too many flies. The corpse had been left behind. And the Priest vaguely assumed that the guards who were returning for the corpse would find the Indian too. Then he was engulfed with the others in the sandstorm and ceased to think at all.

During the sandstorm the Priest pressed his turbaned head against the side of his camel and gave himself up to pent-up desires. In savage humiliation, he depleted himself. Repeatedly he rendered himself weak and weeping. He was grateful for the howl of the wind and scream of the storm and the bad temper of his camel, for these covered his moans. It seemed he could not be more wretched. He even resisted tasting his own tears, despite his now desperate thirst, for he loathed himself. He wished to die in earnest now for it seemed the only solution to his miseries.

At one stage in the storm, the Falasha woman emerged from the *takhteravan* and stood like a wraith before him. She was bearing a load of silk sheets and soiled clothes which leaped out of her arms and twisted violently in the wind. He saw her from behind throwing everything into the storm. Aghast, he thought at first that she was throwing off her clothes; her veil had slipped away and the bones of her skull stood stark against the whirling storm. But he did not see her when she turned around, for one of the wet silk sheets spun out of her arms like a thing bewitched and slapped full into his face. He was choked by the heady perfumes of the sodden silk and the sand which clung like treacle in its folds. He buried himself in its sensations, covered from head to foot and trapped by his ankles. Then he dissolved in his delirium.

When the bandits attacked some two hours later, the Priest had fallen into a stupor. He lay tangled in the sheets which had been thrown out of the bride's *takhteravan*, wrapped like a mummy and rigid with his face down on the sand. The bandits thought him dead. When the chieftain emerged from the bridal *takhteravan* abruptly, cursing foul oaths, he gave the Priest a terrible blow on the head as he killed his camel and set the *takhteravan* on fire. And so it was that the man of God survived the raid.

The questions of life proved more difficult than the answer of death. Resurrection was a painful paradox. He loathed and he loved her. She touched his lips with a trickle of warm blood that both sickened and revived him. She cradled his head like a mother he craved and condemned. He fought against the paradox of this life, fought with her enigmas and interrelationships, fought through the contradictions with which she confronted him, the terrors of self-disgust and self-acceptance. Till he surfaced, drenched with dew under the new moon. He had a throbbing pain in his temples. There was a half-naked woman lying on the sand beside him. And he was alive.

When the Priest understood that it was the Falasha woman who had saved his life, he began to sob uncontrollably with shame. The salt tears stung his sore-encrusted cheeks, burned his cracked and blackened lips. She murmured to him with infinite tenderness. She lifted her hand and wiped away his tears and he felt the touch of her fingers with reverent awe. She wore a single ring, with a carnelian, on her little finger; it caught against his beard and tugged against the fibres of his heart. She took it off and gave it to him.

The love he felt in that moment for the Falasha woman who lay like a broken moth under the mottled moon beside him was like no sensation or experience he had ever known before. It washed over him like waves from the distant sea that had no name; it flooded his dry heart with water from a fountain he had not guessed he contained. When he begged her forgiveness and asked what he could do for her, she murmured her wishes in a voice so low he had to bend down to hear the request. He had to bow his head, unturbaned, to hear and marvel at her. And he kissed her then, with bleeding lips. But she had already drifted back into unconsciousness. Since he had never loved before, he did not know it when it came to him. And so he let the brief beauty go, unquestioned. It needed no further proof of what it was.

He had never seen anyone die before either. When, shortly before dawn, the Falasha woman began to emit harrowing cries, a terrible dread filled his heart. He had brought her back to the ruined shrine, as she had requested. He had laid her down beside the old dried well inside, and had found the place already occupied. The ashes of her fire from the previous day were still fresh and the dervish sat crouched beside them. It seemed that he, as well as the corpse, had remained behind at the well.

The Priest told the mean-spirited man of the raid, brusquely; he was suspicious of this scoundrel who had saved his skin. It confirmed his opinion that the dervish was a thief and probably in league with the bandits. But despite his loathing and his distrust, he found himself ashamed to be found like this, exposed like this, even by such a contemptible creature as this dervish. He was embarrassed to be discovered by this disreputable fellow in the company of a woman whose body was arced like a bow with pain. Even though she was clearly in the last throes of death, he felt compromised.

It was to him, the Priest, that she was addressing her cries. She was trying to tell him something, gasping out

broken words in a language he did not know. She was
pointing to the saddlebag on the mule that had carried her
back to the well. Suddenly he understood that she wished
him to open it, and he did so, torn between his desire to
fulfil his obligations to this woman he had briefly loved
under the desert moon and his dawning sense of self-
consciousness and shame before another man. He shuddered to obey a slave woman under the watchful eye of the
shrewd dervish in the corner of the ruin.

The saddlebag was stuffed with packages. He removed a
narrow one from among the rest, a roll of parchment, and
gave it to the slave. Then he ransacked the saddlebag to find
whether it contained anything other than these packages,
wrapped in silk and rough paper. It did not. The dervish
leaped from his dark corner to inspect the saddlebag too,
but at that moment the Priest suddenly could not bear his
sullying presence and turned on him savagely, holding the
saddlebag close. It was strange how strongly he felt a
revulsion against this man. It was as if, by withholding
the saddlebag from this thief, he could protect the Falasha
woman.

'The saddlebag belongs to her!' he said harshly. 'You
have no right to touch it!'

It was clear that the fellow was itching to get his fingers
on it. As he turned back to sulk in his corner, muttering
about contamination and disease, the Priest felt an intense
desire to kill the man. His rage was astonishing even to
himself, for the dervish was physically much stronger than
he was. But he had been cowed, momentarily, and watched
the Priest with narrow fear. The Falasha woman, however,
seemed unaware of the drama of antagonism before her.
She had only just enough energy for the roll of parchment.
When she managed to tear open the twine around it, she

finally lifted her eyes to the Priest and he read her last request in their fathomless depths.

He was stunned by the invocation he chanted for her in the dawn beside the well. It was couched in the lofty language of the sacred Quran and yet he had never heard such words before. They seemed to lift the sun from the horizon. They reminded him of a voice; he could not for the moment recall whose. The language was familiar and yet forgotten. Musingly, he reached back into the saddlebag and drew out another package. This too contained paper covered in fine calligraphy. He felt the dervish's breathing hot behind him and tried to shrug him away, but his earlier rage had dissipated. There was more fear in his own feelings now as he unrolled the parchment and scanned the words on the paper. His heart shuddered as the first finger of dawn light pointed to the page.

He struggled to keep his wits about him. The dervish was asking questions at his elbow, in a wheedling voice. Brushing him away like a fly, the Priest told him loftily that the calligraphy was of a rare quality of penmanship. That was obvious; even an amateur could see that. The dervish continued pestering him, as he turned away to concentrate on the words forming themselves on the page. It had evidently been written by a master of the art, he snapped. He wished the man would leave him alone. The dervish fingered the saddlebag but at that point the Priest no longer noticed him. To his wonder, he had discovered that the writing on the paper was in Persian and he had begun to read.

And the words whispered to him of mysteries decreed in the Mother Book. They spoke to him of truths veiled in the Mother Book. They called on him to bear witness to blessings ordained in the Mother Book. They urged him to recall all the promises that would be fulfilled by the Mother Book. In ringing tones they told him of the One hailed and expected in the Mother Book.

The Priest flung the paper abruptly from him. He was terrified. With a curse, he threw it into the ruined well. His fingers burned and itched from touching it. He had heard this voice before indeed! The woman in Karbila had echoed words like these. The woman in Karbila had spoken of these mysteries, of these truths, of these promises in the Mother Book; she too had taught the proof of the Mother Book. He had fled from the Mother Book and it had pursued him here, to this derelict ruin, to this abandoned well, on the road between Mecca and Medina! It was waiting for him here, at the shrine of Abwa', the mother of the Prophet! What was the meaning of this?

When the dervish murmured that it was no wonder, given the nature of the woman's disease, that his reverence should be so afraid of touching her belongings, he hardly heard him. When the dervish asked in pliant tones whether the holy sir might consider parting with this piece of horsehide to a poor unworthy beggar to whom contamination was a mercy and whose poverty dictated no discrimination, he turned on his heel and walked out of the dim shrine, trembling from head to foot.

His head was throbbing. He did not know whether it was because of the wound on his brow from the night before, which he had barely had time to attend to, or from hunger and thirst and exhaustion from the long ride till dawn. Or whether it was because the words he had just read filled him with such vertigo, these 'mother words' so pregnant with significance, so full of meanings. He leaned over the side of the well in the early morning sun and drew up the fresh water towards him. Then he plunged his face into it and drank deeply. He drank and drank as he had never drunk before.

When he returned, refreshed, some time later, he found that the slave was dead inside the ruin. And the dervish was in full possession of the saddlebag. The woman had given it to him, he said blandly, before she died. The repulsive fellow had strapped it to his back and clearly had no intention of parting with it. He was excessively pleased with his acquisition and stood tall and ominously defiant. The Priest realized with a jolt that this unpleasant dervish towered above him and was threatening. His earlier thoughts of killing the man had been more than reckless. In fact he was a thug more than a dervish.

Fear, however, was less acute to the Priest at that moment than the stab of regret that followed it. He realized that he had lost his chance to look again at those mysterious papers. He had thrown away the writing that he had unravelled from its twine and now the dervish had all the rest of the bundles inside the saddlebag. But the single invocation he had chanted for the slave woman was still locked in her cold fingers. This at least he could retrieve. If he dared. He drew near her.

'God protect you, she died of smallpox, sir,' the dervish murmured.

The Priest looked at her severed face and saw the same beauty he had glimpsed beneath the moon. He knew that his love for this woman, and the summons of the Mother Book, were locked up together in his heart. He knew too that the words in the saddlebag and the teachings of the woman in Karbila were one and the same. And yet he could not bear to admit the truth of either of them, though he wanted to believe in both. Unable to resist but unwilling to comply, he could not accept, nor could he wholly deny. He hung over the dead woman, his heart yearning towards her and his mind resisting.

In the end he left the paper locked in her grasp, because he loved her too much to deprive her of it and he dreaded just as much the import of the words she clutched so fiercely in her death. He ordered the dervish roughly to come to his assistance and between them, they lifted her body and threw it unceremoniously into the disused well. She felt light and brittle like a dry bird, but a pool of heavy, black blood remained where she had lain. The sound of the rocks and stones falling down the dry well afterwards appalled him.

He tried to wash the contamination of it from his hands, his body, his heart, his soul. But he kept her ring, for it was the colour of her blood. He did not know whether he should return to his studies and dedicate the remainder of his days to the persecution of heresy. Or devote himself forever to the new doctrine of love from the Mother Book of life. He hovered, indecisive, beside the well, and was glad when the dervish went on to Medina without him.

THE DERVISH

When the Dervish saw something falling from the top of the cliffs ahead of the caravan, he was immediately on the alert. He knew it was a signal from the tribe and narrowed his pale eyes to look more closely at the skyline. What he saw confirmed his expectations and sent the adrenaline coursing through his body. There, on the edge of the high escarpment, silhouetted against the early morning sky, were the figures of men. About thirty of them, maybe more.

The Dervish had been on the lookout for the tribe for three days, ever since he had reached Al Jamum, outside the precincts of Mecca. When the caravan had been joined by a convoy of Turkish soldiers at the junction of Osfan, a day's ride further, he had become afraid that he might miss them altogether. With these effeminate jackdaws prancing alongside, sporting their dazzling blue uniforms and pomaded hair, the caravan was likely to be attacked before he could establish any links with the tribesmen. He had therefore begun to hunt for the traces of their passage, independently. He had to keep a vigilant eye out for the codes they used, the signs they left for each other. He made short forays into the wilderness when his absence would pass unnoticed, and searched among the passes and the drifting dunes for several hours at a time as the caravan lumbered its slow way towards Medina.

Six months before, on his first trip in this region, a wild Bedouin had taught him certain paths which had the advantage of speed and perspective on the caravans. He had hired the fellow to be his guide through the mountain range of Dafdaf, a haunt of the savage tribesmen, but he had not entirely trusted the Bedouin. He suspected this lizard of a man to be in league with the notorious nomads, of being a spy who might turn on him at any time, of being a murderer who might deliver him a stab in the back when he least expected it. The fellow seemed capable of picking up signals in the wind and reading codes in the rocks. But he had no proof of his duplicity other than a certain tingling on the back of the neck. He had made a shrewd study of the scrawny devil and had learned to decipher his arts. Since he himself was a secret agent, his susceptibilities were particularly acute when it came to spies.

The Dervish was a young Englishman in disguise who was on a political mission in this region. The sheikh of the Harb tribe, Ibn Rumi, had rebelled against the Turkish rule some months ago, causing considerable disturbance to the Ottoman presence in Mecca, and the Englishman had prevailed upon the British ambassador in Constantinople to send him out as a spy to gather information about these activities. In order for the information to be accurate, it was necessary to establish reliable and independent links with the rebel leader, of course. Cordial relations between Her Majesty's Government and the Sublime Porte naturally required this. He managed to convince the ambassador that it might even prove advantageous to establish cordial relations with the rebels themselves. The whole region was in turmoil and it had always been the policy of Her Britannic Majesty to protect her private interests, whatever her public position might be. He proposed, therefore, to be a secret agent and negotiate an arms deal with the tribe.

The ambassador thought the mission rather far-fetched, personally. Ibn Rumi, in his opinion, was notoriously independent, and would probably want to keep aloof from the British as much as he wished to shrug off the Turkish rule. But he allowed his newly arrived attaché to believe he would be serving his country well if he took it on and calculated that it need not cause too great a diplomatic scandal if an anonymous agent were accidentally killed somewhere in the Arabian Peninsula. What attracted him to the proposition was that it might serve his own interests to get rid of the young upstart, who seemed too ambitious to him by far. He was evidently an adventurer more than a diplomat by inclination and if he did not advance his own career, he was liable to cause a scandal. Besides, the ambassador was privately piqued by his attaché's disinclination for buggery; even the subtlest propositions had provoked little response on the part of the young Hercules. The great man's pride had been somewhat snubbed. He had concluded that the fellow was a fool and suspected that once given the rein, he might usefully hang himself through lack of judgement and be no further threat. And so he agreed to the proposal.

The young Englishman had been eagerly looking for just such a challenge ever since he took up his position. Initially, there had been some talk in Whitehall of sending him as an agent to Central Asia, where Britain and Russia were locked in a cold war for control of the high passes leading to India from Kashgar. It was an area made infamous by stories of reckless subterfuge and spy networks, and his hopes had been raised by the prospects of this exciting assignment, which would have shown how well and with what flair he could serve his country's political and economic interests. But at the last minute someone else had been given the position and he had been assigned instead to the suffocating and sycophantic seat of the sultanate and had found himself subjected to the ambassador's verbal effluvia and his wife's unspeakably boring dinner parties in Constantinople.

Pushing paper around in a dusty office was not his idea of a promising career, and the ambassador's wife had proven to have an awkward temperament that required a certain obliqueness of approach to arouse and was an embarrassment once provoked. She was an ardent Catholic and interpreted all his advances as indications of a spiritual affinity between them, the illusion of which he was hard-pressed to maintain, however useful it might have been to do so. He also had difficulty remaining enthusiastic about what Cardinal Newman might do next, which seemed to be the main topic of her conversations with him. Religious matters were of significance to the young attaché only if they could advance his prospects. As the wife of the ambassador grew increasingly excited by his ardent susceptibilities and flattered herself that his conversion was a matter of mere time, for his own part, he became more and more impatient with their debate over the cardinal's remarkable conscience. It was hard to maintain faith in the notion that this faculty enthroned in Edgbaston had any bearing on his own career.

He wanted to make his fortune; he wanted to return home covered in glory. He wanted to influence History with a capital 'H' and be responsible for some significant political change that would extend the power and prestige of the Empire and be for ever associated with his name. Above all, he wanted to return to his own country trailing clouds and trophies of success. Others of his compatriots, who were also secret agents under the guise of diplomacy, had become illustrious in recent years and had acquired priceless artefacts, discovered deathless carvings and ransacked immortal manuscripts from dark antiquity. They had been knighted and given all sorts of distinctions, so why could not he win fame through his exploits? He was almost thirty, unmarried, and still needed to prove himself.

His eldest brother had been crowned with intellectual honours at the university and had, with the natural arrogance that was his due, assumed his role as heir apparent at the family seat. His younger brother had achieved similar distinctions in the Church and had settled into the meritorious dullness of a parish priest. But this middle son (his sisters did not really count, being mere marriage fodder) had been a disappointment to his father. First he had failed to follow in his elder brother's footsteps and had been sent down from university with ignominious results after a scandalous affair involving his landlady's daughter. Then his career in the army had also ended abruptly and his dreams of procuring a prestigious promotion to India were permanently dashed while he was training mercenaries in Persia. For his discretion had been unequal to his imagination and some of the ammunition for which he was responsible had disappeared quite unaccountably, its whereabouts unknown. This was a dishonour and a disgrace. He had been recalled home at this point, severely reprimanded by his father and told that if he could not conduct himself properly in future, he would be cut off without a shilling and reduced to trade. It was all he was fit for, said that patriarch in disgust. He had now been given his last chance as a minor attaché at the British embassy in Constantinople. If this reprobate son blackened his name at Whitehall too, he would be obliged to emigrate to America.

Much depended on the success of his diplomatic career, therefore. Despite the fact that there was a high level of tedium and a low level of intelligence associated with the duties of a minor representative of Her Majesty's Government abroad, he was determined not to return home until he did so crowned with laurels. His farewells were very dramatic. His two sisters wept copiously over him as he prepared to sail to the Bosphorus, for they thought him wonderfully handsome and wild and daring and believed him to be cruelly maligned by envy. They always took his part against their brothers' scorn. He basked in their attentions and avoided telling them that the most daring exploit required of him in this new position would probably be to keep the pencils of the ambassador permanently sharpened. His brothers, on the other hand, permitted him to understand that though they assumed he would restrain himself from further folly, given his previous record of notoriety, they held out no great hopes that he would come to much in the end. This led to angry scenes and chilling adieus. He told them that he trusted they would live to regret their words and left London in high dudgeon.

Even as he allowed himself to be petted by his sisters, even as he seethed with indignation at his brothers' sneers and damnable faint praise, the young Englishman had a sinking feeling that they were right. He would not come to much in the end. He had always striven to disprove their condescension in the past but perhaps he deserved it after all. A great emptiness opened within him at this thought and he took his leave of his father with a degree of contrite submission that astonished that old gentleman.

But it did not last beyond the Channel crossing. Nor did he dwell on his doubts for long but used them, instead, to fuel his ambitions. His hubris rose from a profound sense of insecurity, and the emptiness soon gave way to bluster. One way or another, he would make the world admire him, he thought. He would show them all that he was a hero!

He had dwindled into a diplomat, therefore, but retained his dreams of glory. He had shrunk into a petty pen-pusher, but still anticipated adventure. And he had been yearning for an opportunity to abandon his stuffy routine, because polo and the ambassador's wife were insufficient as challenges to him. So when news came of the uprisings among the Harb tribe in Arabia, he immediately saw possibilities here of the glory and the drama he craved. He interpreted the ambassador's approval of his plan as a sign of his superior's belated confidence in his abilities. To travel across wild deserts and negotiate deals with the notorious leader of the tribesmen was exactly the chance he had been looking for to finally show to his father, his brothers and himself that he was not a total bounder.

Despite his chequered history, he was a young man not ill-endowed with graces. Tall, blue-eyed, broad-shouldered and an excellent equestrian, he assumed he was irresistible to women. His failure at the university had not been caused by lack of intellect alone, but by dearth of discipline; his disgrace was not due to stupidity merely, but profligacy too, which always has its charms. His immaturity had caused him to squander his money on sexual conquest and waste his time on the races. But he was beginning to grow up.

He was already less foolhardy than the ambassador

hoped or his brothers would have liked to believe. Under the appearance of impetuosity and daredevil courage, he was also less impulsive than his father supposed or he himself would care to admit, for he had become increasingly cautious when it came to questions of personal danger. He took trouble to minimize his risks while appearing to take them. There was a certain calculating and self-serving element in his character which it would have diminished his honour to confess. In fact, it had been easier to admit to incompetence in the army than to be accused of cowardice; there were some, even there, who had called him a cad. Despite his bravado, therefore, he had all the makings of an excellent diplomat.

Another talent which had always served him well was his flair for drama. He was of a rather histrionic bent and the theatre showed him to great advantage. It had made a convincing lover of him in his adolescence and now, in maturity, it served him singularly well as a spy. He had a chameleon capacity for imitation and was able to cover his fair hair and skin, his religious disinclinations and his foreign accent with admirable professionalism. Although, like many Englishmen, he had little gift for languages, his years in the army had not been wasted and he could parrot an adequate knowledge of Persian and Arabic as well as a sufficient smattering of Turkish with a certain authenticity. Acting was second nature to him.

He was also blessed by a complete disregard for theological fastidiousness, and although he had, like his brothers and sisters, received the damp sprinkle of Anglican waters with a healthy howl in the family chapel early in life, he had no difficulty whatsoever in adapting himself to the external mannerisms of the Mohammedan religion. He watched, he listened and he had learned to echo the trappings of Shiite fervour and Sunni solemnity. In fact he rather fancied the way he performed his prayers.

Drawing on all these qualities and skills, he took pains to identify the right mask for this particular mission. It had to be one that provided freedom from restraint and suspicion as well as easy access to acquaintance and disappearance along the road to Mecca and Medina. For there were grave risks entailed in his disguise. If he was to travel on this pilgrimage route, he would have to give others some indication of spiritual motivation: a type of motivation, it must be admitted, that had hardly existed in his life before. He had managed to avoid its rigours for years by mumbling the offices found in the Book of Common Prayer whenever constrained to do so and maintaining the vaguest possible acquaintance with parish churches up and down the land, for he was a young man who did not readily care to identify himself as a miserable sinner. In fact, all that had been required of him until this time was that weak and watered-down expression of spiritual motivation associated with weddings, christenings, and funerals conducted under the placid auspices of the Church of England.

However, the Sufis of Persia had rather impressed him by their anarchic philosophy and he thought their spiritual motivation vague enough to cover a multitude of ambiguities. It demanded so little commitment and consistency as to rather suit than strain his temperament. That was what led him to adopt the disguise of a dervish, therefore, when he embarked on his mission to the deserts of Arabia. He spent several weeks studying the mannerisms, the intonations, the dances, the methods of praying and begging and the general appearance of dervishes in eastern Turkey, and was rather pleased with the impersonation he commanded. He kept his axe and his begging bowl and would often use them, in later years and at the height of his diplomatic career, at fancy-dress parties at the embassy.

It was to his credit, however, that the young agent harboured a niggling fear that his fancy dress might not pass the test of sincerity. His desire for glory did not extend to death, nor did his ability to mimic include martyrdom. There was a certain magic associated with the name of Mecca, but he preferred to be thought brave enough to have been there without actually going. On the ambassador's instructions he passed through Baghdad to be briefed, therefore, but though the consul-general of that city saw him leave in the guise of a dervish bound for Basra where the pilgrim boats embarked, he had no intention of accompanying his fellow passengers on the *hajj*. When he arrived at the sultry and fetid port of Jiddah, he looked around for a trade caravan instead, which would enable him to skirt around the holy city.

There was a bridal party which, it seemed, needed to skirt around Mecca as much as he did, and such an escort would have suited his convenience very well. But it required several days to arrange for the caravan leader to make the detour. A rotund Indian from Karachi, upon whom he recognized the unmistakable marks of colonial corruption, was playing an instrumental role in the negotiations and the Dervish watched him closely, impatient for the haggling to be over. He was sure the odious chap spoke English but he refrained from approaching him and had to place his trust in the fellow's evident venality. Despite protestations among the pilgrims, it seemed likely that the Indian would prevail.

Just hours before they left, however, a consignment of Turkish soldiers suddenly arrived in Jiddah to escort the bride to Damascus, and this changed the Dervish's plans entirely. The bridal train would take the detour in the company of the Turkish escort now, and the pilgrim caravan would head straight for Mecca. He was in a dilemma. He could certainly not travel in the company of the Sultan's soldiers if he wanted to contact the Harb tribe. There was no alternative but to proceed directly to the holy of holies with the pilgrims.

Thus it was that one fear forced him to face another and he was obliged to proceed step by step towards the city of Mecca, much against his will. But he did not participate in any of the preparatory rites or rituals, as they approached, in case his deception might be detected. He lingered instead in the company of those who importuned the pilgrims on the way. Nor did he don the special robe of pilgrimage, because it was so hot, but found he could avoid suspicion better among the indigent. He arrived at Hedda, on the outskirts of the holy city, in the wake of the pilgrim caravan and in the company of beggars.

Once there, he lost his nerve. This was the last cara-vanserai before Mecca and his last chance to avoid the terrors of the *hajj*. Keeping as low a profile as he possibly could, he sat in a cold sweat under the burning sun, mumbling what he hoped would be construed as prayers among the beggars massed along the route, and waited for the caravan to pass. Then he looked for the first opportunity he could to skirt around the city, in the company of tradesmen heading north to Al Jamum.

It took two long weeks, for he travelled by foot, but the delay was worth it for the relative safety it afforded, and a lingering stomach problem caused by the unexpected charity of sacrificial meat from the *hajj* was the most he had to pay for this modest adventure in violating religious propriety.

Later he would describe in vivid detail all the activities in which he had participated in Mecca and would give a very convincing performance of the pilgrimage he never had. His delivery always had an impact on the ladies, who were particularly impressed by his graphic account of facing wild tribesmen on the one hand and rabid fanatics on the other. But what he never mentioned was that his adventures brought him no closer to his goal, for during the two weeks that he spent begging his way around the city, and the one further week he spent in Al Jamum waiting for the caravan bound for Medina, he saw no sign, he found no codes, he discovered no hint at all of the activities of Ibn Rumi or his men.

One day's journey from Al Jamum, his disappointment deepened to dismay. For at the caravanserai of Osfan, he found the bridal train waiting to join the pilgrim caravan again: the same jingling train of wedding women, with its eunuch in attendance and its escort of effeminate soldiers. He had no choice now; he could not avoid the company of the Turks. And since he had not the courage to face the desert alone, he had to take reconnoitring trips on the side to search for the Harb tribe. Once he could track them down, he thought, he would dissociate himself from the caravan immediately. Once he could trace them, he would approach Ibn Rumi alone.

Everything depended on his independent search; everything depended on his vigilance in recognizing the signals en route. It was just a matter of deciphering the codes, like the Bedouin. He knew the tribesmen wrote messages in the sand. They left clues in the rocks. They wrote their secret code so subtly that only one who knew the language of the spider could read the words they wrote on the web across the entrance to a cave. He had to keep his senses alert, therefore, and survey the dunes behind as well as beyond the lumbering caravan. And when, on the fourth morning after leaving the city of Mecca, he saw an object falling – a rock? a load from a camel's back? – when he saw something falling from the high cliff face up ahead and plummeting down into the gully below, he knew it was a signal.

The tribesmen were up there sure enough, on the high escarpment; he saw their silhouetted figures for one tantalizing moment etched against the morning sky. Then they vanished, like dew at sunrise. They had doubtless seen the caravan approaching. They were probably preparing to attack! There was no time to lose; he had to leave the company of the Turks immediately.

But the caravan had stopped. Minutes after the Dervish saw the signal from the tribe, there was a great crying and shouting and heaving and cursing and braying and snorting and spitting as the entire caravan came to a grinding halt in the middle of the desert. He did not linger to find out the reason for it. Even if the caravan leaders had also seen the tribesmen and were preparing a defence, he knew he had to reach Ibn Rumi before his men attacked. Even if the blue serge coats of the Turkish soldiers with their glittering bayonets poised in perpetual readiness were not sufficient enticement, the wealth on board this caravan was worthy of a raid. He slipped away as the pilgrims began to complain and the guards began to protest. He slipped into the dunes to the northwest of the road above the caravanserai of Khulays where he had been subjected to a cruel attack of fleas the previous night, and cut swiftly on foot across the rocky valley towards the cliffs up ahead. The terrain was rough and the hidden paths he had learned from the Bedouin required goatlike assurance.

He had been scrambling through the valley for barely half an hour when he suddenly heard the unmistakable bray of a mule behind him, down among the lower dunes. Someone was following him! Hiding in the rocks at a vantage point just above the road, he saw a figure ambling along towards the cliffs of Dafdaf. It was the Indian from Karachi! What was this oily fellow doing on his mule ahead of the caravan? Why was he heading for the cliffs?

The Dervish had not trusted the Indian from the time he found him to be closely associated with an old man who travelled at the back of the caravan among the pack animals and beasts of burden. The suspect pilgrim seemed shrivelled enough and toothless enough to pose no threat, but he was wily, he was sharp. He had eyes like pins. On several occasions, the Dervish found himself under the uncomfortable scrutiny of this fellow, who spoke thick Turkish and clotted Persian that the Indian claimed to understand. The Dervish concluded that this so-called pilgrim was from the very region where he had hoped to make his name: from the high passes of Kashgar. Doubtless he came from the murderous mountains to the north of India where many a brave officer and British surveyor had lost his life. Doubtless he was a spy of the tribes from those treacherous regions who were armed by the Russians. The frequent conversations of the Uigur and the Indian merely confirmed the Englishman's suspicions of the old fellow, who had been eyeing him narrowly since they had left Mecca. He wondered whether he had been recognized as an agent, and whether the old spy had not sent the Indian out to murder him.

The Indian was not proceeding along the valley road to Medina as if in pursuit of anyone with the intent to kill, however. He was rolling along on his mule in a very casual fashion. From time to time he pulled out a drinking bottle of some sort and proceeded to gulp down something that caused him to produce a series of liquid burps. Once he even broke into snatches of faint song. It was high noon and the shadows were minimal. As he drew near the hidden Dervish, the fat fellow craned his neck about and stared to the right, the left, in all directions, as if on the lookout for someone or something. Perhaps he had seen the tribe and was also searching for them. Maybe he was a secret agent too!

Suddenly the Indian wiped the sweat off his face and belched loudly with a crude oath. The Dervish froze. Was it a signal? Would the tribe come swooping down, called by a curse? Panic thundered through his veins; his composure and the Empire's hopes hung by a thread. He waited, beaten by the hammer of his broken pulse.

But there was no response to the Indian's belch, other than the faint cry of distant desert birds above them, other than a certain thickening of the air as the weight of the sun bore down against the rocks about them. There was no response and whether or not there had been any meaning in the oath, its significance soon became irrelevant for there was not a breath of air around them. The Dervish permitted himself to exhale, slowly. Whatever the Indian's purpose in riding out into the madness of the noonday sun, it could not be well planned, he concluded, for the fellow had a vacant and rather unsettled air, more like the object than the agent of a plot.

The Indian clopped past and continued along the road in the unforgiving heat towards a small ruin in the distance. The Dervish watched him for a few moments and then plucked up his courage to start again, picking his way cautiously from one outcrop of rocks to another, moving closer and closer to the cliffs on the other side. He wanted to scour the whole valley of Khulays for the signal dropped from the clifftop, for it must surely be close at hand. He wanted to scrutinize every rock and dune shadow for the presence of the tribesmen, for if they had not dispersed down the other side of the mountain slopes, they should be within a stone's throw and waiting in ambush. He had to move cautiously so as to see them before being seen.

He had hardly gone more than a few hundred yards when he suddenly heard a distant yelp and a series of muffled cries behind him. Ducking quickly out of sight behind a cluster of rocks, he squinted against the blaze of heat to glance back towards the road which he had left behind.

But there was no one on it any more. No one at all. The Indian and his mule had vanished! It was very strange. Had he been dreaming? The Indian had been there a few moments ago, dwindled by distance but still clopping along the road. Now he was nowhere. Had he gone into the ruin? The sun, directly overhead, was driving down like a nail between the agent's eyes. Was he imagining things? The Dervish blinked the sweat away from his brows and stared uncomprehending towards the ruin for a few moments. Had someone just moved there between those stones, a dark shadow? The crumbling walls seemed to surge and separate in the heat and distance. There was nothing; he must be seeing mirages. Or was that a cry he had heard? And there it was again! But no, there was silence only. And he felt a flickering shadow pass over him. High over the cliffs, in the vast immensity of sky, the carrion birds wheeled in slow down-spiralling circles above him. It must have been the cry of birds he had heard, he decided, and rubbed the sweat off his burning eyes.

He progressed slowly, due north and east of the cliffs, searching for signs of the tribe. Every rock might be a potential message, placed just so, to signify departure or return. Every ripple in the sand might betray their presence or spell out their absence. As he combed his way across the rocks and stones and shifting sands of the valley and arrived, step by step, closer and closer to the menacing cliff face, he began to suspect that Ibn Rumi and his men had decided to remove themselves after all. They must have driven hard round the farther side of the escarpment. They had vanished into the passes of Dafdaf in order to lay an ambush for the caravan further up the road towards the caravanserai of Towal. There was no one here.

But even if he was obliged to search still further before he found the tribe and its leader, nevertheless somewhere, at the foot of this tall cliff, must be the object he had seen falling. Somewhere nearby, surely, he should find the signal they had dropped: the rock, the stone, the mule, the man. He kept the road behind him and pressed on in the perpendicular heat, his brain boiling in the sun and his ears throbbing with a murmurous drone that grew louder and louder. He shook his head but the thickening hum was still there. He cupped his ears, but the sound increased. He wondered if he had a touch of sunstroke perhaps, and briefly closed his eyes.

He did not notice the cloud of flies hovering in the air until he was almost upon them. He did not notice the Indian either, coming upon him from behind, until he saw the mess of blood and bone before him. He saw the dead man exploded like ripe fruit on the rocks almost at the same moment as he turned to see the living one riding towards him with a gaping hole of a mouth in his face into which the flies were pouring. And he knew from the glazed eyes of both the living and the dead that neither saw him. With his heart pounding he ducked behind a massive rock which stood like a sentinel against the cliffside and watched in horror as the Indian approached.

The man stopped some yards away from him and slid off his mule. He seemed barely conscious as he collapsed among the rocks. His chest and belly were covered with blood. His face had caved in and he was wheezing and gasping, emitting a strange combination of gurgles and moans. He seemed to be fumbling on the ground in front of him, searching for something among the rocks. He had not seen the dead body, apparently. This lay oozing and festering in the heat a few paces away from the sweating Englishman, a mass of bubbling flies and broken bones. Horrible sight! The Dervish kept his eyes off the face. He could not bring himself to look; it was too revolting to be human. And the carrion birds that had been wheeling overhead were coming closer now. Cawing and cackling like hideous geese. Some had alighted near the body already and were stabbing and pecking at it viciously.

The Indian seemed to be in a state of shock. He sat hunched in a heap among the hot rocks, staring into the burning space before him, under the thunderous sun, with that dreadful wheezing, gulping noise coming out of the bleeding hole in his face and the flies building up a storm around him.

Should I go to him? thought the Englishman. The man needed help, that was evident.

But what could I do for him? he thought. The poor chap's past help anyway.

And then, as his thoughts raced to put the pieces of his puzzling suspicions together, he thought, Ah! And what if this is just a trick? A decoy?

The Indian seemed obsessed with something in front of him. What was it? As he lifted up the saddlebag from among the rocks, the pieces of the puzzle all fell into place. The Dervish saw and understood at the same instant. There it was! The very object he had been searching for! The Indian was opening the saddlebag now on his knees. He was drawing something out of it which looked like a bundle of paper. He was unrolling the package, swaying like a drunk man as he bent over it.

The Dervish knew immediately that this was the signal dropped from the clifftop by the tribe. It was the signal and the Indian had found it first! He too had been searching for it because he was obviously a spy. That was it! He was in collaboration with the old man, who was a Russian agent, and now they had found the message from Ibn Rumi before him. He had to retrieve it! Immediately!

The thoughts of the Dervish were racing. The Indian was in no condition to fight. He was dazed and weak from loss of blood. Nor was he in command of his faculties, for how else could he sit so close to a festering body buzzing with flies and not notice it? How else could the Dervish watch him and remain unobserved? The man was clearly out of his mind. Whoever had butchered his tongue had taken more from him than met the eye. He seemed to be bereft of his senses. Even now, he was raving. He was groaning and swaying about from side to side, uttering incoherent noises. It would take no effort at all and little courage to snatch the saddlebag from him.

But at the very moment the Dervish decided he was going to come out of hiding and grab the saddlebag from the dumb Indian, he heard a whistle. It was a piercing whistle, so near that it shook him physically as he crouched in his hiding place, so loud that it bounced off the cliff face north of him where the outlying rocks lay closest to the ruin on the other side of the valley. A clean, sharp whistle which sent a shiver of terror up his spine and cut through the heat like a knife of ice. It was a signal from the tribe.

And suddenly, even as he grasped its fatal import, he saw a troop of men rising like phantoms, like mirages, like spirits exhaled from the very rocks, rising and riding as they rose. The tribesmen! Men and horses, hidden so well on the two sides of the valley that the naked eye could never have seen them. There were fifty of them at least, hidden among the ruined buildings and the rocks north of the road. Ghosts of the desert armed with guns and knives. And at the signal they rose up like a cloud of locusts and drove hard, with the sound of lashing whips, along the road towards Medina. Within a few seconds, the entire troop had vanished into the distant heat, in a thunder of hooves and a cloud of dust as the vultures settled down. The sound of the whistle was still echoing in his ears as the dust of their hooves settled on the Dervish's lips.

And then he realized what he had missed. He had walked right through the hidden tribesmen and not even seen them! He had wasted the last half-hour and lost his chance to find the very man he had been looking for. He must follow them immediately; he must at all costs intercept them. Suddenly, with a flash of insight, he understood what had happened to the Indian: the man had probably stumbled upon Ibn Rumi by mistake. He had an offer from the Russian agent but had come upon the tribesmen unawares and his offer had not met with their approval. All the more reason for the mission of the Dervish to succeed!

Without another thought for the saddlebag, the Dervish slipped out of his hiding place. The Indian never raised his head or noticed him, and the flies above the festering body merely heaved and swelled as the Englishman brushed past. Even the ugly birds barely budged in their gorging. A hurried glimpse of the blossoming face brought a rush of nausea to his mouth; he thought it strangely familiar. And then he began to run, panting, through the rocks and shallows of the valley towards the ruin on the other side. He ran breathlessly, and by the time he had reached the ruined shrine, the caravan too had arrived.

He did not even notice that there was a well there at which the pilgrims were gathering with festive joy. He took no time even to drink, and disregarded the row that had started around the caravan leaders, where all the pilgrims had gathered and were gesticulating wildly. Feverish with fear lest he be seen by the too bright eyes of the old pilgrim who was forever watching him, he unhitched one of the fine Arab horses from the back of the mule train, grabbed a water skin to sustain him, and within minutes was galloping furiously up the valley road towards Medina in the direction taken by the tribesmen a short while before.

The Englishman would never tell anyone of the futility of his search for the next several hours. He would never tell anyone how he lost himself and wandered almost to Hamama, how he panicked there in the empty desert because he could not find the road to Towal. He would not tell of his shameful behaviour when he stumbled upon three travellers among the dunes, how he became hysterical imagining he was pursued by bandits, how he panicked completely on glimpsing a green turban and the gleam of a pearl in the ear of a slave. He had fled in terror at the sight of them, floundering among the rocks in the opposite direction, and had lost the road entirely as a result until he came to Buraykh. He would never admit to what he drank then after he drained the last dregs of the tepid ooze of the water skin dry in the middle of nowhere or how he wept before rediscovering the road again in the windy mountain passes of Dafdaf. He rode back towards Mecca at that point, because he was totally disoriented, and he found himself by pure luck meeting the caravan head on, barely three *farsangs* from the caravanserai of Khulays which he had left that morning. And he did not have a single glimpse of the tribe of Harb or its leader in all his fruitless wanderings.

He never told anyone about this episode, and he even convinced himself, in later years, that it was a fortuitous detour, because by the time he rejoined the caravan, the guards of the corpse had mutinied, had defied the caravan leaders, and were turning back. They were turning all their pack animals around, half the way from Towal, and were heading back towards the well. And he went with them.

The reasons he gave in later years for his return to the well masqueraded as cool logic. He said it was because he had to avoid association with the Turkish escort of the bride so as to have a chance to contact Ibn Rumi. Had he stayed he would have been killed along with all the other pilgrims, he said, at the hands of the marauding tribesmen who laid waste the caravan some three or four *farsangs* beyond the well. What he did not say was that the bandits who raided the caravan had nothing to do with the Harb tribe, as he discovered later. But it made the adventure more dangerous to gloss over this distinction. He also said that he returned with the muleteers to retrieve the saddlebag which he had last seen in the possession of the Indian across the valley from the ruin, under the cliff. Perhaps that was his reason, after all, for he had lost all trace of the tribe. Since the last he had ever seen of them had been there, as he thought in the valley, between the tall cliffs of Dafdaf and the well of Abwa', he was driven by a kind of blind instinct to return to this spot, as though it retained some message for him that he had not clearly deciphered, as though it needed further decoding. But there was no logic in his decision. This, of course, he did not admit, even to himself. What he said was that the success of his mission depended on his return to the well.

And so it did. He rode back in the direction of the well with the quarrelsome muleteers, keeping up a fair banter with them about the corpse all the way, which involved some jokes in rather bad taste and a certain amount of winking and nudging of a rather crude suggestiveness on their part. They had apparently misplaced the corpse at the well and that was their reason for returning, they said. Its rank odours had accompanied the caravan for the first three days of the journey from Mecca and the Dervish had always been rather relieved, when he made his little forays into the surrounding hills, to get away from the cloying smell, which had increased abominably from day to day. The habit of these Mohammedans to traipse about the country-side with their dead seemed both bizarre and barbaric to him. But while it was an offensive custom to travel with a corpse, in his opinion, it seemed even more objectionable to leave one behind. The guards were supposed to be conducting this one to Medina for burial and had already been paid a fat sum, by the dead man himself, to safeguard his goods all the way to Damascus. Whether by accident or design, however, the defunct proprietor of the valuable mule train filled with a costly load of indigo had been mislaid.

The Dervish suspected that the guards had some plan to abscond with the dead man's goods and were actually heading back to Jiddah. He guessed that they had little or no intention of retrieving the corpse. He supposed this was what the nudges and the winks were all about, but he was wholly unprepared for their attack on him. Despite his acute sensitivity to the nefarious motives of others, he had not considered that his own might be suspect. When asked why he had chosen to accompany them, he had told the guards he preferred their company to that of the caravan leader, and had used as his excuse the fact that he had not offered his songs and dances to the jinn and ghouls in the ruin. He had constructed a fair jumble of superstitious nonsense, larded with references to dreams and portents and to the love of wine and women, in order to give them the impression he was a religious simpleton with epicurean appetites. He had thought his reasons and his lilting accents plausible enough, and their crude jokes had led him to believe his performance so convincing that he did not realize that they had not believed a word he had said. They had seen through his disguise fairly rapidly, and although they could not guess what had brought this foreign charlatan into their midst, they interpreted his decision to return to the well with them as being motivated by pure greed. They did not care a dried fig for his blasphemous presumptions but they were certainly not going to let him get away with a share of the stolen goods.

Within a brief *farsang* from the well, the guards turned on the Dervish with knives and sticks. If it had not been for the pistol he kept concealed inside his belt, and the excellent reflexes of his high-spirited stallion, he would have been dragged from his horse and that, as he never tired of telling his female audiences in later years, would have been the end of him, for they were a savage lot. But though they were violent, they were unarmed. Consequently, he was able to disperse them with a few well-aimed shots. He caused panic by killing a couple of their mules and then broke through their ranks and raced towards the distant ruin, even as the sandstorm came upon them.

The Dervish spent the entire sandstorm inside the abandoned well in the ruin. Partly from fear and partly to protect himself, he left his fine Arab steed to the storm and the frustrated fury of the guards and then clambered down into the well as fast as he was able. The storm howled through the broken arches of the ruined shrine and turned the air into a boiling foam of hot sand above him. He heard no more than its scream and whine for the next several hours, and was deafened by the clamour of its thousand tongues of vengeance in the funnel of the well. He imagined at every second that the guards were clambering after him in hot pursuit. The well echoed and boomed and gonged with the eddies of trapped wind. It was so fierce and he was so scared that he did not dare to emerge into the open until the storm began to abate. And by then he was parched and spiritless. It was thirst that finally drove him out of his hiding place, for hours had passed since he had drunk anything, and his soul was spittleless with disillusion.

He would have climbed out of the well immediately, when the howl of the wind died down, had he not suddenly heard a curious sound somewhere nearby. It was a strange high-pitched call, almost a song, in a voice he dimly thought he recognized. It lifted, like a bird, and hovered in the air close to him. And then, just as suddenly, it was gone. He waited, tense and desperate, for some further minutes to hear any signs of possible pursuit before he dared come out. Following the direction from which he heard the sound, he found a sort of crevice leading out through a narrow channel at the bottom of the dried well. And when he finally had the courage to crawl through this, he found himself emerging into the narrow gully, just below the ruin. Since he was afraid of walking across to the road which lay exposed beneath a sick-looking moon, he chose instead to climb up the rocky slope towards the north wall of the shrine. Thus it was that he was saved from the quicksand at the bottom of the gully, and found the new well, filled with clear water under the evening star.

By then, night had fallen. The wind had lulled and there was no sign of the guards or their mule train. His horse too had disappeared. But at least he had escaped with his life intact, although there was something unredeemed about the nature of his deliverance. He felt a curious kinship with the disowned corpse, which he found by its smell. Its sweet stink of putrefaction, as he climbed up towards it from the gully, was familiar enough almost to be a comfort to the Dervish. For he felt his desolation keenly that night.

It was a terrible night, the night he spent in the company of the corpse in the ruined shrine beside the well. It was a night of emptiness, a night in which he had to confront all his failures, all his cowardice, his mediocrity, the loss of all his hopes of going home triumphant with his mission accomplished. He had never felt so stripped of strategy, so depleted of plans. What should he do now? Where should he turn? What kind of hollow thing was he?

Some time in the middle of that night, the Dervish saw the dance of far flames in the direction of the cliffs. He had been unable to sleep, for the mouldering odours of the corpse penetrated his fitful dreams and caused him to toss and turn where he lay in the corner of the ruin. He had leaped to his feet with a suffocated cry after a terrible dream in which the corpse had reached a rotting arm towards him from beyond the north wall of the ruin. It had laid hold of him with putrid fingers and pressed pure slime into his throat. He tore himself from sleep to escape its touch and ran out of the ruin, shaking with dread. After drenching his head and shoulders in the cold water of the well to banish the nauseating smell of the dream, he was somewhat restored to his senses. And that was when he saw the blink of far-off flames beneath the cliffs.

A fire under the cliffs? It must be a signal! The tribesmen had gathered again where he had seen them earlier that day. He even fancied he heard the sound of voices drifting across the valley, as though they were carousing round their fires, as though they were celebrating their raid. They were undoubtably there! But did he dare approach them in the dead of night? Did he have the courage to creep across the treacherous valley in darkness, under the fitful glances of the sickly moon? Was he brave enough to try to find them, stumbling into rocks and quicksands on the way? What if they caught him and killed him without questioning him?

No. He did not dare. He was mortally afraid. Much as he would have liked to see his mission accomplished, he was more frightened of meeting the knife of Ibn Rumi in the night than of imagining how to meet him in the day. That admission marked the lowest ebb his dishonour had yet achieved. He realized he had failed to retrieve the signal thrown from the clifftop that morning, he had failed to follow the tribe when they left like thunder at noon and now, finally, he failed to face them at night. He crawled back into the ruin, which stank of the rotting corpse, and knew then that he would face ignominy on his return and prove his brothers right in their opinion. His emptiness engulfed him.

When he was woken, in the dark hour before dawn, by the arrival of another seeming corpse carried on the back of a mule, the Dervish thought at first he was still trapped in a nightmare. He crouched low in the shadows, beside some ashy embers in the corner of the ruin, and strained to see in the semidarkness. The woman, for it was apparent now from her groans that she was not yet a corpse, was carried into the ruin by a turbanless priest whom he recognized as one of the pilgrims in the caravan. It was clear from the condition of both that they were, perhaps, the sole survivors of a raid. The priest had an ugly gash across his temples but seemed otherwise unhurt. The woman, however, would not survive for long. Her condition was more grave. He guessed she would be dead within the hour.

What caught the attention of the Dervish was the saddlebag strapped to the side of the mule. Could it be the same saddlebag that he had briefly seen in the possession of the Indian that morning? An impossible coincidence! One saddlebag is much the same as another, he told himself. He was doubtless imagining things and the light was too poor to distinguish anything clearly. He did not attempt to speak to the couple, and they seemed unaware of his presence, so it seemed safer to lurk in the shadows. But when the woman called out urgently for the saddlebag to be opened, and when he saw the priest draw a bundle of papers from it, he shuffled to his feet and came closer to look.

At that point the priest turned on him. 'Keep your filthy hands off, you dog!' he snarled. The Dervish drew back in surprise; he was disconcerted by the man's violent energy. Who did this puny cleric think he was? But his diplomatic instincts caused the Englishman to restrain himself. Stifling a desire to punch the brute between the eyes, he summoned his thespian powers to his assistance and gave a very creditable performance of a cringing, beggarly dervish who craved forgiveness for his presumption, but he just wished, if the scholarly young gentleman would be disposed to grace this illiterate one, he just wished to know what Holy Words lay in these priceless bundles, for surely it was the Hand of God that had brought them here to illumine this Dark Night and bring a wretched sinner to the Threshold of Enlightenment . . .

Mollified, the priggish priest allowed the Dervish to glance at the page he had been given by the woman. It was a single line of writing, an invocation, he said, to satisfy his curiosity. He then delivered a brief dissertation to the Dervish and the listening dawn on the high quality of penmanship of this calligraphy, saying that it was doubtless written by a master, couched in a language which echoed the sacred verses of the most holy book. Which was strange, continued the priest in his nasal tones, because it was utterly different from anything found in the Quran. He appeared to take his own scholarship very seriously. He chanted the words and then fell into a profound silence. The Dervish flattered him on his excellent delivery and waited, expectant; what else did the saddlebag contain? Clearing his throat nervously the priest fished around and drew out another package. He opened it and yet another wad of paper fell out, covered in the same fine calligraphy.

The Dervish peered over the priest's shoulder, rather bored. High quality of penmanship? Rare calligraphy? It was double Dutch to him of course, all this fine stuff, but he found the writing rather pretty and delicate in the light of the rising sun. His imitation of the language did not reach even the remotest borders of literacy, but he sometimes liked the shape of the words. Maybe this was a find after all. He stared more closely at the scribbled writing. It seemed to dance across the page. Even if he had not succeeded in contacting the Harb tribe and winning immortal fame for himself as a political agent, he could at least return with something like a trophy. Maybe he could make his name as the discoverer of a master calligrapher whose style was hitherto unseen in the West and unknown even to the British Museum. Others brought back cuneiform carvings and the ruins of Nineveh, so why could he not astonish the Western world with a rare example of Persian calligraphy?

But even as the Dervish began to contemplate this possibility, the priest suddenly crumpled up the paper he was reading and threw it with a violent oath into the dried-up well. Then he turned and strode out of the ruin. The Dervish hovered for a moment, uncertain. What did this mean? Was the quality of penmanship less significant, then, than the pedantic fellow had first thought? Was the style less lofty? Or more so? There were tantalizing possibilities here.

The saddlebag remained half-open, bulging with its mysterious contents on the ground beside the dying woman. The Dervish waited for a second to see if the priest would return. He did not. Slowly, softly, he bent to retrieve it and had just closed his hand about its straps in order to pull it towards him when the woman stirred to uncertain consciousness. She turned her immense eyes on the Dervish. He saw with a shudder that her face was cruelly marked with the pox and that she was an African. He had not realized this before. She had been lying in shadow, and he had noticed only the blood seeping from her in an ever-widening pool. She was on the verge of death from who knew what disease. Quickly, without a word, he pulled the saddlebag from her side. He held it tightly in his arms as he withdrew rapidly into the shadows. Perhaps it was contaminated, but he would take the risk. This stuff could be valuable.

She had kept her eyes fixed on him brightly. As he turned back and looked at her again, like a ray of sunrise she smiled on him most beautifully. And died.

The Dervish returned to Constantinople through the Gulf of Aqaba and Damascus, accruing his triumphs at every step. He had contacted the Harb tribe. He had succeeded brilliantly in his mission. He had exchanged oaths with Ibn Rumi, he said, sealed with blood. Her Britannic Majesty, he had averred to that champion against oppression, would defend the cause of liberty, would rush to the defence of the downtrodden everywhere, would support the cause of right against the cause of wrong. It was just a question of the price, and this, he claimed, had been the fruit of his mission to affirm. He had survived the most terrible hardships and endured the most daunting dangers for this cause; he had suffered thirst and burning heat to this end. He had faced the fearful terror of the *hajj*, and moreover he had managed, by a fluke, to come upon this trove of manuscripts, written in a rare and exquisite penmanship, echoing the lofty language and the mystic utterances of the Quran. And to the wonder of all, he had found these samples of calligraphy in the middle of the desert. They were unique, for no one had ever seen such a quality of art or poetry before. Those who had read this stuff affirmed that its beauty could strike terror in the soul . . .

The ambassador leaned over the desk and leafed through some of the bundles and packages that had been opened in front of him with a trembling hand that had been reddened and dried by long years in the sun. He was intensely irritated with his attaché. The confounded fellow had not only come back alive, looking like a golden god with his damned muscles rippling irresistibly, but his wretched mission in the middle of the desert had attracted a great deal of attention. There was even some talk in Whitehall of promoting him. And what was all this rubbish he had brought back? The ambassador prided himself on his Persian and Turkish scholarship. He donned his pince-nez and stared blankly at the pages in front of him, his right temple throbbing. He could not see for jealous rage.

'Oh dear, I'm afraid you've been awfully gypped, old chap,' he murmured between set teeth. 'I never saw such rubbish in all my life.'

The young attaché looked somewhat crestfallen, but not for long. 'I've been told by the very best authorities that this is an unusual find, sir,' he began again. 'It's a quality of penmanship so rare –'

But the ambassador had run out of patience. 'That it'll serve to curl my wife's hair,' he snapped. It was an unfortunate blunder, because he knew his fool of a wife had embarrassed herself by trying to convert the young man recently in one of her confounded crusades. He flushed a lobster red and indicated that his attaché was dismissed.

The young man smiled smoothly as he gathered up the bundles and packages and stuffed them into the saddlebag. An excellent diplomat. Even as he bowed and left the room, he knew that his own career was confirmed and his name made.

The contents of the saddlebag were widely distributed.

The wife of the ambassador claimed a fair portion of

them as her own and shared them with ladies of a mystical inclination when her husband retired to London shortly afterwards. She had been quite taken by the way the handsome young attaché had snatched the saddlebag from the jaws of certain death. When some of the writings were translated for her by a Venetian dragoman at the embassy (who also evinced great interest in the penmanship and managed to steal a specimen or two without her ladyship's knowledge), she had the pieces beautifully framed and circulated, during the decade that followed, among artistic friends with a predilection for the Pre-Raphaelites. She often exclaimed that these scraps from the desert were an authentic reminder of the truth of the Gospels and echoed the Song of Songs. Wonderfully passionate, she said.

An English doctor who was travelling back to Tabriz through Constantinople a decade later hazarded a guess that he might have met the author of these writings, whom he remembered as a mild-mannered madman with a melodious voice. A German orientalist was so inspired by some of them that he started a commune in Freiburg – after he returned from his researches in Persia – where it was said that women had equal rights with men and lived without any obligation to consummate their marriages. Several other packages from the saddlebag were scrutinized by a famous French philosopher who passed through Constantinople in later years. He found them remarkable for their audacity and considered them quite the best example of the influence of French philosophy on Middle Eastern thought. They gradually made their way from Paris to gallery cellars and storage attics in museums all over Europe.

One was traced in the early years of the twentieth century to a library in St Petersburg, where it was permitted, even after the Bolsheviks came to power, to remain permanently exhibited under a phosphorescent light, to the wonder of the liberated.

A large number of bundles festered in the British embassy and were forgotten until a fire almost destroyed the building, shortly before the Young Turks' revolution at the turn of the century, at which point they were salvaged and identified, by one of the undersecretaries, as a code containing vital state secrets that should be sealed in a strong-box for posterity.

Some found their way to the basement of the British Museum, where they survived blackouts and air raids in the company of old mops and brooms, only to be discovered after the war, by a janitor looking for forgotten ration stamps, who sold them for a pretty penny to a man who kept a stall in the Portobello Road. Others, saved by a blunder on the part of a badly paid archivist, were sent to New York via Naples on the steamship *Cedric* instead of the *Titanic*, thereby escaping the wreck to be marooned in a row of antique shops in a certain quarter of New York which today specializes in fake Oriental penmanship.

At the turn of the century, a young Falasha from Ethiopia, converted to Christianity by a man who had lived in Constantinople during the decades before, came across a document among his dead teacher's papers which bore a seal he instantly recognized as belonging to the returned Messiah. He insisted on emigrating to Palestine, where he tried to convert the monks of the Carmelite monastery to his opinion, much to the embarrassment of the Society for the Conversion of Jews as well as the leaders of the German Templar Colony established in that region. The Zionist groups ignored him and his claims, and despite his ardour, the affair was hushed up and never reached the Western press.

It is difficult to know how many other people may have encountered the contents of the saddlebag. But what is indisputable is that the bag itself, emptied of its load, was kept for many years by the English attaché as a souvenir of his historic exploits in the Arabian Desert. He hung it on the wall above his desk at the embassy in Constantinople, together with his axe and begging bowl, as a memento of his adventures as a dervish. And then, when he was promoted to higher offices, he kept it in his study at home, to the intense irritation of his wife, who looked for the first opportunity to throw the nasty thing away.

THE CORPSE

M y smell is like a name, thought the Corpse. It is linked to my identity and I cannot remember when last I did not smell. I have been smelling so bad for so long that my memory is saturated with myself, he thought as he mounted the steps.

Then he tried letting some of himself go. It was hard, because he had not practised these steps when he was alive. But it worked.

We live, thought the Corpse, as if we would live forever. And when we die, we think we will smell forever. But neither is true; it is a question of detachment.

He had not wanted answers to this question during his life. During his death, however, the answers required addressing.

The Corpse thought without the benefit of his own brain cells. He passed like a bad odour through the minds of others. He lived briefly for a moment in the memory of others. He was remembered, fitfully, as a result of irritation. But at this point he was grateful for anything. He used these subtle interfusions to belong to others. He used these hidden interactions to conjure life with others. These arts, though not well developed, were not entirely atrophied in him. But he was a long way from being able to dance.

There was help, of course. The starlight assisted. The sheer beauty of the desert dunes bore witness. Angels of every denomination quietly affirmed. The Corpse was not alone in this difficult transition but he had not mastered it by any means. He wished ardently that he had been better prepared for the steps of this dance.

This wish, he realized with astonishment, was a kind of prayer. Although he had preferred a cruder bargaining in life, during his death he knew with absolute certainty that the prayer of the merchant was a blessing. It rose out of the well forever and always and in his long decaying he envied the thief who had deserved it. Would that he might receive blessings instead of curses!

The steps he was mounting led to an upper chamber, the coloured fragments of whose windows caught the sun and brought a mosaic of dancing colours into curious relationships.

If we had only lived as if we would die forever, the smell would not be such an impediment, thought the Corpse. We would be free to obey the dance.

He had not done so, however. Quite the contrary. He had mounted those steps without the benefit of prayer and had stumbled. He had accredited himself with the kind of blessing that could not countenance annihilation of personal identity. He had missed the significance of infinite transformations, of discovery beyond his own boundaries, of the delicacy of this dance of immortality. And so he lingered: a bad smell.

Would that I had no name and no identity, he thought, since it is worth so little. We should live as if we would die forever. There's more of it.

But this was already becoming too difficult. From 'I' to

'we' was further than he had been willing to extend himself. As a tradesman, he had developed a strong sense of weighing his expenditures against the value of his returns, but these subtle interfusions, these enigmas and interrelationships that stretched the interest beyond the imagination of anything conceived in the original down payment, were already beyond the means he had developed. He needed more than starlight, more than moonlight, to arrive at such fluid transitions between personal pronouns.

The sun glancing through the coloured window panes in the upper chamber confirmed the dance but he could not follow the steps without anguish. They leaped backwards to a particular moment that filled him with excruciating pain. It was only with the greatest effort that he could fit the pieces together. There was an answer of connection to this question of detachment, he realized.

He was in a small courtyard where grew a single laden orange tree beside a pool. The air was redolent with orange blossom grown from a single seed of infinite freedom. There was a door across the courtyard and he could see the steps beyond, leading upwards. Always further upwards. The Abyssinian servant at the door told him his master waited in the room above. His master.

He had given the young man some merchandise to sell in his absence. On his return he had found that the prices had dropped radically, and the value of his goods had been much less than he had originally agreed with the merchant. But the merchant insisted on paying him the sum he had expected, far more than the goods had actually fetched. He had insisted. To do otherwise was contrary to the law of trustworthiness, he had said.

He had thought the fellow a naive fool. They all thought him a naive fool. Prayed too much, that was his trouble.

You can't do business with your eyes closed. Later, over that matter of the indigo sales, he had tried to take advantage of this naivety. It is easy to cheat when you evoke trust. But the law dictated reciprocity. And though the merchant was a *sayyid*, he was no fool. It looked as if he was praying with his eyes shut but he saw through them all. Before going on his pilgrimage, he had completed all his business transactions and exposed the cheat.

His steps stumbled as he mounted towards the upper chamber. Something was in the way, blocking access, which he was obliged to name. He tripped over a shadow with a smell. Himself. He had broken the pattern. He had violated the covenant with the merchant. His failure filled his steps with pain. Pain, thought the Corpse, is when the dance stops.

The excruciating pain was somewhere in the region of his chest. It appeared to have collapsed and no longer supplied him with the breath required to allow his brain cells to keep functioning. So the other means took over. Limping interfusions. Crippled interactions. Weak because dependent on the bonds he had not built, the connections he had not made, the detachment he had not achieved. Feeble. But they took over. Not exactly dancing, but moving at least. They had no choice.

This is the way it is, he thought, as his stench attracted the curses of the pilgrims. You cannot escape the law of trustworthiness. You have no choice. Even when you break the terms there are severe consequences. Pain is a broken covenant. They were circumambulating the Kaabih when it happened, he remembered, and in such a place, to break a covenant is fatal. They said he had a heart attack.

At the top of the steps where the Abyssinian slave had led him, he found the young merchant sitting in the upper chamber to the right, surrounded by his papers. There were rush mats on the floor aglow with the sunlight shining through fragments of coloured glass. The verdant equinox, the ardent ruby tender and vibrant, clusters of amethyst on shores of pearl. An ocean, indigo blue, on which the boat tossed towards his pilgrimage: a sea of affirmation and negation. The rich old man stood at the door and removed his shoes with an obsequious show of humility and deference. The young merchant of modest means did not even acknowledge him. His pen case and ink lay at hand and he was engaged in composing a treatise, an invocation, or was it a poem?

It was quite evident that he could not be interrupted. His green-turbaned head was bent over the page. He was chanting in a low voice as he wrote, swiftly and with exquisite penmanship, across the delicate blue paper. His script was like breath covering the page. The words unfurled like feathers from the tip of his reed pen. And he dipped again and again in the blood-dark ink and hardly paused for the dots. The speed at which the words flowed was astonishing; it matched exactly the rhythm of his melodious voice.

The rich merchant from Bushire who had come to speak to him on a personal matter regarding their trade relations was obliged to seat himself in the corner of the room beside the door, with his bare feet tucked up beneath his robes. He was obliged to wait. It was awkward because he felt dishonoured, unclean. He wanted to be done with the matter of indigo and go home quickly, but that was impossible. The contract of courtesy did not permit it. He had already broken the law of trustworthiness and had to abide by the consequences. He could not break any more covenants. He found himself presented with a bowl of rose water by the same Abyssinian servant. To wash his hands. To partake of tea the colour of carnelian. The merchant was fastidiously clean.

I cannot remember when last I did not smell, thought the Corpse as he mounted the steps forever, thinking of indigo. How long it took him to mount these forever steps.

He was upset because he had tried to cheat the young man and the young man had refused to be cheated. He had claimed the common discount after the sale of indigo and the young man had refused to allow it. He called it unjust. He said it was untrustworthy. He refused to lower his prices once they had been agreed to, just as he had refused to lower his payments after they had been promised. But everyone knew it was the custom, surely! You pressed your bargain, you made the deal, and then, when it was all signed and sealed, you demanded a discount too. This young merchant did not. He called it dishonesty. He called it cheating. Why was he changing the words? It was just *baksheesh*, that's all! A common custom!

You will have to change your words, he said. Trustworthiness transcends such customs.

But everyone did it!

You will have to change your customs too, he said.

Who was he, this young upstart, who thought he could change words? By whose authority did he believe he could alter the customs of the land? His naivety was dangerous! The first time, the old man had thought he was dealing with a fool; the second time, he realized he was the fool himself.

He was climbing the steps then, to argue with the young merchant who had changed the colour of indigo. But with each step he felt himself falling lower and lower.

Then the bottom dropped out of his world. When he looked towards the Kaabih using the means beyond the reach of brain cells, he saw someone standing there with the ring of the stone in his hand. My memory is saturated with myself, thought the Corpse. My vision is dimmed with myself; I cannot see or tell beyond it. But surely I know that young man?

The young man standing there beside the black stone was uttering words that pressed against the cracked chest of a groaning world. He was uttering words that burst like blood through the eardrums of the world. It was the young merchant who had killed the customs and resurrected the law of trustworthiness in the land. It was the young *sayyid* in a green turban who had changed the words of the world in Shiraz. And his name was fragrant. His master!

He heard the words across the seething, surging ocean of a crowd, as clear as birds calling at dawn through an open window, like a black curl of hidden meaning moving across the cheek of creation in the morning breeze. He heard the words spoken by the merchant beside the Kaabih clear as water from the forever filling well, even as he was always dying.

Would that I had no name and no identity, he thought, and could become a syllable of such words as these! Would that I could be part of this! The prayer was melodious under the merchant's flowing pen and he listened with growing wonder as he sat there, with his horny feet tucked under his travel-stained robes, in the upper chamber. He listened with growing awe, as he sat with an empty tea glass in his hand, while the merchant chanted the words he wrote with marvellous swiftness and beauty across the pale-blue page of dancing coloured glass. It was then that he decided to go on his pilgrimage too, with the young man. His last pilgrimage.

He forgot about the indigo discount. He forgot, momentarily, about himself. He ceased for a second to smell, so tender was the fragrance of the rose water on his open palms.

So this is our story, the Corpse pondered as he leaned in

gentle dissolution against the north wall of the ruin. A story
of delicate rottenness and subtle decay unwinding its
bobbin from day to day. A story of trust, a story of change,
a story of detachment and connection, like perfume in the
desert which lingers in the memory of men saturated with
themselves. And where, as we step wider, do the odours
disappear? Where are we when the smell has ceased? They
said he was to be honoured by a burial in al Baqr because he
had died on his last pilgrimage. Was that where it would
end? What then was the beginning?

He knew, from the moment he saw the young man
holding the ring of the Kaabih in his indigo-blue hand, he
knew from the moment his personal identity collapsed
inside his chest, that this was the beginning of the story.
Whatever was the young man's fragrance in the kingdom of
names, it was clear that he had been uttered by the spirit of
spirits. The birds flew like arrows from his mouth and were
destined to plant seeds in all the deserts of the world. They
wheeled thrice about the Kaabih and departed with the
sound of a rushing torrent.

When the old man died, he had not yet learned the steps.
He could not follow the pattern without falling. His connections were atrophied. But after some days of dissolution
he was beginning to arrive at the transition between personal pronouns. And who shall water these my orchards
after they are gone? And who shall watch over our apricots?
And what can sweeten this subtle and unfolding fruit
within you? thought the Corpse.

We are thirsty, whispered the seeds inside the Corpse.

It was difficult to begin learning the steps, parched as
were his meanings, atrophied as were his pronouns, till he
heard the water in the well. The well was summoning him
to prayer. It was no bargain, but a gift: gratis they called it,

the opposite of bribery. The well had been filled with the merchant's morning prayers and they were bubbling to the very brim. The Corpse knew then that he had no wish to be carried beyond this boundless point.

If we died as if we could live forever, the story would be endless, he realized.

He knew, with the bride, that the prayer of the merchant was his very soul's salvation and had stood before him like a shudder when he rose in the mornings and bent over him like a kiss when he slept at nights. He knew, like the chieftain, that it lay within him like the fragrance of a rose. He knew too, with the thief, that the God to whom the merchant prayed was the God of the pure wind and the desert voices, the true One burning the heavens by day and treading the moonlit dunes by night. He knew then that the honour he preferred was not to be buried in the dead sands of al Baqr but to dissolve at this very point, with the pilgrim in the quicksand, near the well.

And his prayers were answered. He was easily forgotten after all.

Connected and detached, he flowed in pity towards the dervish scrambling up the slope from the gully at his feet. Tenderly he cradled the slave through the crumbling ruin beyond his head and lingered an eternity with the priest between the old well and the new. Wondering, he mingled in the smoke of the funeral pyre cherished by the Indian which drifted quietly across the valley and settled like a memory on the stone lip of the well. And finally, with the prayer, the Corpse dropped himself like a hundred-petalled rose and hovered gratefully among them all.

They began to drink their fill.

When the point is sure, the circle shall be wider and the dance complete, thought the Corpse, as he ceased to smell.

GLOSSARY

Ahriman   the Evil One, the 'Hostile Spirit' symbolized by darkness, according to the teachings of Zoroaster

Ahura Mazdah   the God of infinite goodness, the Supreme Being, symbolized by the light of the sun and fire, according to the teachings of Zoroaster

anderun   the private part of the house or women's quarters in Persia

arak   a distilled alcoholic drink

ashrama   the stages in the life of an individual, of which there are four in the Hindu tradition

'Atabat   the Shi'ia Muslim shrine cities of Iraq

avatar   an incarnation of God in the past or future, according to Hinduism

Avestas   the holy scriptures of the Zoroastrian faith, written in four parts, including liturgical writings, songs, hymns of praise and a detailed code of ritual purification

baksheesh   an expected bribe or tip imposed in addition to an agreed price

bhakti   the path of love and worship followed by Hindus

biruni   the public part of the house for men and male guests in Persia

caliphate   the ruling institution in Islam accepted by the *Sunnis*, based on the theory of the elective principle. Caliphs (successors) were designated to govern the community from the time of Abu-Bakr who succeeded the Prophet

chaffiyeh   a square head cloth worn by men and kept in place around the crown by a black rope

dervish   a wandering holy man associated with the Sufi traditions

254

Dharma   the universal law, moral order, the 'right way' to live for the Hindus

Dhu'l-Hijjah   the 12th month in the Islamic lunar calendar during which the pilgrimage or *hajj* prescribed by Mohammed takes place

druj   the People of the Lie, a reference to those, in the Zoroastrian world view, who opposed the peace and harmony of *asha*, the People of Righteousness

duhkha   the suffering that exists in this contingent world according to Buddhism and Hinduism

Falasha   the name given to an immigrant population of Ethiopians who professed to be Jews and claimed to be of the House of Israel. According to some theories they were converted to Judaism during the period of Jewish slavery under the Pharaohs of Egypt; according to others they are the legitimate descendants of Solomon and the Queen of Sheba

faqir   a dervish, literally 'poor'

farrash   an attendant or footman

farrash-bashi   a head guard or attendant

farsang   a unit of measurement: approximately three or four miles, the distance which a laden mule will walk in an hour

Gebr   the name given to Zoroastrians of Persian background and culture (pronounced 'gabr')

Gita   the Baghavad Gita or collection of holy scriptures of the Hindu religion

hajj   the Islamic pilgrimage to Mecca prescribed by Mohammed. Every adult Muslim should undertake this pilgrimage, if s/he can afford it, at least once in a lifetime

Hajj-i-Akbar   the greatest pilgrimage, during which the Festival of Sacrifice, which takes place on the tenth day of the *Dhu'l-Hijjah*, falls on a sacred Friday

haoma   a narcotic intoxicant, traced to former, corrupted practices in ancient Persia, used in times of prayer among some Zoroastrians

haram   a forbidden area, including the sacred enclosure surrounding the *Kaabih*

Harb   One of the Saudi tribes whose leader, Ibn Rumi, had revolted against the Ottoman pasha of Mecca in a bid for independence in the mid-19th century

Haurvatat   the archangel of salvation, or wholeness and health, one of the six divine attendants of *Ahurah Mazdah* in the Zoroastrian pantheon

Hijaz   the province of Saudi Arabia containing the cities of Mecca, Medina and adjacent territories

'Id al-Qurban   the Feast of Sacrifice on the tenth day of the *hajj*, to commemorate Abraham's intended sacrifice of Ishmael/Isaac, during which animals are slaughtered during *rajim* and the meat distributed among the poor

ihram   a special white robe of raw cotton worn during the pilgrimage at Mecca

Imam   the term applied by most *Shi'ias* to the twelve legitimate apostolic successors of Mohammed, based on the hereditary principle of succession from the house of the Prophet through his cousin and son-in-law 'Ali. Also applied to the founders of the four schools of *Sunni* jurisprudence

Imam-Jumih   the person who leads the *Shi'ia* congregation to prayer on Fridays

jellaba   an Arab dress consisting of a long shirt

jñana   the path of enlightenment in the Hindu scriptures

Kaabih   the most holy shrine of Islam in Mecca round which circumambulate the pilgrims. According to Islamic tradition, this square room with the sacred black stone at one corner, said to have descended from heaven, is the spot from which the promised *Qa'im*, or Mahdi, will one day proclaim himself, holding in his hand a ring of iron that is fixed in the stone

kad-khuda   a local chief or headman of a small township or village in Iran

Kali Yuga   the dark or iron age of history according to the Hindu scriptures

Kalki   the incarnation of God ordained to appear at the end of the dark age according to Hindu scriptures

khan   a caravanserai, in which travellers and their animals took refuge throughout the Middle East until the early years of the twentieth century. Also, in a different context, a term of respect applied to a man

khanum   a term of respect in Persian, applied to a lady

Krta Yuga   the golden age according to Hindu prophecy

madrasih   a religious school where the sciences are taught to Islamic scholars

maya   the illusory nature of the physical and material world and the veil that hides reality, according to Hindu scriptures

maydan   a market area or central meeting place in a town

memsahib   a term used by Indians to refer to a European woman or lady of the house *mojaver*   a resident of the holy cities of Mecca and Medina

moksha/mukti   liberation or salvation from the cycles of suffering for the Hindus

mubahala   a form of mutual execration based on sincere prayers which appeals for divine arbitration between right and wrong

mujtahid   *Shi'ia* scholar or priest who has achieved the level of competence necessary to apply judgements on points of religious law. Also the term applied by *Sunnis* to the founders of the four schools of law

mullah   a *Shi'ia* priest

Parsee   the name given to Zoroastrians of Indian background and culture

punkah   a fan used in India made of cloth strapped to a pole and sometimes wettened. It is pulled back and forth to produce a cool breeze

Qa'im   the Twelfth Imam, or Mahdi, who is expected to return in the 'fullness of time' according to Islamic prophectic traditions

qualun   a water pipe, sometimes called 'hookah' or hubble bubble

rajim   a special ritual of the *hajj* which consists of casting stones at the 'idols' identified with Satan

sahib   the term used by Indians to refer to a European male authority figure

samsara   the cycle of rebirth or successive lives which certain Hindus believe enables some individuals to progress on the path towards salvation (*moksha*).

Sanatana Dharma   the universal law, moral order or right way of living at the cosmic level. The *Sadharama Dharma* is a general code of ethics at the human level. The *Varnashrama Dharma* sets out customs and duties at the social level. Everyone also has a personal *Dharma* or right way to live.

Saoshyant   the saviour who will appear in the fourth epoch of the universe according to Zoroastrian prophecy and will raise the dead for their final reward or punishment, after which good will reign eternally

sayyid   of the lineage of Mohammed, in Shi'ia terminology

Shaykhi   a follower of a *Shi'ia* sect with messianic leanings founded by Shaykh Ahmad-i-Ahsai in the 18th century in Iran

sheikh   Arab leader or head of a tribe or group in the Middle East

Sheol   the name for hell, the gloomy place of everlasting doom, according to the Jewish Torah, where unhappy souls wander eternally. Also called *Tophet*

Shi'ia   one of the two great forms of Islam (the other being *Sunni*).

THE SADDLEBAG

Most of the *Shi'ias*, found principally in Iran, uphold the succession of 'Ali, the cousin and son-in-law of the Prophet, and his sons Hassan and Hussein through a line of twelve hereditary imams

Sunni the majority tradition of Islam, upholding the theory of the elective principle for the Prophet's succession from the first caliph Abu-Bakr

Superior Man as distinct from a sage, who has the capacity to transform others, a superior man, or *chün-tzu* in Chinese tradition, is one whose nobility and virtue one should try to emulate

takhteravan a wooden travelling litter for women carried on the backs of mules or horses

T'ien the Chinese definition of Heaven or God whose mandate rules over man and the world, a transcendent and immanent source of creativity working incessantly in the universe

Tophet (see *Sheol* above)

'ulama the Islamic learned class

Vedas the Hindu scriptures

wadi a valley

Wahhabi a *Sunni* sect founded by 'Abdu' 1-Wahhab in the 18th century which sought to reform the spurious accretions in Islam associated with the extreme veneration of saints and the ostentation of worship and which emphasized the Prophet's human rather than divine attributes. The Wahhabi won converts among Saudi tribes and waged holy war against the Ottomans.

xiao ren the definition of an ignoble and self-serving man invented by Confucius for purposes of comparison with the Superior Man, or *Chün-tzu*

zibh cutting the throat of animals for the sacrifice of *Id al'Qurban* on the tenth day of the Islamic pilgrimage

SOURCES

This work is inspired by the language, the metaphors, the symbols and traditions of many holy books of different major religions of the world. It includes references from the Hindu scriptures of the *Bhagavad Gita*, sayings attributed to Buddha, quotations from Confucius' *Analects*, and *The Book of Changes*, echoes from the traditions associated with the *Quran* and from the Bahá'í writings. While the archetypal circumstances depicted here are much influenced by religious history of the Middle East, none of the characters and actions of this fictional work, however, are intended to represent historical figures or actual events.

ACKNOWLEDGEMENTS

My thanks are due to dead and living friends, and in particular to Soheil Farhad and Moojan Momen for their invaluable scholarship, Farzaneh Milani and Amin Banani for their sensitive advice, Helenka and Mark, for their practical support, Helen and Mimi, for their example and the Bloomsbury people for all their encouragement and the patience of angels. I would also like to thank my mother and my daughter who listened and my sister-in-law who allowed me, so generously, to hear.

A NOTE ON THE AUTHOR

Bahiyyih Nakhjavani is a Persian writer educated in the UK and the United States. She now lives in Belgium where she teaches European and American literature. She has also written for documentary film, and lectures internationally on the arts and the Bahá'í faith.